Horsing Around with Murder

A Senior Sleuth Mystery - Book 1

MAUREEN FISHER

Horsing Around with Murder
by Maureen Fisher

Copyright © 2019 Maureen Fisher

ISBN 978-1-9995755-1-9

Edited by Stacy Juba
Cover by Streetlight Graphics.

Discover more about Maureen Fisher
http://www.booksbymaureen.com

PREVIEW

"Zeke?" I yelled over the wild neighing that went on and on.

Nothing. Something was terribly wrong.

Lancelot reared up, pawed the air, and crashed down again. The stall door swung open. The fact that I didn't have a coronary on the spot testified to my heart's excellent health.

With Zeke's appearance in the doorway, instinct told me to remain silent. He grunted a little while backing out of the stall. I could tell he was dragging something limp and heavy. Once in the corridor, he gently lowered his load and straightened, his face a mask of shock. As he ran his fingers through his hair, I noted his hand shook.

"I was too late to save him," he muttered in a tight voice.

I studied the inert object and shuddered. It was a man—a man who was either unconscious or dead. His head was turned away from me.

My throat tightened. "Oh, Zeke," I said softly.

His eyes vacant and haunted, he used an arm to swipe sweat off his forehead before closing the stall door. Remaining silent, he averted his gaze and crouched beside the body.

I glanced again at the still form, my heart galloping in my chest. "That's Luc Lacroix, isn't it?" I clenched my fists, dimly aware of my nails digging into tender flesh.

Zeke nodded.

My heart bounced around in my chest. "Is he ..." I stopped talking.

Zeke checked Luc's pulse while I shifted from one foot to the other. Seconds ticked by until he stood and faced me, his expression grim. "Yeah. He's dead."

Chapter 1:
Last Chance for Success

IT ALL BEGAN THREE DAYS earlier when I, Abby Foster, sat in my office staring at our annual profit and loss statement. Daunted by the prospect of financial ruin, I grabbed my squishy stress ball and gave it several killer squeezes. Unless we increased our revenues, Grizzly Gulch Guest Ranch was toast. Worse, my two sisters and I would be collateral damage at an age when most sane people contemplated retirement.

In an attempt to lower my blood pressure, I stretched and gazed out the window at the long ridges and rolling terrain of the Alberta foothills. How could I leave this vast beauty?

The answer was, I couldn't and wouldn't. We desperately needed five-star reviews. Our week-long equine breeding symposium was our only hope.

Scowling, I chucked the useless stress ball at my office door, which simultaneously flew open.

The ball bounced off my younger sister's forehead.

"Hey," Dodie said, rubbing her brow. "What the fudge, Abby?"

"Sorry," I said. "A little advice? Try knocking."

A sinus-clogging cloud of Chanel No. 5 filled my office as she teetered inside on four-inch spikes, ridiculous shoes for a sixty-two-year-old woman. Brilliant flowers splashed the plus-size muumuu top, which should have hung loose. Instead, it clung like shrink wrap to quadruple-D boobs before encasing a bulging muffin-top and belly pooch. The hem landed a scant inch below crotch-level.

"Huh, I figured you'd be in a decent mood since you've been holed up in here for hours with your best friends—numbers and spreadsheets." Dodie's eyes lit up as she zeroed in on a low filing cabinet where I'd stashed a plate of Chef Armand's cookies, telling myself they were for visitors, not myself. She selected an oatmeal-raisin and bit down.

I rolled my eyes. "Don't stand on ceremony. Help yourself."

Through a mouthful of crumbs, she replied, "Don't mind if I do," and crammed the rest of the cookie into her mouth. Bending over to scrutinize the plate, she presented me with a disturbing view. She'd encased her plump legs in black leggings, a feat as miraculous as stuffing a bucking heifer down a drainpipe. Her queen-sized butt-cheeks bulged, straining the wafer-thin fabric in an alarming manner.

Before she'd retired, Dodie had accumulated years of experience in the food industry. Along with an avid interest in food, she also knew her beverages, especially the alcoholic kind. Those talents, combined with her people skills earned her the dual titles of Food and Beverage Manager plus Head of Guest Services and Housekeeping.

Straightening, she faced me, giving my eyeballs a chance to heal. Holding two thumbprint cookies on a napkin, she minced over to a visitor's chair and parked herself.

"Nice outfit," I said, cringing at her eye-popping getup.

"Huh. Wish I could say the same for yours. You dress like a nun. Loosen up a bit, Sis, wear something snappy." She chomped into another cookie.

I ignored her jab about my work attire. Hey, I liked the no-nonsense look of a button-up blouse and tailored pants. "So sue me. I look elegant and professional."

"Why so grumpy?"

"I've spent the better part of a glorious May morning studying spreadsheets. Bottom line? We're in deep financial trouble. Our survival hinges on next week's horse breeding symposium. It's gotta be a success. Unless we attract a lot more guests we'll default on our loan and the bank will re-possess Grizzly Gulch." I gave her a hard stare. "I don't know about you, but I'm too old to become a bag-lady."

"That bad?" she asked around a mouthful of crumbs.

At the thought of losing Grizzly Gulch, a sharp pain knifed between my shoulder blades. "Today is the two-year anniversary of Uncle Benny's passing." I fought down an unexpected burst of emotion. Uncle Benny had left the three of us all his worldly goods, including Grizzly Gulch Guest Ranch.

"Don't go all weepy on me." Dodie raised her cookie in the air. "Here's to our favorite uncle. It's a sure bet he croaked happy. Hey, when they found him, his feet were in his boots and his hindquarters firmly lodged in his ATV's heated seat. He was doing what he loved most—riding fences in Grizzly Gulch's northwest pasture."

I gave a watery smile. My sister had a knack for putting things into perspective.

Initially, owning and operating a dude ranch in the foothills of the Canadian Rockies had sounded idyllic. Two years and a ton of renovations later, the reality of running a money pit like Grizzly Gulch missed the mark by a country mile.

"We got carried away with our renovations," I said. "The upgrades to convert a rundown dude ranch into a deluxe vacation destination overstretched our finances—and that's putting it mildly."

"The renovations will pay for themselves. Our place is fabulous."

I couldn't help but agree. We'd made massive changes.

"Hey, it'll be fine," Dodie assured me. "The Foster sisters will never end up as bag ladies. The three of us survived a whole lot worse than a cash flow problem."

Yeah, we'd survived a dysfunctional childhood and, in my case, a dysfunctional adulthood, emerging as survivors.

Dodie shifted in her chair, a sure sign she had more to say.

Placing my forearms on the desk and leaning forward, I scrutinized her face. "Okay, enough about our money problems. What brings you to my office when you have high-maintenance chefs and hysterical housekeeping staff to manage?"

"This may knock your bra off, so please stay calm," she said.

My blood pressure spiked into the red-alert zone. "Of course," I replied.

"Clara has to take a couple of weeks personal time, maybe more."

My tongue glued itself to the roof of my mouth. Clara, the youngest of the Foster sisters, was widowed twenty years ago at age forty. She has turbo-charged people skills and the kindest heart in the world. She also produced Wendy, our beloved niece. Because of Clara's ability to interact with guests without getting up their noses, she holds the vital position of events manager, and is currently in charge of our horse breeding symposium.

5

Although not in her job description, she also smooths any feathers Dodie or I may have ruffled.

I shook my head. "No way." As the impact sank in, I increased the volume. "Clara handles our events. She can't leave us high and dry two days before the symposium."

"I'm hungry." Dodie stood and eyed the cookies. "I need a snack to tide me over."

Sensing my sister's next move, I averted my eyes while she bent over to make another selection. She scarfed down two more before returning to her chair. A mouthful of cookie muffled her next words, but I made out, "Clara has already packed, booked her flight out of Calgary, and is writing notes for you as we speak."

I tried not to hyperventilate. "What can possibly be more important than a symposium that's our last chance to save the ranch?"

At that point, Clara burst into my office, her curly gray hair, normally elegant, scraped into a messy ponytail. She wrangled a rolling suitcase behind her and stopped long enough to blurt, "Wendy needs me! I'll be back as soon as Eric returns from Paris. I left you notes about the symposium." She flung a yellow pad covered with her barely legible handwriting on my desk, then whipped her suitcase around to flee.

"Stop!" Panic gave my command a sky-is-falling quality. "What happened?" Wendy was Clara's daughter and my beloved niece who lived in Vancouver.

Clara actually stopped.

A horn blared outside.

"What's wrong? Where are you going? You can't leave like this."

The honking grew more insistent.

Clara ticked the details off her fingers. "Wendy was thrown off her horse. Hubby's gone for two weeks. Kids are frantic and so are the neighbors who took them in. Gotta go." And she left.

In my distress, I nearly said a word no nice woman repeats. Two, actually, but I restrained myself. Clara had insisted Dodie and I stop splashin' the Big F around, explaining how guests don't appreciate staff who curse a blue streak. Seeing the wisdom of her objection, we agreed to stop swearing.

Remembering our pact, I settled on, "Holy moly. That's terrible. I hope Wendy's okay. I'll phone Clara tomorrow morning." In a reflex motion, I reached over to grab a cookie and popped half of it into my mouth. A burst of buttery sweetness improved my perspective. After weighing my options, I said to Dodie, "We'll get along fine without Clara. You can step in for her. If necessary I'll help with staff issues."

Dodie's eyebrows drew together. "Nope. This upcoming symposium is too important. You need to do it."

"I'm too old," I shot back.

Although I was pushing sixty-four, I'd agreed to fill two positions at Grizzly Gulch. My background as an accountant made me the logical choice as the chief financial officer for our new venture, but general manager, not so much. I suspected my sisters had confused bossiness with leadership skills. I'd accepted the GM position because I'd be safe from public speaking and horses. The events manager, on the other hand, was expected to give speeches and make nice with trail horses on a daily basis.

"We need an events manager and you're best suited for the job."

I shuddered. The stench of manure always triggered my gag reflex, and those hooves and long, equine teeth could inflict untold damage. Not to mention I would rather have my eyes poked out with a blunt stick than deliver the daily spiel about upcoming activities.

"It's sweet of you to ask, but thank you, no," I said, pretending I had a choice in the matter. "I'm no fun. You're perfect for the job. Guests love you."

"Except when they hate me. You do remember what happened last time I covered for Clara, eh?"

Dodie had a point. Cornered by a guest who'd grumbled about manure in the stable, she'd smiled sweetly and assured the guest she'd be delighted to housebreak all thirty-eight horses. In the meantime, she would instruct the wranglers to diaper every single one of those hairy manure-machines at bedtime. Old tablecloths and duct tape should work nicely. The conversation had thundered downhill from there.

"You've gotta take one for the team, Abs," Dodie said. "I already told Clara you'd replace her. It's not like it's forever."

A chill ran down my spine. We sat there, quiet, my brain darting to and fro like a caged ferret, seeking a way to avoid acting as the events manager.

Dodie's voice shattered the long silence. "Meditating, are we?"

I narrowed my eyes. "My arthritis is acting up."

"Anyone fit enough to join the Hale and Hearty Karate League can handle a few guests." She paused. "Got any real excuses?"

Even in my terror, I recognized that parachuting Dodie in as events manager was a bad idea. As GM, it was my duty to place the ranch's welfare above personal phobias. Resigned to my fate, I suppressed a sigh and even forced a wobbly smile. "Very well. Events manager it is," I said evenly, unwilling to show weakness, even to Dodie, by confessing that horses and speech delivery scared me spitless.

I planned to take those secrets to the grave.

"At least I won't need to get too involved with the symposium," I said, trying to find a nugget of optimism. "Clara's been collaborating with Muffy Walton. Seems Muffy plans to do all the heavy lifting. She'll even be staying here in case guests have questions. I don't want to tread on her toes."

Muffy owned a nearby ranch, a phony smile, and a millionaire husband. I was convinced she hid dark secrets behind her mask of perfection.

Dodie gave an impressive eye-roll. "Muffy's a spoiled socialite pretending to be a rancher. Does she know the basics of horse breeding?"

I shrugged. "She studied animal science at the University of Alberta. It was her idea to collaborate with us on the equine breeding symposium, with us providing the guests as willing students for her workshops. She invited her classmates to attend, even placed ads in the *Big Sky Equine News* to target all the horse ranchers in Alberta. We should be grateful to her."

"What's in it for Muffy?"

"Now that she's rich, she owns racehorses. Horse breeding services are a bonus spinoff. Muffy needs customers for the semen she collects."

Dodie snickered. "That's not a sentence you hear every day."

I frowned. "It's a win-win. We get off-season guests and, hopefully, great reviews leading to more bookings. Muffy publicizes her horse breeding business and drums up new clients for her artificial insemination service."

"Somehow, I can't picture Muffy delivering a semen collection demo."

"Her trainer's helping with the hands-on workshops."

"The broody but gorgeous Luc Lacroix?" Dodie waggled her eyebrows. "Word is he's amazing with the hands-on stuff, and I don't mean with horses, if you get my drift."

I frowned. "You shouldn't talk that way about a business associate."

Dodie grinned, displaying an excellent set of choppers. "You're such a serious puppy, Abby, but I love you anyway." I found myself enveloped in a warm, fragrant hug. "It'll be fine. Clara asked me to remind you about a meeting she's scheduled with the owner of an outfit called The Crazy Cow."

"What's that about?"

"No idea. It's in her notes. She also mentioned that Zeke offered to help in every way possible."

My face warmed up. Zeke Robinson was our sexy silver fox of a barn manager. As I imagined all the ways he could help, my pulse skyrocketed. Try as I might, I was unable to forget he'd placed the Big O within striking distance, an event I'd thought was no longer achievable. As if to remind me, my fun parts gave a mighty throb.

"Great," I said weakly, standing to relieve the pressure.

Oblivious of my inner turmoil, Dodie headed for the cookies on her way out. When she bent over, her lycra-clad buttocks quivered, exerting immense pressure on her poor leggings. The fabric thinned, then parted, a horrifying yet fascinating sight.

The rip started slowly, widened, and accelerated, until ground zero was exposed.

"Oh, look. I can see the full moon," I managed to choke out. "Crack me a smile."

Clasping her hands to her ass, Dodie straightened with a lurch that made her wobbly bits—in other words, pretty much everything—jiggle. She slitted her eyes at me. "Stop making fun of me, or I'll—"

"What? Show me Uranus?"

We both doubled over with mirth.

Gasping for breath, I recovered enough to say, "You'll need new leggings for Saturday. You can't subject our guests to the trauma of a repeat performance. Imagine the reviews."

Next week had to be perfect. Our future hinged on achieving glowing reviews.

Chapter 2:
The Big Day Arrives

T wo days later I catapulted out of bed. Saturday was Day One of our equine breeding symposium, and we expected thirty-eight participants. After a quick shower followed by a quicker breakfast of bran buds and coffee, I fussed with my shoulder-length bob, boosting its volume with extra product and ruthlessly wielding a curling iron. Satisfied my ash blonde highlights and caramel-toned lowlights disguised those pesky white strands, I tackled my outfit. First, I selected a freshly-ironed plaid shirt, which I tucked into black designer jeans containing plenty of lycra. I buckled on a tooled leather belt and slipped into a black leather vest. After adding hoop earrings and ankle boots with a heel high enough to slenderize my legs but not so ridiculous as to cripple me, I assessed myself in a full-length mirror.

Not bad for an old broad, if I did say so myself. Definitely un-nun-like. I looked like a successful owner, CEO, and GM. Although my poundage had hit a new peak, black was slimming, and the vest camouflaged a thickening waistline. Better still, my legs were long enough to fool people into thinking my ass and thighs verged on normal.

To ensure a smooth check-in process, Dodie and I were registering everyone ourselves. Since most of the regular guest services staff were rookies, we assigned them alternate tasks, such as parking lot greeters, flower arrangers, or spa attendants.

I reached the reception area at 9:10 a.m., twenty minutes early. Hey, promptness matters. Dodie was nowhere in sight, likely primping in her apartment on the second floor of the main lodge, sandwiched between Clara's and mine. I seated myself behind the check-in counter and surveyed our newly-renovated lobby. A cathedral ceiling soared above terra-cotta tile flooring and subtle-hued area rugs. Floor-to-ceiling windows along the front admitted plenty of natural light. Chandeliers and recessed wall sconces added soft illumination.

The few items we'd kept from the original lobby were a jarring note in a five-star establishment. I'd begged my sisters to sell these trophies on eBay, but Clara insisted Uncle Benny would turn in his grave. Consequently, glassy-eyed animal heads, mainly elk and deer, dotted the walls along with a fish that sang *Don't Worry, Be Happy* when you pressed a button. A moose head with a colossal antler spread occupied the spot of honor above the stone fireplace.

I doubted Uncle Benny, being dead, gave a hairy rat's ankle about what we did with the heads.

I surveyed the check-in area. Hallelujah. Dodie had remembered to set a bowl of my favorite chocolate truffles on the counter. Unwrapping one and letting it melt in my mouth, I savored the sweet creaminess. Next, I stacked four notepads, aligning the edges with precision. After firing up both computers, I arranged a box of pens in a mug and made sure everything else was ready for guest check-in. Seeing no sign of Dodie, I pulled out my horror novel, hoping to calm my nerves.

Fifteen minutes later, the lobby door opened. After a long pause at the threshold, Dodie grimaced then hobbled inside. She wore skin-tight jeans, amazing knee-high boots, and another flowy top, this one tie-dyed in shades of magenta. On noticing me behind the counter, she switched on a bright smile and straightened. Her heels made little clicking noises on the tiles.

"Whatcha reading?" she yelled. "*Financial Planning for Dummies?*"

"Nope. *Hard, Hung, and Horny: A Tender Love Story.* You can borrow it."

"Groovy." She sucked in an audible breath and kept on walking with an odd stiff-legged gait, flared nostrils, and fixed expression.

"You look like you're passing a kidney stone," I observed.

"You have a ... remarkable way with ... words," she said, staggering the last few steps. Once behind the counter, she flung herself into her chair with a grunt.

"That was a geezer-grunt," I said. "What's wrong?"

After a lengthy pause, she said, "Turns out cramming this year's booty into last year's jeans is the mistake that keeps on punishing."

Once her words sank in, my effort to swallow my laughter resulted in an explosive snort.

Dodie scowled at me. "I always suspected you were a heartless bitch."

"Those skinny jeans are the reason you're late. Am I right?"

"Yeah. I'd planned to arrive early, but it took me half an hour and every muscle I own to close the zipper. I had to lie flat on my back. Came close to blowing an artery. Luckily my top hides the overflow." She grabbed a handful of flesh to illustrate.

"Uh-huh."

"I bought this at *Happy Hippy Clothing Co*. Cool, eh?" She adjusted the tunic top over her rippling mid-section and finger-fluffed her white hair, which was gelled into spikes with a magenta streak added.

In spite of her weight, she looked fun, funky, and much younger than her age. Maybe I should consider changing my hairdo, too. I'd had the same one for forty years.

"You look great and so does your matching hair. Why are you limping?"

"I didn't have time to buy new leggings. These jeans are tighter than Spanx on a Sumo wrestler. My feet and ankles have ballooned two shoe sizes due to compression. The boots were snug to begin with, and now they feel like mediaeval torture devices."

"God help you if you have to pee."

"Didn't think of that. I'll need your help."

"There are some lines I won't cross. That's one." Frowning, I studied Dodie's face. "You're sweating, beet-red, and breathing hard. What else is going on? It's more than the jeans."

Dodie hesitated a beat and muttered, "It's my good parts, eh? Those fancy bits we never mention in polite company."

"What about them?"

"They're, um, stimulated." She gave a slight squirm and winced. "Yowza. Remind me to sit still. What if they never return to normal?"

My screech of laughter echoed off the cathedral ceiling. When I got myself under control, I said, "I'm sure your lady-parts will settle down once you wear looser pants."

"Great beauty comes with great sacrifice," she said loftily.

I fought the urge to snort. "I have a teeny-tiny favor to ask," I said, steering the subject away from her beleaguered lady-parts to a matter of greater concern to me.

"Ask away."

"If Zeke walks in, help me make conversation. I get tongue-tied around the man. Mostly all I can l think of is how much I want to jump his bones, and that would be a huge mistake. It's been fifteen years since my divorce. Thanks to my therapist, I'm finally feeling normal. I have no wish to get serious with anyone again."

Professor Elliot Fitzgerald Hutton was my gorgeous, brilliant, and charismatic ex-husband. He was also a high-functioning alcoholic who delighted in slapping his wife around, with a little strangulation on the side for variety's sake.

Dodie raised a skeptical eyebrow. "We've discussed this. Many times. Zeke's a far better choice than your ex-husband and those other control freaks you dated before your marriage. They all reminded me of our late daddy."

Her Freudian implication didn't escape me, but I wasn't up to examining it. I folded my arms across my chest. "Mixing business with pleasure is a huge mistake."

"You sound exactly like Dad. He only said that to throw Mom off the scent. Too bad he didn't practice what he preached."

Since I couldn't bring myself to discuss my father, my ex-husband, or any other abusive, controlling, and cheating man from my past, I responded, "I can't date an employee. It wouldn't be right."

She examined my face. "Did you and Zeke finally get it on?"

Fudge nuggets. Was it that obvious?

Dodie and I had similar man problems. After years of therapy, I'd finally recovered from an abusive childhood and a handful of bad dates followed by a toxic marriage that nearly destroyed me. Dodie, too, had left home and gravitated into the arms of unsuitable men, but she'd never been dumb enough to marry. She now claimed that family, friends, and career were all she needed. Clara was the only one of us who'd enjoyed a happy marriage and children. Ironically, she was now a grieving widow.

I uncrossed my arms and confessed, "Let's just say Zeke and I got carried away after last week's line dancing." I explained how, as a grand finale, I'd let him sweet-talk me into viewing his new living quarters off the barn. One thing had led to another. After he'd rounded third base and we were halfway to home plate, closing in on the point of no return, my phone chimed with Clara's ringtone. Fearing trouble, I made the mistake of answering. All she wanted was some girl-talk, but the call restored my sanity. I'd broken my self-imposed rule—never, ever, date an employee. Worst of all, my time with Zeke had been wonderful, even effortless. But involvement would be another mistake.

Dodie said, "I fail to see the problem."

"I can't date a younger man who's an employee to boot. What if we break up? What if I'm too old for him? What if I want to fire him? What if I refuse him a raise? What if I double his salary? I can go on and on."

"Please don't. You're over-analyzing again. I'm sure you two can work it out. Zeke's kind, loyal, and seriously hot. I bet he's all sinewy muscle under those cowboy getups he wears. And he's the perfect age for you. Old enough to have stuff in common, young enough to get it up without chemical assistance."

I was so busy picturing those sinewy muscles, I paid no attention to the front door opening. Even the gust of unseasonably warm air swirling through the lobby and around my ankles failed to distract me.

With a sharp nudge, Dodie whispered, "It's the power couple of Moose Corner."

Muffy and Franklin Walton were approaching the check-in desk. Well-worn jeans and a nondescript sweatshirt couldn't disguise Franklin's careless confidence that spelled wealth and power. His rumpled hair, graying at the temples, emphasized his appeal. Muffy was as glamorous as a movie star. She wore western chic, paired with boots to die for, a wide leather belt studded with turquoise stones, and gobs of chunky turquoise jewelry.

Because Muffy was instrumental in the symposium, both for the vision and the delivery, I dug deep into my acting skills to give them a warm welcome. "Muffy, Franklin. Good to see you again."

"Abby," Muffy said, her voice cool. "Dodie, too. How nice. I was sorry to hear Clara won't be attending the symposium."

I forced myself to be gracious. "I realize I'm a poor substitute for Clara, but you have no idea how much I'm looking forward to working with you on the symposium. And Franklin, I didn't realize you were joining us. What a lovely surprise."

Franklin's smile displayed perfectly capped, unnaturally white teeth. "Much as I would love to attend the symposium, I'm off on a business trip."

With a toss of blonde tresses, Muffy explained, "I'm driving Franklin to the airport. I wanted to stop here first to make sure Clara told you the semen collection demo is tomorrow afternoon."

"She did." I fully intended to skip the demo seeing as how it involved horses.

Muffy appealed to her husband. "I wish you'd cancel the trip for once, dear."

Franklin's chuckle sounded forced. "Duty calls, my love. The oil industry doesn't manage itself. I'll call you from Riyadh to let you know my return date. If all goes well with the Saudis, I'll be home within the month. In the meantime, don't forget you're going to dismiss that horse trainer you hired."

Muffy glanced at us and pulled Franklin aside, presumably to talk privately. I didn't inform her of the acoustical anomaly, possibly caused by the cathedral ceiling, that carried the faintest whisper to the check-in counter with remarkable clarity. Bursting with curiosity, I strained to listen, certain Dodie did the same.

"I can't fire Luc for no reason," Muffy said. Although she kept her voice low, every word came through, loud and clear. "You never listen. He's the best in the business, and we're old friends. I trust him."

We pretended to be busy scribbling notes and fake-typing.

Franklin voice didn't carry as well as his wife's, but I made out, "*Mumble* … I don't trust him one iota … *mumble* … want him gone by tonight."

"Are you out of your mind?" Muffy hit high-C before she caught herself and lowered her voice. "I need Luc for the workshops, especially tomorrow's demo."

Franklin frowned. "*Mumble* … was charged with horse drugging … *mumble*."

"There was no conviction. Luc swore the charges were bogus."

Her remark must have pushed a button because he roared, "Then please explain why our racehorses only started winning after you hired him."

"Because he's the finest trainer in Alberta." Muffy paused, then asked,

"Are you accusing me of letting Luc drug my horses?" In my peripheral vision, I noted her face had whitened.

I couldn't make out Franklin's next words, but her reply carried, loud and clear. "I would never hire a horse drugger. You know how much I love those horses, but I love you even more."

He quirked one eyebrow.

Seemingly unaware of the avid audience, she gripped his arm. "If any tests proved our horses were winning races due to Luc's drugging, the scandal would ruin your reputation. I would never do that to you."

He removed his wife's hand from his arm and leaned closer. All I was able to I make out was, "*Mumble* ... divorce ... *mumble* ... iron-clad prenup."

As if Franklin hadn't just threatened Muffy with divorce, he raised his voice and said pleasantly, "I'll call once I arrive, dear. The trainer had better be gone. And don't bother driving me to the airport. I'll call a cab." After a quick glance at his Rolex, he pulled put his phone and strode away, leaving her standing in the lobby.

Misery aged Muffy by a decade. She blinked away tears.

I felt an unexpected connection, especially when she displayed a hint of vulnerability, saying, "I'm sorry we aired our dirty laundry in front of you."

"We all go through rough patches," I assured her, having experienced more than my share.

"Franklin could easily have stayed home, but he'd rather work. All he thinks about is the bottom line, business decisions, and his precious board meetings. That's why I pulled together this horse breeding symposium, to impress him, maybe prove I'm not an airhead. Without Luc, I can't go ahead with the demo. Lancelot—he's the stallion we're using for the demo—won't let anyone else near him."

Luc was crucial to our equine breeding symposium. The last thing I wanted was to lose him before the semen collection demo. "Riyadh's on the other side of the world," I pointed out. "Gives you a couple of days breathing space, yes?"

Muffy's smile looked forced. "You're right. Thank you. Please have a porter take the luggage to my quarters. I need to unwind and prepare for the symposium. Since you don't need me for the guided tour, I'll skip it."

She marched away, leaving me feeling unsettled. Muffy's guests, particularly her classmates, would expect to see her smiling face as soon as they arrived.

Dodie murmured, "Hunk alert," causing me to jump.

Slanting a glance at the door, I felt my pulse quicken. "Zeke," I whispered, suddenly breathless. "Remember, you promised to help with the conversation and keep me in line." I studied my computer screen, ignoring the lanky cowboy slouched in the doorway. It was difficult because my good parts throbbed in a merry conga rhythm.

Dodie whispered, "You're outta your mind if you let this one get away."

"What part of, 'I don't need another man in my life,' did you not understand?" I said under my breath, continuing to fake-type like crazy.

Dodie whispered, "In that case, stop drooling on the keyboard."

"Can't help it," I murmured back. "He's got everything I like rolled up into one smokin' hot package."

"Speaking of package—"

"Shhhh."

"Ladies," Zeke drawled.

Heat rose in my cheeks as I met his penetrating gaze. Zeke had a rugged face, not classically handsome, but definitely appealing. Lust coursed through my body, leaving me limp and speechless.

His piercing dark eyes softened under craggy brows. Fine lines radiated out from his eyes, testament to a life spent outdoors. He removed his Stetson, revealing dark hair liberally streaked with white. "Hi, gorgeous. Clara explained everything before she left for Vancouver. I understand you're helping with the symposium." He clasped my hand in both of his. His hands were a little rough, nicely warm, and a whole lot strong. He was too close, his touch far too sensual.

"Uh ..." I said, Rendered inarticulate by lust.

Dodie rescued me. "Abby's happy to step in."

Zeke leaned toward me, oozing sex appeal. "I'll stay real close," he murmured. "If you need anything, and I mean *anything*, day or night, you call me."

My lady-parts respond with such enthusiasm, I feared I would achieve solo liftoff.

"I'll make sure she does," Dodie advised Zeke, ignoring my glare.

"Thanks." He winked at her and angled toward me once more. "You look real nice today."

His killer smile fried several million of my brain cells. The husky quality of his voice made me feel as though I was the sexiest creature in the world. If not already seated, I'd have melted onto the floor.

"Abby thanks you," Dodie said helpfully.

He nodded. "A wrangler reported a downed fence, so I'd best get moving." He tipped his hat. "Shouldn't take more'n an hour. I'll be back in time for the guided tour."

His departure left me limp and quivery.

Dodie stretched and wandered over to the window. "I wonder where all the guests are." She peered outside. "Oops. I spoke too soon. Here comes someone now."

"I need a moment," I mumbled.

"Pull yourself together," Dodie ordered. "Zeke's having words with some dude who waylaid him, but I can't hear what they're saying."

I snapped out of my lust-induced trance to join Dodie at the window. Zeke was nose-to-nose with a tall, sharp-featured cowboy at least two decades his junior.

"Who's Mr. Hot-Dark-and-Broody?" Dodie asked.

"Luc Lacroix. He's the trainer Franklin ordered Muffy to fire." I strained to listen.

Vibrating with impatience, Dodie nudged me. "What are they saying?"

Triple-glazed windows muffled the voices, but my hearing was top-notch. "You really need to get your hearing tested. With you yapping in my ear, I didn't catch everything, but Luc's yelling at him about problems in the barn where Lancelot is stabled, something about intruders and security issues." I paused to listen. "Zeke's telling him to go get some sleep and sober up."

After another acrimonious exchange, Luc strode off, his long legs carrying him out of my line of sight. Zeke headed in the opposite direction.

"You gonna tell Muffy?" Dodie asked after we returned to our chairs.

Before I had a chance to respond, Luc burst into the lobby through the door from the kitchen area. Clearly he'd fooled Zeke by circling around the main lodge and entering through the delivery entrance.

He swayed in the doorway and steadied himself before staggering toward us. The air grew heavy with whisky fumes, testosterone, and Hugo Boss.

I slipped my hand into my pocket and clutched my ever-present canister of bear spray, which is pepper spray on steroids. We women of a certain age know how to protect ourselves.

"Ladies," he said, slurring the word. "Luc Lacroix, Ms. Walton's trainer."

"We know who you are," I answered, unsmiling

"Do either of you know where Muffy is?" he asked. "I need to talk to her."

I shrugged. "I'm sorry, but Ms. Walton isn't available."

Dodie leaned forward and sniffed the air like a hound. "You smell like a distillery. Go sleep it off."

Using the counter to support his weight, he leaned closer to get in her face. "Mind your own business, lady."

In spite of the fact that Luc was drunk and possibly dangerous, Dodie said, "Does Muffy know you drink on the job?" She was clearly ready to rumble.

"Relax. Both of you," I ordered, elbowing Dodie.

The air crackled with anger. Luc's hawk-like features contorted as he went nose-to-nose with Dodie. "If I were you, I'd listen to your geriatric sister."

Dodie's complexion matched her magenta top. I gave her a warning kick.

Too far gone to heed me, Dodie rose from her chair. "You're tap-dancing on my last nerve, buster, so do yourself a favor. Go sleep it off."

A muscle in his jaw bunched. It crossed my mind he'd have no problem hitting a woman. Under the counter, I eased the canister from my pocket and ever-so-gently flipped its safety clip. This geriatric would give him more than he bargained for.

I was raising my hand to aim the spray at Luc's eyes, when a woman's musical voice penetrated the red haze clouding my brain.

"Luc Lacroix. You haven't changed. Not one little bit. Remember me?"

Chapter 3:
More Suspects Arrive

A T THE WOMAN'S WORDS, SANITY returned. I, who preferred to analyze a situation rather than overreact, had been a mere finger-twitch away from pepper-spraying Luc Lacroix, one of our symposium's key players. I replaced the canister and stood to greet the woman.

Oblivious of his narrow escape, Luc gaped as the most beautiful woman in the world approached the counter, her hair a cascade of burnished bronze that caressed sculpted cheekbones before tumbling over her shoulders.

"Wow," Dodie said softly. "I wonder who she is."

The woman was tall, slim, and curvy in all the right places. I sighed with envy as she glided toward us, her impossibly long legs making short work of the distance.

She stopped directly in front of Luc. "Do you recognize me now?"

Luc scrutinized the woman's face. "You look familiar. Give me a clue."

"Animal Sciences, class of '99."

"Impossible. I would remember someone as beautiful as you." He offered her a lazy smile.

"I imagine Muffy will have no problem remembering me," the goddess murmured.

Muffy's name seemed to trigger a spark of recognition. His eyes widened. "Veronica Melville? No way." He backed off a step, all trace of flirtation erased.

"Bingo. Muffy sent me an invitation. I own a breeding ranch near High River. The symposium sounds fascinating."

"You look … different."

She ignored his comment. "The invitation mentioned you were a presenter, and I thought to myself, wouldn't it be fun to play a game of catch-up with Luc and Muffy?"

He turned pale under his tan. "Fun. Yeah. That's one way to describe it. Great to see you again." He made a speedy getaway.

Veronica's gaze followed his exit, a trace of bitterness twisting her mouth. "Once a jerk, always a jerk. Someone should teach him a lesson."

Guessing Dodie's intent to quiz the woman, I thwarted a grilling by starting the check-in process, asking for a credit card and explaining about the buffet lunch followed by a guided tour. Dodie was forced to quit eavesdropping and process the next guests.

"Where's Muffy?" Veronica asked me.

"She's taking care of some last-minute details," I hedged.

"I expected her to greet her classmates, especially after issuing a personal invitation for the symposium. Seems she hasn't changed a bit either."

"I'm sure she'll return soon. She was looking forward to seeing everyone."

"Will Luc accompany the guided tour?"

Veronica's questions indicated a woman on a mission rather than fun and games with old friends. I replied, "He's participating, yes."

"In that case, I'll be there."

"Wonderful. A porter will bring your luggage to your cabin." I beckoned to a young man, who hovered near the entrance, and gave him the cabin number.

Veronica bestowed a brilliant smile on him and sashayed toward the door.

Dodie had finished processing three middle-aged couples and started in on another while I checked in a party of four in record time. Once the rush was over, Dodie sank to her chair and said, "I don't think Veronica's here for the symposium."

"Me, neither. Maybe—" I stopped in mid-sentence, distracted by a towering colossus of a woman wearing a slouchy bush hat jammed over crinkly orange hair. The fabric of her khaki safari shirt and cargo pants strained to contain her bulky frame. She stomped toward us bearing a pair of suitcases.

"I'm Harmony Parrish," the woman announced, her stony gaze bouncing from one severed animal head on the walls to another. Who knew the human mouth had the ability to pucker up in a remarkable imitation of a beagle's butt?

Hearing my sister's shaky intake of breath beside me, I didn't dare look at her for fear a bray of laughter would explode. I rushed through the check-in process. "Do you have any questions while we wait for the porter?" I asked, sliding a glance at Dodie. My heart sank. Her scarlet face signalled repressed mirth.

Harmony studied the moose head over the fireplace for a long beat. Every pore of her body oozed condemnation. "You bet your sweet patootie I have questions. Do you realize some psycho-loser shot these magnificent animals to bolster his ego?"

Remembering the importance of the symposium, I opened my mouth to make a soothing statement, but Dodie jumped to her feet, the fire of battle in her eyes. "And here I thought it was because natural predators disappeared, shoved out or killed by humans, allowing the remaining wild species to overpopulate the environment. A clean shot saves them from starvation or disease and prevents untold car accidents." Clearly, Dodie had forgotten the customer was always right.

Harmony's brows slammed together. "Hogwash. Guns are the penis-extenders of the under-endowed."

I'd never thought of guns that way, but it was a notion worth considering. Dodie found her voice first. "Aren't women allowed to own guns too?"

"I get it. You're a pair of penis-wannabes." Harmony's mouth pursed again, imploding into a tight 'O'.

The young porter wandered in at the exact moment Dodie responded using her outdoor voice, "I never, *ever*, wanted to own a penis, thank you very much. Unlike some, I'm more than happy with a vagina."

The word "vagina" reverberated throughout the lobby.

"Cabin 15-B," I told the porter.

His face turned bright scarlet as he tossed Harmony's suitcases onto a trolley and wheeled it out the door at lightning speed.

I transitioned into damage-control mode, laying a hand on Harmony's freckled arm. "Dodie didn't mean to offend you by defending hunters, hon. Arguing is her hobby." I gave my sister the stink-eye. "*Isn't it?*"

Picking up on her cue, Dodie had the grace to look abashed. "Yeah. I'm sorry I got carried away. See, I'm practising for the local debating club.

Truth be told, I hate guns, love animals. I even capture spiders and transfer them outside."

"It's all true," I confirmed. "You're an animal rights activist, yes?"

"Yeah, I'm a volunteer for PETA," Harmony said more calmly. "People for the Ethical Treatment of Animals."

"How wonderful," I said, intent on salvaging an awkward situation. "I've already notified the chef you're a vegan. Instead of steak tonight, you're getting marinated tofu with quinoa pilaf and a medley of braised veggies."

Harmony's expression grew less ominous. "It sounds delicious. Thank you."

"You're most welcome. We try to accommodate everyone's needs."

"Too bad Luc Lacroix didn't get the memo."

"Excuse me?"

"He had the gall to kick me out of the barn when I was monitoring the wellbeing of the horses. I'm betting his boss didn't check out his shady past before hiring him."

"What do you mean?"

"Haven't you heard?" Harmony lowered her voice. "Luc Lacroix has a reputation for horse drugging to win races. If he tries any more funny stuff, you'd better stand back because I intend to nail him." With that declaration, Harmony departed.

As soon as she'd disappeared, I turned to Dodie with a straight face. "Think that'll be before or after the lad recovers from the trauma of picturing your vagina?"

We wheezed with laughter. Once we subsided, we sat. Dodie was quivering for a good gossip. "Do you think it's true? Is Luc drugging Muffy's racehorses?"

"She's sure had a lot of wins recently."

"And what about—" Dodie chopped off the question when another guest, approached the lobby door. "Incoming. We'll talk later."

The guest dropped two suitcases onto the floor and swept a melted chocolate gaze around the lobby. His body was buff, his jaw chiseled, and his hair mostly pepper with an attractive sprinkle of salt. He looked expensive, and, as he drew closer, I discovered he even smelled expensive. Yet I felt no twinge of attraction. Bad sign. Zeke had spoiled me for other men. I stood and welcomed the man.

He removed his Stetson. "Clay Davis. Nice place you have here." He smiled, proving he still had all his teeth. "I'm here for the horse breeding symposium."

"Let's get you checked in, Mr. Davis. I'll find someone to bring the luggage to your cabin right away."

"Call me Clay. Please."

While Dodie ogled, I did what needed to be done and buzzed for a porter.

Clay was halfway to the door, when he turned and said, "One more thing. I'm acquainted with one of the presenters. Name's Luc Lacroix. I have a business matter to discuss with him. Is he around?"

Although burning with curiosity, I kept my reply professional. "You might catch him at the stables. If not, he'll join us after lunch for the guided tour."

"I'll mosey on over to the stables right now." He nodded to us. "Ladies."

"I wonder what that's all about," I mused as he walked out the door.

For the next fifteen minutes, we registered more guests, explaining the fun that lay ahead, taking their credit card, and sending them off to their cabins. When the last of a group of three friends departed, a petite woman paused inside the doorway.

"Hello-o-o," she trilled, smoothing down a miniskirt which, in my opinion, was better suited for a twenty-something. "If I'm late, I apologize for being a nuisance." She tap-tapped toward the check-in desk on a pair of four-inch stilettos.

Women who trilled generally headed my to-be-avoided list, but this one seemed friendly. Noting Dodie's curled lip, as if she'd detected a bad smell, I stepped in hastily. "No problem at all. Welcome to Grizzly Gulch."

"I'm Tess Jenkins," the woman chirped. "My stars, the cowboys around here sure are handsome. I plan to enjoy every single second of this fabulous week."

Although she was relatively wrinkle-free, I gauged her to be around my age. The highlighted hair, crêpey neck, and sun-spotted hands were dead giveaways.

"That's wonderful, Tess." I grinned at the newcomer's enthusiasm and went into my spiel. Dodie redeemed herself by reciting details of the afternoon ahead. It might have been my imagination, but she seemed out-of-sorts.

"Everything sounds fantastic." Tess's smile encompassed the whole lobby in its brilliance. "I must tell you, this place is even lovelier than your website made it sound. Good golly, I'm ready to burst with excitement." Suddenly silent, she studied my face.

Self-conscious, I brushed back my hair. "Is everything okay?"

"Oh, my, yes. It's just that, well, you're a stunning woman. Those gorgeous blue eyes take on a green tint in this light, and I adore your outfit. Plaid is so versatile."

Dodie turned her head away to mutter, "Gag me," under her breath.

I kicked Dodie on the shin while saying, "Aren't you a doll? It's so nice someone around here notices." Ignoring what sounded like a low growl, I smiled at Tess. "What brings you to our little slice of cowboy paradise?"

Her giggle made me feel like the wittiest woman on earth.

"You're too cute, Abby. I'm here because I own the prettiest, gentlest mare in the whole, wide world. Ever since Duke—he was my darling husband—passed, Morning Glory is the love of my life. She deserves to experience the joys of motherhood, but those stallions can be so fierce. I was trying to decide what to do, and the next thing I knew, God answered my prayers with an advertisement about a horse breeding symposium in the *Big Sky Equine News*."

Seemly oblivious to Dodie's eye-roll, Tess said, "I hate to mention this, but I filled out the 'Special Needs' section on the intake form with 'Diabetes'. I know it's a bother, but I do hope the chef is aware of my condition."

I assured her the chef was, indeed, aware of her health issues and understood the dangers of hidden carbs to a diabetic.

While Dodie ignored us, Tess and I chit-chatted about the ranch. I found myself describing Grizzly Gulch's deluxe facilities, activities, and was starting in on the special equestrian programs when Dodie interrupted with, "I've called a porter."

Tess jumped guiltily. "Oh, dear. I'm monopolizing your time. You're both such fascinating women, I forgot you have other guests."

"Not at all," I assured her. "Do you have a credit card?"

"It's in here somewhere." Tess placed her purse, which was the size of a carry-on suitcase, onto the counter while she rummaged in it, muttering, "Where's my wallet?

Being nosy, I stood on tiptoe and craned my neck to peer inside. Because our aunt was diabetic, I recognized insulin paraphernalia such as boxes of glucose tabs (strawberry-kiwi soft chews), insulin pens, a blood glucose meter, and a box of spring-loaded lancets. I also glimpsed a flashlight, clippers, a collapsible saw, duct tape, containers, bottles, and more items I was unable to identify.

Tess looked at me, and a bright pink crept into her cheeks. She fished out the wallet, and snapped the clasp shut, saying, "Don't mind me. My purse is an extension of my medicine cabinet plus tool shed. I like to be prepared for any crisis."

Smiling, I dealt with the credit card and handed it back.

Tess walked away, turning to give us a cute little wave before disappearing.

Once she was gone, I whirled on Dodie, who was seated again and massaging her calf. "What was that about? And don't pretend you don't know what I mean. Our goal is to make guests feel welcome, not like intruders."

"What are you talking about?"

I parked myself in my chair. "Tess. You hated her."

"I didn't hate her. I don't trust her. She was buttering you up. Did you notice she didn't put her wallet away? I swear she didn't want you to see the weird stuff she carries in her purse."

"You're jealous because she complimented me."

"There's something 'off' about her."

"She was just being friendly." Actually, I liked her, and I don't usually warm up to people right away.

"I don't trust her, and you shouldn't either."

"Aw, you care. That's sweet." I scooted my chair over to Dodie and gave her a squeeze. "I may like Tess, but I *love* my sister."

Dodie turned a fiery red and shoved me away. "Don't go all gooey on me."

But I saw right through her. Dodie loved the hug.

A flurry of other guests captured our attention. We registered a group of women on a getaway, followed by several young couples who expressed more interest in partying than the symposium. I figured they would change their minds when they learned what was on tap for tomorrow's hands-on demo.

While I sent them off with the porter, Dodie examined the registration list. "Only one more set, a family of four," she crowed. "I hope they take their time, because we have a million things to discuss."

Our discussion, however, never got off the ground due to the sounds of squabbling, shrieks of childish laughter, and a deeper voice admonishing, "Boys, we're gonna turn around and go home if you don't stop farting."

"Hold that thought. Here they come," I said as a family of four exploded into the lobby. Leading the charge were two identical boys, who were around ten years old. The twins pretend-galloped around the lobby. The parents darted after their offspring in a futile attempt to corral the pair.

While I was considering the best way to eject them without incurring a lawsuit, Dodie stood and greeted the parents with, "Welcome to Grizzly Gulch. You must be the Wright family."

The mother said, "Yes we're the Wrights. I'm Sheila, my husband's called Big John, and the twins are Wes and Coop."

Big John roared, "Wes, Coop. Park your asses on those chairs." His voice was tremendous, unlike his tiny stature. He made a grab for his sons. The twins escaped and went their merry way, giggling and yelling about boobies. Women's boobies, horses' boobies, cows' boobies, boobies in general. It seemed boobies were a hot topic with ten-year-old boys.

Dodie lost no time dealing with the registration while Sheila engaged me in conversation. "I hope the mean cowboy from the stable won't be on the guided tour." She flipped her ponytail. "If he works here, he should be fired." She went on to describe the twins' confrontation in the stable with someone who could only be Luc. Naturally, her sons bore no part of the blame.

The boys, who were using their armpits to generate pretend-farts, darted outside. Big John stood at the door, yelling about tanning their hides, then swaggered to the reception desk in time to hear Sheila wrap up her complaint about Luc.

I eyed Big John warily. "I'm so sorry Luc frightened the boys. He's part of the symposium, not one of our employees, but I'll be sure to talk to his boss."

Sheila closed her eyes and moaned. "This is gonna be one very long week."

For everyone, I thought.

Sheila turned on her heel and pounded after her sons, with Big John close behind her.

With a simultaneous groan Dodie and I locked gazes. The week ahead promised many challenges.

"We need to discuss how to handle difficult guests," I said. "I want everything to be perfect."

"Maybe later," Dodie replied. "To achieve perfection, I need to slip into comfortable pants so my fun bits and I can recover before the guided tour begins."

Chapter 4:
A Rocky Start to Perfection

I T WAS A GLORIOUS AFTERNOON, warm with the pine-scented whisper of a breeze carrying the promise of spring. Thirty-eight guests were trickling onto the lawn to gather in clusters beside the main lodge. From my vantage point on the porch beside Dodie, I scanned the crowd for Zeke. Without him to lead the tour, we were in trouble. And if Luc didn't sober up and show his face by the time we reached the barn, guests who hadn't met him would feel short-changed. On the bright side, Dodie was wearing boots and jeans that actually fit. Her feet and lady-parts were happy, minimizing the possibility of X-rated comments.

I reached for my phone.

"Stop checking your phone," Dodie said. "It makes you look worried."

"I *am* worried. It's not like Zeke to be late. The fences must be in bad shape."

My anxiety increased when we overheard the gorgeous Veronica ask Big John, "Have you seen Luc Lacroix? He's going to wish he'd never messed with me."

"Get in line," Big John said. "I've got a bone to pick with him, myself."

His wife added, "You wouldn't believe how the jerk flipped out when he caught our kids exploring the barn. He terrified our sweet little boys. All they wanted to do was pet the horses."

"Speaking of boys," I murmured to Dodie, "have you seen them?"

"Not since check-in. I hope they're not tearing the place apart."

Harmony, who was clearly unaware we could hear every word from our vantage point on the porch, said, "Luc Lacroix was horrible when I checked out the horses." She lowered her voice. "He's a sly and devious man, you know."

Harmony's accusation triggered an outburst of questions, which Clay's arrival halted. He glowered at the group and said, "If this is a Lacroix-bashing session, I'm in. The bastard screwed me over in a business deal."

Just when I thought it couldn't get any worse, Big John hollered, "Boys. Where are you? Come here or you're getting a time-out."

"Yeah, like that'll work," Dodie whispered.

"Nothing's going right," I said in an undertone. "I wanted our guests to get a good impression of Grizzly Gulch, but it's *so* not happening."

She shrugged. "It might help if you apologized for the delay. I'm surprised you haven't done it already, seeing as how you're Canadian and all."

"Listen to you. Who said you didn't have people skills?" I summoned the guests.

Once they'd gathered around, I stood on the top step and raised my voice. "I apologize for the delay. We're waiting for Zeke and Luc to join us. I'm sure they'll arrive any minute."

"Where are they?" someone wanted to know. "We want to talk to Luc."

"Zeke's off repairing a fence. He'll be back soon," I said, hoping I was right. "Luc was up all night with a sick horse, so he took a quick nap." It was almost true, and sounded better than sleeping off a morning drunk.

Pouting prettily, Veronica massaged her temples. "A nap. That's a great idea. A half hour is all I need to get rid of this nasty headache." Her lips parted in a smile, revealing perfect teeth. She turned and sauntered in the direction of the cabins, her slim hips swaying so gracefully she seemed to float. I surmised she'd gone to find Luc.

A moment later, Tess blasted onto the scene, all smiles and panting as if she'd been running. Her energy and enthusiasm were a welcome change from everyone else's negativity.

"Sorry I'm late, Abby," she announced, "but tell me, pretty please, who is the older cowboy with those yummy brown eyes and lanky build?"

I raised one eyebrow. "That sounds like Zeke."

"Is he spoken for?"

I made a noble effort to maintain a neutral expression while squeezing my answer past the lump in my throat. "Not to my knowledge."

I assumed Tess hadn't sensed my discomfort because she babbled on. "I can always tell when a man likes me, and Zeke does. He smiled at me when I arrived. Woman to woman, the men I date are usually younger, but I'll make an exception in his case. Good golly, I could eat him up."

Fudge nuggets. Tess was planning to seduce Zeke. "Knock yourself out," I said through a clenched jaw.

Dodie nudged me. Too softly for anyone else to hear, she murmured, "You still feel Tess is a kindred spirit?"

"Not so much," I whispered back.

Tess started listing more of Zeke's attributes, but the arrival of Chef Armand, a man of great girth, talent, and temperament, curtailed conversation as he stormed from around the back of the building. He halted before us, a struggling twin dangling under each beefy arm.

"This cannot be tolerated," he announced, plopping the wriggling boys down in front of the porch while maintaining a tight grip on the scruff of each scrawny neck.

I descended the steps and walked toward them. As I drew near, the acrid odor of smoke tickled my nostrils.

"It was an accident," one twin whined, flailing his arms and kicking out. His sneakered foot connected with Armand's shin.

"*Merde*," the chef roared, exhibiting remarkable restraint. "These boys, they try to burn down the building. The parents, they must deal with these … these … *petits délinquants*." He inhaled deeply and bellowed, "*Immédiatement*."

Mottled red crept into Big John's face as he grabbed each boy's arm. Sheila offered parental apologies and promised her offspring wouldn't indulge in any more pranks.

Under my questioning, the full story emerged. Chef Armand had nabbed the boys behind the kitchen where they were stomping out flames licking the wooden steps. A line cook doused the fire while Armand, using unspecified methods, extracted a confession from the boys. They figured smoke from the pork ribs self-basting in the outdoor smoker would hide the smell of the stolen cigarette they'd shared. It might have worked too—if only they hadn't accidentally set some scattered wood chips alight.

At least, they claimed it was an accident.

Dodie opened her mouth to express her skepticism, but I frowned and whispered, "Don't make me give *you* a time-out."

"You're no fun," she countered. "You sound just like Mom."

I forced my rigid muscles to relax, but it was obvious the crowd was losing patience. Without physical restraint—and I suspected hog-tying guests was a lousy idea—I was helpless to stop an imminent exodus. As it was, five young couples and a family with three teenage girls slunk away, headed for the tennis courts. Several more couples straggled toward the bar.

I addressed the remaining guests. "We've waited long enough. Let's get this show on the road, eh?"

For the next twenty minutes, Dodie and I led guests around the ranch's most impressive features—a state-of-the-art conference room on the mezzanine level of the main lodge, followed by the campfire area, cookout and outdoor eating sites, and the racquet courts laid out beside the shuffleboard area. While recognizing that sooner or later, guests would demand to see the stables, I was pulling for later, so I made sure we avoided areas containing horses.

In spite of my mounting anxiety, I feigned serenity. Tess, on the other hand, was so jumpy she reminded me of a downed electric wire. She talked non-stop, barely stopping to breathe, and darted around bombarding everyone with questions and commentary.

Once the guests had wandered ahead to examine the luxury spa, which contained all the requisite bells and whistles, I figured it was safe to speak bluntly to Dodie without danger of being overheard. "You thinking what I'm thinking?" I asked, flicking a glance at Tess.

"Yep," Dodie answered. "No woman her age is that bouncy without chemical assistance."

By then, everyone had reached the swimming pool. We caught up with them at the moment Tess flung her arms into the air and hollered, "That pool sure is tempting." She promptly undid her belt and started in on her blouse buttons.

Wes yelled, "Hey, we're gonna see boobies," before Big John hustled his sons away.

I rocketed forward to the tune of my left hip's protest. Before Tess's girls swung loose, I took a firm grip on her arm and warned, "No swimming without a bathing suit."

"It's the rule," Dodie agreed.

"Party poopers," Tess said, scowling as she buttoned up.

This was beyond mere bounciness. Momentarily forgetting the guests strolling ahead after realizing the strip-tease was cancelled, I scrutinized Tess's dilated pupils.

"You been smokin' whacky-tobaccy?" I demanded.

Tess gave an eye-roll. "No, silly. Smoking's bad for the health." She giggled.

"She's definitely on something," Dodie said in an undertone. "Might be cocaine."

"Pluck a duck," I lamented under my breath. "I'm liking her less and less with each passing moment."

We each took an arm and half-carried, half-dragged Tess to re-join the group. I described the next attraction—a herd of dwarf goats we used for goat yoga, one of our most popular activities, though why people allow goats to bounce on their backs during Downward Dog escaped me. The goat pen was out of sight, directly behind a steep embankment. A dirt path zig-zagged to the top of the ridge.

"We'll take the road," I said. "It's roundabout, but a lot easier."

"Goats? Cool," Wes said. "C'mon, Coop."

Coop darted off to join his brother in a race for the hilltop.

"They'll be fine, dear," Big John said, clasping his wife's hand. "They can't get into mischief out here in the country."

Sheila, who looked relaxed for the first time since her arrival, said, "Okay."

"Famous last words," Dodie mumbled. "I hope he seized their lighter."

Reminded of the danger, I swung around to ask the parents to follow their offspring and keep an eye on them. They'd disappeared.

I frowned. "Where are Big John and Sheila?"

Brimming with indignation, Harmony snorted. "They took off. Those spoiled brats shouldn't be allowed near those poor, helpless animals. You must stop them."

Son of a beach. Ten to one, the parents had snuck off for afternoon delight. Or, more likely, a couple of stiff drinks. The lack of parental guidance triggered a flash of pity for the twins, who'd scrambled up the embankment to stand at the summit, silhouetted against the brilliant blue Alberta sky.

A child's voice hollered, "Hey! Cute goats."

"And a weird horse!" the other yelled.

"That doesn't look like a horse."

"It's a horse, doofus. I'm going in."

"Me, too," his brother agreed. "Ride 'em, cowboy."

They bolted over the rise and disappeared.

A trickle of apprehension skittered down my spine. I gripped Dodie's arm. "That's no horse. It's Larry the llama. We have to stop the boys before there's big trouble."

"How?" she asked.

"Like this." Raising my voice, I addressed the guests. "Excuse us, folks. Dodie and I will take the shortcut to make sure the boys are safe. I suggest you take the road." I wasted no time hustling Dodie toward the embankment. We started to climb.

"This is harder than our karate class," Dodie said, puffing along behind me.

I paused to catch my breath. "We need to hurry. I have no idea how dangerous llamas are, but I don't want to learn the hard way."

Llamas were supposed to be fantastic guard animals, protecting goats and sheep from coyotes, dogs, foxes and such, or at least warning owners of a larger predator like a bear or cougar.

Voices behind us prompted me to check over my shoulder. Tess was closing in fast. Unwilling to miss the action, the rest of the guests straggled up behind her.

Worried Tess, who'd overtaken Dodie, would trample me, I pumped harder to stay ahead. Once I reached the summit, I groaned. Below us, the twins fiddled with the gate while bleating goats clustered around a large white animal.

Tess halted beside me and squinted at the scene laid out below. "That's one humongous goat."

"It's not a goat. It's a llama," I informed her.

Tess doubled up with a case of the giggles. "There are no llamas in Alberta."

The high-pitched, pulsating call of an enraged llama pierced the stillness. Clearly, Larry detested boisterous twin boys.

I pounded downhill toward the enclosure, aware that the others followed suit. I stopped midway to wave my arms and holler, "Don't open the gate."

A twin opened the gate. Both boys grinned and waved at me before stepping inside the pen, debating about who would ride the weird horse first.

Goats scattered, bleating in alarm. Larry, his neck outstretched, advanced on the boys.

While running, an activity I was certain doctors didn't recommend for a woman nearing the far side of sixty and carrying extra poundage, I bellowed, "Stop."

The pair ignored me and ramped up their argument, ignoring the thunder of hooves as Larry bore down on them.

Maybe it was the long eyelashes, fuzzy topknot, and cute buck teeth, but Larry didn't terrify me the way horses did. Adrenaline helped me reach the gate in record time. Once inside, I halted to consider the best twin-extraction strategy. I released an involuntary squeak when a sinewy arm clamped around my waist, dragging me against a warm wall of muscle. I sucked in my tummy in a big hurry.

"I'd stay back if I were you, gorgeous," an amused voice said. "Don't worry about those two little hellions. Larry won't actually hurt them."

Staring up into Zeke's kind brown eyes, I got lost for a beat. Lust extinguished my fear for the twins' safety. Panting, tongue-tied, and hornier than a crateful of bunnies, I fantasized about jumping his bones. Never mind there was an angry llama stalking the boys, or that I'd told myself I wouldn't date Zeke, or that guests were surging toward the pen. I wanted Zeke, and I wanted him *now*.

Collecting my wits, I pushed him away. "We need to talk."

"We need to do a whole lot more than talk. Sorry I'm late. The fence was worse than I thought. Someone cut the wire. Know of any angry neighbors?"

"None. Clara might have some ideas, but she's in Vancouver." I eyed the llama advancing on the boys. "You sure Larry won't attack?"

"Larry's a sweetheart," Zeke assured me, "but he spits when he's peeved."

Larry had the boys wedged into a corner. Silent now, they'd finally clued in.

"Dad?" Coop yelled, his voice shrill. "Help."

"You'd best calm down, boys," Zeke shouted to the twins. "The llama's working up a good wad of spit, so you don't want to rile him."

From where I stood, Larry looked plenty riled already, with his ears back and tail aloft. His emphatic snort confirmed my suspicions.

The boys tried to slink away, but 400 pounds of irate llama blocked their escape.

Larry blew out some saliva along with air, making a little "pfffffpth" noise.

"Mommy," Wes managed to squeak out before a frothy jet of spit the color of regurgitated grass shot from Larry's mouth, coating both boys in goo. It was a double-header. Both twins started to cry.

"Yuck! We smell like dog poop covered in barf," Coop yelled through his tears.

"It stinks," Wes said, gagging.

Thinking fast, I dug into the bag of treats I'd had the foresight to beg from the kitchen, planning to bribe the horses into letting me leave the barn alive. I yelled at the twins, "Walk slowly to the gate. I'll distract him." I pulled out a chunk of apple. When the boys didn't budge, I bellowed, "Run."

The twins exchanged a glance and raced for the gate. Once outside, they dashed toward the pool area.

Nose twitching, Larry zeroed in on me. Zeke pulled a carrot from his pocket and nudged me back toward the gate, where Dodie stood beside Tess. "He's agitated. Go. He knows I always bring carrots. I'll bribe him and be right along."

"Sure thing." I tightened my grip on the goodie bag and bolted from the pen.

I leaned on the fence beside Dodie while Larry crunched a carrot. The goats nudged Zeke's knees, bleating for their share of the action. He scratched the llama's silly topknot before shifting his attention to the goats. My throat tightened at the moving scene. Zeke's innate kindness extended to animals as well as people. A wave of regret washed over me. Hanky-panky with Zeke was out of the question. It would be all too easy to lose myself again.

The rest of the group closed in on us, and I caught Tess eying Zeke hungrily. I didn't blame her. His easy confidence was shockingly attractive.

Harmony distracted me from my distressing thoughts. "Those kids are lucky you followed them. You're a brave woman."

I shrugged. "It's all in a day's work."

Dodie wrapped an arm around my shoulder and squeezed. "Harmony's right. You *are* brave, and in more ways than one."

I marvelled at Dodie's easy understanding. She was referring to my gut-wrenching decision to let Zeke go.

Zeke approached us at a lope. I edged away, trying to be inconspicuous, but he stopped in front of me, gazing into my eyes as if sending an unspoken message.

Tess interrupted the moment. "Good golly, you must be Zeke. Abby, where are your manners? Aren't you going to introduce me to this sexy cowboy?"

Fudgy, fudging, McFudgster. I had no choice but to make the introductions.

Zeke flashed his killer smile, bathing everyone in its glory. "The goats are nervous, and our llama's had enough excitement. You can visit them again tomorrow. For now, let's go down to the barn and I'll introduce you to the horses."

Tess trotted forward to suction herself onto Zeke's arm. "Oooooh. I adore riding. Especially with the right mount." She slid him a flirty glance while moistening her lips with the tip of a pink tongue.

I clenched my fists but managed to hold it together. Barely.

ChaptER 5:
A FRisky GEldinɡ

AS A GROUP, WE STOOD in the barnyard, a light breeze ruffling our hair. The achingly white peaks of the Canadian Rockies reared their heads above the undulating folds of the Alberta foothills. Mile upon mile of grasses, lodgepole pine, and spruce unfurled their finery in the early May sunshine. The stream, an indescribable blue-green due to silt from glacial melt, danced its way across fertile meadows. Closer at hand, sunbeams created crystals on the partially-frozen surface of Foster Lake, named after my grandfather. The glorious scenery formed a storybook backdrop for the gabled roof and overhanging eaves of our barn. No matter the season, it was a view I never grew weary of.

I'd hoped to avoid entering the barn until, well, the end of time, seeing as how it was home to multiple half-ton, hairy owners of huge teeth, sharp hooves, and bad attitudes. Yet here I was, prepared to run the gauntlet.

Twenty immaculate stalls lined each side of a long corridor. At the far end, a brand-new addition consisted of two larger stalls for sick animals (or special guests like Lancelot), a combined tack room and storage area, a washroom, an office, and the rear entrance. Overhead, a loft provided storage space for hay bales. Last but far from least, a short corridor ended in a sturdy door, the inside entrance to Zeke's living quarters—a cheerful open space with a kitchen at one end and a combined living and dining room at the other. But most of all I remembered the bedroom with its king-sized bed.

The sight of Tess skin-grafted to Zeke's arm was unsettling to say the least, and impending contact with horses dampened my mood even more. I seized Dodie's arm, slowing her down to let the others pull ahead of us as they walked across the barnyard. Let the horses wear themselves out by attacking someone else, hopefully Tess.

"Eat," Dodie ordered, gauging my mood, if not the cause. "Food always cheers you up, eh?"

"Yes, ma'am." I retrieved a quartered apple from the goodie bag I carried, and crunched down vengefully. "A lemon Danish would be better," I mumbled between bites.

To prove my strength of character, I chatted with Dodie, ignoring the way Tess clung to Zeke, touching his hand, flipping her hair, and acting like a bitch in heat. Which made me feel guilty because Zeke deserved to enjoy life, even with someone else.

Once the group was inside the barn and out of sight, I let Dodie drag me through the double doors for the first time since we'd inherited the ranch. The smell of hay, horse, and manure, although faint and not exactly unpleasant, tickled my nostrils as we stood on the polished concrete. The stable area was bright, airy, and spotless. The stall doors and upper grills were all painted white. Sunbeams poured in from strategically placed skylights and upper windows. Based on the neighing and restless shuffle of hooves, most stalls contained occupants.

"You look kinda green," Dodie said. "You okay?"

"Dandy," I lied.

She gripped my arm. "Your teeth are chattering."

"Are not," I muttered through a clenched jaw.

"You're terrified. What's up?"

Dodie wouldn't quit until I spilled my guts, so I huffed out a resigned sigh. "Fine. Horses scare me to death, always have. Only Mom knew. It all started after breakfast the morning of my eighth birthday. Mom was out shopping with Clara, so our daddy got into the whisky. After the first quart, he decided to give me a riding lesson as my birthday gift."

"I don't remember that."

"You were at a sleepover. Anyway, Mom wasn't around to protect me, and I wanted to make him happy so he wouldn't hit her again, so I pretended to be excited. He took me to a ranch owned by one of his drinking buddies, picked a nasty brute for me, and boosted me onto its back. The beast bucked me off. I landed hard, and—"

"Cheezits. That's how you broke your arm. Daddy told us you fell down the stairs."

"It gets worse. After we got home from the hospital, Mom was so worked up, our old man smacked her anyway."

"No wonder horses scare you. I hope you don't feel responsible for our daddy hitting Mom."

I avoided a direct answer by saying, "No biggie. My arm healed."

"But not your heart. A father is supposed to protect his family, not hurt them."

To my utter humiliation, tears filled my eyes. If Dodie hugged me now, I would start to howl, so I turned and sped down the corridor. The sooner this nightmare ended, the better. Zipping past the first six stalls, I avoided eye contact with the occupants, who shoved massive heads out openings in the grills.

Every one of those suckers was munching on whatever horses chew when they're not, say, taking a chunk out of someone's ass. I'd reached the halfway point when the largest horse in the world whinnied, revealing long, yellow teeth. I skidded to a halt, certain the beast's eyes shot red sparks. The sign over the stall door proclaimed "Alamo."

I was about to dart past when Dodie said, "This one seems friendly. Here's an opportunity for you to master your fear."

"Easy for you to say."

"You can do it."

"Fake it till you make it," I muttered as I approached Alamo. "Nice horsie."

Alamo stuck his head out and snuffled my hair, leaving a string of warm drool dribbling down my neck.

I shot backward, crashing into Dodie. Hanging onto her arm, I addressed the horse. "My, what big teeth you have, Grandma."

Dodie said, "She is clearly a he, and teeth aren't the only big things he owns. Maybe we should re-name him 'Porn Star Willie'."

"Huh?"

"He sure is happy to see you, if you get my drift."

I examined Alamo and retreated a step. "Well, pluck a duck. He's *way* too frisky for a gelding."

"Aren't you the sudden expert on horses?"

"Zeke told me all the trail horses are either girls or geldings. This one's no girl."

"I read it happens, but rarely. With the right incentive, even a gelding can become a hornball," Dodie explained. "Obviously, he finds you irresistible." She snickered at her own wit.

Alamo's stiffy was lengthening at an alarming rate. Looking pleased with himself, he thwapped his impressive wang-dangler against his belly.

"Dodie, if you don't stop laughing so hard, you'll pee your granny-panties. Seriously, how do we get him to put that thing away?"

Thwap.

Between gasps and snorts, Dodie managed, "I once heard of a horse ..." *snort*, "whose stomach thumping was so bad ..." *giggle*, "its owner tied a brush to his belly to make him stop."

"I bet the horse stopped beating *that* drum in a hurry."

"I wonder if studdish geldings have happy endings," Dodie mused.

"I don't want to find out."

"Let's skedaddle." She grabbed my arm and hauled me onward. "You, my dear, have a guided tour to finish, and I want to take a gander at Muffy's famous stud."

"I imagine Luc's still sleeping it off." Feeling slightly better, I trotted beside her.

Dodie's glance was withering. "I meant Lancelot."

Luc had insisted Lancelot be housed well away from the other horses to protect his fragile nerves. The stallion would remain in isolated splendor for the duration of the symposium. If Harmony was right about Luc's horse drugging, he'd have plenty of privacy to administer drugs to the stallion.

"I've seen enough horses to last me a lifetime," I said. "Let's catch up with the rest and get everyone out of here before Lancelot freaks out."

Dodie sighed. "Stop worrying. I don't hear anything. Zeke must have sweet-talked everyone into staying quiet."

The sound of Alamo's belly-thwacking followed us as we zipped past some empty stalls until we reached the gang standing silently in front of Lancelot, the temperamental star of our symposium, who was housed in solitary splendor in one of the special stalls in the new addition.

The racehorse was edgy, moving around with an occasional snort.

A quick glance told me neither Veronica nor Luc was present. It crossed my mind they might be together, but I forgot about them at the sight of Tess, apparently a permanent attachment on Zeke's arm.

With a bright smile, I concentrated on ignoring the happy couple, and turned to face Harmony and Clay's accusing eyes. Both were disgruntled at Luc's absence and wanted to know where he was.

I was fabricating an excuse on Luc's behalf when the twins blasted into the barn, their wet hair plastered to their heads. Both boys streamed water. As one, the group sidestepped a growing puddle. Some crowded against Lancelot's stall.

Despite Zeke's soothing words, Lancelot's eyes rolled back in his head as he did a nervous dance.

"Did you turn off the hose, Wes?" Coop asked.

"No. I told you to do it." Wes took stock of the crowd of onlookers. Slowly, his face split in an endearing grin. "Hi. We used the shower beside the swimming pool so we wouldn't smell yucky."

Using my finely tuned peripheral vision, I noticed Zeke unpeeling Tess's grip from his arm. His approach made my heart do a little happy-flutter.

"I'd best go turn off the hose," he advised me. "Keep an eye on the group. Make sure everyone stays quiet."

Tess closed in on Zeke. "I'll wait right here for you, hon. We can have a little stroll, all by ourselves, when you get back." She emphasized her suggestion with a flirtatious side-glance.

"Sorry," Zeke replied. "I won't be able to get away. I'll be rounding up the wranglers and student helpers to do their chores." He leaned closer to me and lowered his voice. "You. Me. Later."

I nodded and watched him walk away, my heart heavy with sadness. He had no idea I planned to break up with him as soon as we were alone. The twins' happy shrieks yanked me back to reality. One of the boys—I thought it was Wes—had boosted his brother on top of Lancelot's partition, where he sat astride the gate, an accident waiting to happen. Both boys giggled and hollered at the top of their lungs.

Lancelot expressed his displeasure by rearing up with an urgent neigh. His hooves pawed the air within a hairsbreadth of Coop's head. I put on the second burst of speed today. Sweeping an arm around the boy's middle, I dragged him away from danger. Simultaneously, the back door burst open causing Lancelot to scream.

"What's going on here?" Luc charged inside. Everyone stopped talking. Several couples and a family with teenagers backed away.

From the accompanying whisky fumes, I gathered he hadn't slept nearly long enough. To defuse the situation, I said, "The twins are over-excited. I'll deal with them." Ignoring Luc's dismissive gesture, I lowered my voice to address the boys. "We must stand back and talk quietly because Lancelot is afraid of strangers. He might hurt you by accident. You don't want to frighten him, do you?"

Wes and Coop shook their heads.

"Use your indoor voice and say you're sorry."

"Sorry," they said in a stage whisper.

Luc disregarded their apology. "Someone should tan their hides. Where's Zeke? I warned him not to let anyone near Lancelot without supervision."

"I'm supervising here," I said. "Zeke went up to the pool to turn off—"

Luc's roar cut me off. "You there! Stop. What are you feeding the horse?"

I whipped my head around in time to see him slap a plastic baggie from Tess's outstretched hand. Pink tablets flew everywhere as Lancelot went wild, neighing and circling in the stall.

Tess flinched. "It's only my glucose tablets. I ... I was trying to calm him down with a treat." She averted her gaze as she scrambled to pick up the tablets littering the corridor. I suspected most had landed in the stall.

While Lancelot rooted around and came up munching, Luc yelled, "You're rewarding bad behavior and turning him into a dangerous horse around people. Get out, and don't go near Lancelot again."

Wes piped up, "Mommy says the brute and his rotten trainer should be shot."

Not to be outdone, Coop said, "Yeah. Our mommy packs heat."

Harmony sniffed her disapproval. "I can't believe your mommy would want to shoot an innocent animal."

Good grief. Never mind that Sheila carried a gun, possibly loaded, or that she'd hinted at shooting Luc, Harmony's focus was the horse.

I whispered to Dodie, "Am I the only one who feels like I've jumped through the looking glass?"

"Nope."

Wes, or maybe it was Coop, echoed my thoughts. "This is weird. Let's go." They sprinted away at top speed.

I gazed wistfully after them, yearning to follow them, but I couldn't. Another crisis was brewing and needed my attention.

"We need to talk," Clay said, getting in Luc's face. "Now."

"Is this pick a fight day?" Luc snarled. "Because before I even have coffee this morning, I find those two little brats harassing poor Lancelot, followed by this nasty bitch," he jabbed a thumb in Harmony's direction, "warning me she's out to nail my ass and will be watching me like a hawk. But does it end there? Nope." Luc cast a baleful glance in my direction. "Next, our gallant barn manager tries a power trip on me, then my nap's ruined by a foxy sex kitten, who wakes me up only to tease me, leaving me hanging, and now you." He glared at Clay.

Luc was so surly, I'd bet money that he and Veronica had hooked up and she'd done a number on him.

"Yeah, me." Clay scowled at Luc. "You'd better listen to what I have to say."

Something in Clay's voice must have caught Luc's attention, because after a curt nod, he said, "Yeah, yeah. Don't go gettin' your frillies in a twist."

No one commented as the men departed, scowling and oozing testosterone and hostility, but I caught shock and distaste etched on several faces.

Making an effort to hide my distress at Luc's drunken tirade, I plastered on my brightest smile and addressed the group. "I'm so sorry you had to hear that. Luc's a gem with horses but miserable whenever he hasn't had enough sleep. His attitude today certainly didn't capture the warm and welcoming spirit of Grizzly Gulch, and I have every intention of reporting this incident to his boss. To make up for both our late departure and Luc's unspeakable rudeness, my sister and I are offering each of you a free massage or facial in our deluxe spa. We'll be along directly to schedule them."

The gang met my offer with exclamations of surprise and gratitude. Lively discussions ensued over which spa treatment to choose while Dodie and I coaxed everyone out the back door in case Luc returned.

Once we were alone in the barn, Dodie enveloped me in a bear hug. "You're a genius. I was worried about the one-star reviews those guests would likely post. Free spa treatments are a wonderful idea. There's plenty of time before dinner. I'll help."

A moist nudge against my neck made me squawk and withdraw from

Lancelot's long, furry snout, which was studded with bristly whiskers. Two gaping nostrils quivered as the stallion craned his neck to get another whiff.

"You sure have a special way with horses," Dodie said. "Take a gander at *that*." She pointed to Lancelot's massive erection.

"Oh, snap. Let's leave before someone else notices his condition." We dashed outside and into the sunshine, where I sucked in a deep, cleansing breath of fresh air, one blessedly untainted by manure. "That's better. Let's go schedule those spa treatments so I can get back and find Zeke."

All morning, our inevitable breakup had weighed heavily on my mind, and I wanted it over and done. Delay only prolonged the pain.

Chapter 6:
Troubles Mount

DODIE AND I CAUGHT UP with the guests halfway to the main lodge. Once we finished scheduling their free spa treatments, everyone was smiling. Dodie stuck around to field questions or complaints while I hurried back to the barn to meet Zeke.

By the time I reached the barnyard, I needed a time-out to find the strength to proceed with my breakup with Zeke. I lingered in the shade of a towering pine until my breathing slowed enough to permit brain function. Once recovered, I scanned the barnyard. Several students and a couple of wranglers razzed one another while chopping and shoveling, raking and hauling. Zeke was nowhere in sight. We'd crossed paths on my dash to the main lodge, so he was likely inside the barn.

A horse's frantic neighing sliced the afternoon's stillness. Lancelot was one unhappy camper. Why didn't Luc or Zeke tend to the stallion?

I hurried across the yard and entered the barn. Immediately, several large heads emerged from the stalls, their furry faces aimed in my direction. I skidded to a halt.

Okay, still terrified. I picked up speed again, dodged Alamo's inquiring muzzle, and dashed down the corridor to the new addition, slowing near Lancelot's stall. There was no sign of Zeke or, for that matter, anyone else.

"Zeke?" I yelled over the wild neighing that went on and on.

Nothing. Something was terribly wrong.

Lancelot reared up, pawed the air, and crashed down again. The stall door swung open. The fact that I didn't have a coronary on the spot testified to my heart's excellent health.

With Zeke's appearance in the doorway, instinct told me to remain silent. He grunted a little while backing out of the stall. I could tell he was dragging something limp and heavy. Once in the corridor, he gently lowered his load and straightened, his face a mask of shock. As he ran his fingers through his hair, I noted his hand shook.

"I was too late to save him," he muttered in a tight voice.

I studied the inert object and shuddered. It was a man—a man who was either unconscious or dead. His head was turned away from me.

My throat tightened. "Oh, Zeke," I said softly.

His eyes vacant and haunted, he used an arm to swipe sweat off his forehead before closing the stall door. Remaining silent, he averted his gaze and crouched beside the body.

I glanced again at the still form, my heart galloping in my chest. "That's Luc Lacroix, isn't it?" I clenched my fists, dimly aware of my nails digging into tender flesh.

Zeke nodded.

My heart bounced around in my chest. "Is he …" I stopped talking.

Zeke checked Luc's pulse while I shifted from one foot to the other. Seconds ticked by until he stood and faced me, his expression grim. "Yeah. He's dead."

"I'll call 9-1-1," I offered, barely recognizing my calm voice.

Patting my pockets to find my phone, I came up empty, then remembered I'd used it in the reception area to book the guests' free spa treatments. I forced myself to think. After the chaos of last-minute requests and changes, I'd placed one final call for a pedicure before putting the phone down and hustling the guests outside.

"I left my phone at reception," I said to Zeke, picturing my pink phone lying beside a vase of fresh-cut flowers at the end of the check-in counter.

He handed me his. While I made the call, he disappeared and returned with a sheet, which he draped over Luc's body, making sure to tuck it underneath. Ten-to-one it was the 1,000-thread-count sheet I remembered from Zeke's bed.

Catching me watching, he flushed. "To protect his privacy," he explained.

I fought the tears jamming my throat, but a shuddery breath escaped.

"It's okay if you want to cry, Abby. A violent death is a terrible shock."

Zeke's gentle voice combined with his understanding made me tear up in earnest. Taking comfort from the way he wrapped his arms around me,

I leaned into him and sobbed against his chest. My tears lasted forever, or so it seemed, until the reassuring beat of his heart against my cheek calmed me. I pushed away, mortified to see a large, damp patch on the front of his shirt.

"It's so horribly sad," I said, sniffing. "No one, except maybe Muffy, liked Luc."

"Here," he said, fishing out tissues from his pocket. "They're clean."

Nodding my thanks, I blew my nose as quietly as possible. Mission accomplished, I said, "Y-you're the first man I've met who carries tissues."

"Sometimes a horse's nose runs or its eyes drip. They're not so different from people. I want them to feel comfortable, so I use tissues to help them out."

Surprising myself, I felt a faint touch of, well, non-hatred for horses. I stuffed the tissues in my pocket. "Sorry. I never cry. It's embarrassing."

"No apologies necessary. Let's sit until the police arrive. I don't like to leave Luc alone." He led me away from the body, and into the tack room. I'd never been inside it until now. A narrow window ran the length of the room near the ceiling. Equipment covered the walls—bridles and bits, stirrups and halters, reins and harnesses. One entire wall was devoted to saddle racks draped with saddles.

We collapsed onto a short bench. I tried not to notice that he smelled good, a combination of soap and the outdoors.

After a lengthy silence, I spoke first. "How did Luc die?"

He shrugged. "No idea. After I turned off the hose and rolled it up by the pool, I headed back here. You passed me going in the other direction with the guests."

I nodded. Tess had seen Zeke first. She'd darted forward to cozy up to him, rubbing her boobs against his arm while whispering in his ear. He'd replied in such a low voice I didn't catch his answer, but from her scowl, I gathered it was a brush-off.

"By the time I got here," Zeke continued, "Lancelot was screaming, trying to destroy his stall. I went closer to find out what was wrong. That's when I saw Luc, sprawled in the stall. He must have returned from his meeting with Clay and tried to quiet the horse. I'm guessing he died under Lancelot's hooves."

We sat in silence for several minutes. Out of the blue, Zeke said, "I'm not interested in Tess, you know."

48

A blast of hope surged through me until I remembered the impending breakup. I must be a horrible person. Who worried about personal difficulties when a man lay dead on the far side of a flimsy partition? "None of my business," I muttered.

"Abby, I want you to make it your business." Without missing a beat, he went on, "Once I returned, I didn't go into the barn straight off. The student helpers were raking, splitting wood for the bonfires, shoveling manure, that sort of thing. It was such a pretty day, I decided to help them. Next thing I knew, your text arrived."

"Whoa. What text? I didn't send any text."

"You sent me a text saying there was a brush fire out in the back pasture. I figured the twins were messing around again."

"I don't know anything about a fire."

"Now that you mention it, there was no sign of smoke. I assumed it had burned itself out, but you can't be too careful. Some of the wranglers were inside, mucking out stalls and forking hay. I figured they needed a break, so I sent them off on ATVs to take care of it, told them to grab the fire extinguishers just in case. They're not back yet."

"Someone must have seen my phone lying on the front desk and used it." After pausing to think, I asked, "Was anyone else in the barn when you told the wranglers to fight the fire?"

"Not that I'm aware of," he replied.

"Do you know when Luc returned from his meeting with Clay?"

"Nope. He generally uses—used—the rear entrance, so I wouldn't have seen him from out front."

I chewed my lip trying to put the pieces together. "What happened after the wranglers left to fight this brush fire?"

"Let's see. The students and I were working, chatting, enjoying the early springtime sun. Everything was nice and peaceful, but not for long. Pretty soon, Lancelot was pitching a fit, but that's not unusual, so I didn't worry. I assumed Luc's meeting with Clay was finished, and he would take care of settling the horse. But the stallion screamed harder than ever, so I went into the barn to see what was riling him."

"Did you see anything suspicious?"

"Not right away. When I reached Lancelot's stall, the poor beast was in a terrible state, stomping and snorting, his ears pinned to his head. I thought maybe he was hurt, so I came closer. He shied away. That's when I saw Luc sprawled on the floor. It's a good thing I had more carrots, because I tossed them to Lancelot while I dragged Luc into the corridor. That's when you arrived."

The rear door banged. A moment later, three wranglers tromped into the tack room. I jumped to my feet, while Zeke unfolded his long frame.

"You weren't gone long," Zeke said, stepping forward. "Did you find anything?"

"False alarm," one of them said, and glanced at me. "No offense, ma'am. We were happy to check it out for you."

"Abby left her phone up at the main lodge. Someone else used it to text me," Zeke explained. "Must have been a prank."

Or a hoax. The thought blindsided me. A text from my phone had conveniently emptied the barn of potential witnesses to Luc's death. I gave a mental headshake. No, it must be a joke. A bad one, but a prank. It would have been easy for anyone, even the twins, to text Zeke.

The alternative was murder, which was unthinkable.

At the mere suggestion of murder, the ranch would be crawling with cops. Guests would demand a refund before they packed and headed out. Bookings would dry up and cancellations would roll in. Before long, Grizzly Gulch would fold. Dodie, Clara, and I would end up bankrupt as we neared retirement.

No, the call had to be a joke.

Lancelot, who'd remained quiet for a few minutes, renewed his efforts to trash the barn, bucking, plunging, and uttering high-pitched squeals. The wranglers had no idea Luc was lying dead in the corridor, only a few feet away. This was so, so wrong.

Fighting another upsurge of hot tears, I unglued my tongue from the roof of my mouth. "I should warn you that ..." I broke off, but couldn't bring myself to say the words. The wail of sirens pierced the sudden silence.

Zeke mercifully stepped in. "There's been a terrible accident. Luc is dead."

I exchanged a glance with Zeke and mouthed, "Thanks."

The wranglers started talking at once, asking questions, speculating on the cause of death. Ignoring the uproar, Zeke held out his hand to me. "Ready?"

I nodded and gripped his hand, grateful for its solid warmth. Together, we headed down the corridor to face the RCMP.

Chapter 7:
Whole Mess o' Trouble

AFTER THE BARN'S COOL SHADOWS, the afternoon sun made me squint. Dropping Zeke's hand, I shaded my eyes to study the cavalcade entering the barnyard, sirens blaring. The RCMP cruiser crunched to a halt near the barn. Thankfully, someone switched off the siren, leaving behind a throbbing silence. The deputy medical examiner parked beside the cruiser, while the ambulance made a three-point turn and backed up to the barn's main entrance. All occupants exited the vehicles.

I couldn't make out who'd responded to my 9-1-1 call. Beside me, Zeke muttered, "Just our luck. Harrison and Calvin Perkins."

The Perkins brothers had been mediocre cops in their day. Now, they were terrible, marking time until their retirement. If they thought Luc's death was murder, which it absolutely wasn't, they'd bungle the investigation, no doubt about it.

To make matters worse, Harrison and I had a history of sorts. I'd refused to date him. Twice. He'd never forgiven me. The Mountie demonstrated his displeasure by issuing me speeding tickets. In my opinion, only one had been valid.

Staff, guests, and neighboring ranchers streamed into the barnyard to watch the unfolding drama. I scanned the crowd for my sister and found her standing alone looking confused and worried.

Leaving Zeke to deal with the Mounties for a few minutes, I edged through the crowd and tugged Dodie aside. When I'd finished an abbreviated description of Luc's death, her first words were, "Was he murdered?"

"Shhhhh. I hope not. If the Perkins brothers decide to conduct a murder investigation, it'll be a disaster." But Dodie's question about murder resurrected my fear.

I surveyed the crowd, my gaze moving from face to face before fixing on Muffy. She looked as anxious as I felt. She must be wondering what sort of emergency required the RCMP, an ambulance, and the Medical Examiner.

I glanced over Dodie's shoulder. The two Mounties had collared Zeke. "Uh-oh. Gotta go. Zeke needs my help. You circulate and talk to guests. In case you're right about a murder, try to find out as much as you can about motive, means, and opportunity. Start with Muffy. With the symposium starting tomorrow, we don't want her to fall apart. Be tactful."

"I'll try, but it won't be easy." She disappeared into the crowd.

I tunneled my way between chattering spectators. Catching sight of Zeke striding toward me with Harrison hot on his heels and Calvin following, I pressed forward. Harrison's eyes glinted with malice when I reached him. He further endeared himself to me by opening with, "Nice of you to greet us when we arrived."

Zeke towered behind him, his expression thunderous.

"Calvin," Harrison yelled at his brother, never taking his narrowed gaze off my face, "get over here, pronto. There's work to do, eh?"

Calvin, who'd dawdled to gawk at Veronica's porcelain beauty, shoved through the crowd to arrive slightly breathless. "I want to interrogate the foxy lady." He jerked his chin at Veronica.

Harrison gripped his brother by the shoulders and shook him twice. "Focus."

"Right. Luc Lacroix is dead."

Harrison swiveled his gaze to me and stretched his lips in a grim smile. "Seems you've got yourself a whole mess o' trouble here, lady." His eyes remained frigid.

The full weight of Zeke's arm fell around my shoulders, silencing a snarky comeback. I soaked up the feeling of being protected. Not that I wasn't self-reliant.

Zeke bent his head to go nose-to-nose with Harrison. "Watch my lips, Perkins. Luc Lacroix had an unfortunate accident, end of story. There won't be any more talk of, and I quote, 'a whole mess of trouble.' Got it?"

He'd spoken softly, but his voice held a ring of authority, making something deep inside me quiver.

Harrison broke eye contact first. "Got it." He nudged Calvin. "You hear that?"

"Eh?" Calvin, swung his gaze from Veronica to us, and slowly downward, to encounter Zeke's blood-spattered shoes and jeans. "Look at you," he said. "Aren't you the image of Leatherface in *The Texas Chainsaw Massacre*? I bet that's how you looked during your stint in Afghanistan, at least before—"

"Enough." Zeke's low, threatening growl boded nothing but trouble. "Take that back or you'll regret it."

Harrison bared his teeth. "Did Calvin strike a nerve? Guess you'll feel right at home in a jail cell."

Goosebumps popped out on my arms. What dark secrets was Zeke harboring?

I refused to consider Harrison's insinuation that Zeke was a killer. On the contrary, he'd tried to save Luc, and was broken up over the trainer's death. You can't fake the depth of emotion I'd witnessed.

I glared at the Mounties. "You boys should be ashamed of yourselves."

"Ouch," Harrison said.

"Why?" Calvin asked.

"If I hear of either of you so much as hint that Zeke harmed Luc, I'll take out a full-page ad in the *High Country Tribune* explaining how I refused to snort a line of coke the pair of you offered me behind the Seniors Center last month. Everyone in this county and the next will be fascinated to learn how you handle proceeds from your drug busts."

"That's not fair," Calvin whined. "We were just being sociable."

"You wouldn't squeal on us," Harrison countered.

"Try me," I said. "I can vouch for Zeke's innocence because when I arrived, he was inside the stall trying to drag Luc out. If Zeke was the killer, why risk his own life to save the victim?" Every muscle in my body quivered with outrage.

"That true?" Harrison asked Zeke.

Color returned to Zeke's cheeks. His gaze settled on my face for a long moment. "Yeah," he said slowly, "Abby arrived while I was pulling Luc out of the stall."

"I guess you're off the hook," Harrison muttered.

Calvin scratched his head. "So if Zeke didn't kill him, how did he die?"

Zeke massaged the bridge of his nose as if rubbing away a headache.

"Something must have spooked Lancelot—he's the stallion Luc was training. The animal was bucking and kicking to beat the band. I waited for Luc to come settle him down, but nothing was happening. I went to see what all the ruckus was about, and found Luc inside the stall. He was unresponsive."

Harrison removed his hat and scratched his head. "That don't sound right. I heard tell Luc Lacroix was some sort of horse whisperer." He jammed his hat back on.

"He is, uh, was," I replied, "but accidents happen, even to horse whisperers. We're using Lancelot for our horse breeding symposium. He's so high-strung Luc didn't want any guests near him without supervision."

From the sound of things, Lancelot was pulverizing the wooden walls of his stall.

Calvin eyed the twins, who were racing around, brandishing plastic swords and shrieking in an excellent imitation of homicidal maniacs. He said, "Those kids probably snuck into the stable and spooked the horse, eh?"

Zeke shook his head. "Nope. I would've noticed them. And seeing as how Luc scared the bejesus out of the boys for hassling the stallion earlier today, I doubt they'd be dumb enough to try it again."

"A rattlesnake might have spooked Lancelot," I offered. "Diamondbacks are out early this year. Only last week, one of our wranglers shot a huge rattler sunning itself on a flat rock beside the pond. This far north, their poison may not be as potent, but they still terrify horses."

"Weather's been unseasonably warm and dry this spring," Harrison said. "Makes 'em livelier than usual this time of year."

At his easy agreement, my conscience got the better of me. The Mounties deserved full disclosure. "There's more you should know. It may be relevant."

That caught everyone's attention.

"Yeah?" Harrison said.

"After lunch, I left my phone up at the main lodge. Someone used it to text Zeke about a fire in the back pasture. Turned out it was a prank. There was no fire."

"You think a prank text message is related to Luc's death?" Harrison asked.

I shrugged. "Maybe. It's out of the ordinary. I think it warrants investigation, don't you?"

Harrison narrowed his eyes. "You still have the text?" he asked Zeke.

"Nope," Zeke replied. "I deleted it when we learned it was a prank."

"You find your phone?" Harrison asked me.

"Not yet."

"Probably stolen by now," Calvin pointed out. "It was most likely one of those kids, but there's no point in asking them. They'd lie through their teeth."

The Perkins brothers' laziness was legendary, and so was Harrison's reluctance to accept advice, especially from a woman who'd spurned his advances. But at least I could live with myself. I'd pushed for a police investigation.

A new voice floated over the enraged stallion's screams. "Hey, Abby. Long time no see."

While wondering if Lancelot intended to demolish the entire barn, I turned and recognized the Deputy Medical Examiner, Atticus Lightheart. I waved. "Hey, Atticus. How are you?"

"Better than the last time we met," he said with a wink.

I laughed. "That wouldn't be difficult." The last time we'd met was at a summer party in Banff. Atticus was so drunk he'd fallen into the glacier-fed Bow River. Luckily, the water was so cold we heard him howl back at the barbecue, and hauled him out before he went over the falls.

Chuckling, he addressed the Mounties. "Harrison, Calvin, you gonna make me do this alone, or ya wanna see what's what in the barn?"

Zeke said, "I'd better come too, make sure Lancelot doesn't claim another victim."

The Perkins brothers, Atticus, and two paramedics wheeling a gurney bearing a neatly folded body bag all followed Zeke into the barn.

Once they'd departed to examine the corpse, take photographs, and hunt for clues, I welcomed the opportunity to stay behind and learn as much as possible in case Luc's death proved to be murder. I'm a terrible schmoozer, never did master the art of small talk and empty compliments, but I did my best, chatting up guests, focusing on those acquainted with Luc.

After I'd interrogated as many people as possible, my energy faded. Needing a breather, I strolled over to the hay wagon conveniently parked in preparation for the evening hayride. It was a low-slung affair with portable steps beside it. I climbed aboard and perched on a hay bale, enjoying my breather until Coop and Wes bounced over.

"Can we look at the corpse?" Wes implored, gazing at me. "We've never seen one."

"Please?" Coop wheedled. "I bet it's bloody and scary."

Before I had a chance to refuse, a voice roared, "Boys. Get over here. Now."

"Uh-oh," Coop said. They darted away seconds before Big John emerged from the crowd and halted in front of me.

"Which way did they go?" he asked, panting from the exertion. "You'd think they'd be exhausted after playing volleyball for the past hour. Lord knows, I am, and so are the others."

So there was no way the twins spooked Lancelot as Harrison had insinuated. Their parents were ruled out too, maybe others.

I pointed Big John in the direction his sons had taken.

He'd barely disappeared into the crowd when somewhere nearby, Neil Diamond belted out *Sweet Caroline*. I recognized my phone's ringtone and spotted my pink phone resting at the front of the wagon, no doubt where the texter had discarded it.

With an awkward scramble down the length of the wagon, a feat I was glad Zeke hadn't witnessed, I grabbed the cell but not before the ringing stopped.

I examined the phone. Except for the marketing call I'd missed, there was no record of any phone calls or text messages. Someone had deleted the text and erased the call log.

The squeak of metal wheels announced the conclusion of the death scene examination. The paramedics left the barn first, wheeling the gurney with its body bag, which clearly contained an occupant, toward the ambulance. I shoved the phone into my pocket and hopped down to face Zeke, Atticus, and the Perkins brothers.

Atticus took the lead. "We found Luc's body was bruised and cut. From the gash on his skull, I'd guess a hoof caught him. It's probably the cause of death, but I won't be certain until I conduct a post-mortem."

Not to be outdone, Harrison added, "There was no sign of an altercation, but we found blood on the stall floor and on Lancelot's hooves. I'm guessing the horse lashed out, caught Luc off-guard."

Yeah, Lancelot wasn't what you'd call docile. "How were you able to examine the stall?" I took care to avoid the words "crime scene".

"Zeke was great," Atticus said, ignoring Harrison's scowl. "He used a carrot to distract the horse while we examined the stall. Lancelot even quieted down enough to let Zeke check him for suspicious marks or wounds.

The more I thought about it, the more I believed someone had murdered Luc. "It sounds like you believe Luc's death was accidental," I said.

Harrison nodded. "Sure looks that way."

I blew out the lungful of air I hadn't realized I was holding. Thankfully, the cops wouldn't be crawling around Grizzly Gulch conducting a murder investigation, spooking guests, suppressing business, and killing our hopes of success. Once everyone dispersed, I'd tell Zeke and Dodie I believed Luc's death was murder.

Atticus took his leave to follow the ambulance, which was pulling out. They sped off in the direction of the nearest hospital, leaving the Perkins boys to wrap things up.

Harrison asked, "Is there next of kin we should notify?"

After conferring with Muffy, who'd pulled herself together, we learned Luc's parents were dead, his ex-wife was re-married and living in Alaska, and his brother, Tommy "Mad Dog" Lacroix, was in jail for armed robbery. He also had a sister who was married to a municipal politician and living in Toronto. Harrison ordered Calvin to notify the deceased's sister and tell her to pick up the body once they released it.

At that point, Clay, who sported a black eye, sauntered over in time to hear Harrison's comment. I'd noticed Clay earlier, nose-to-nose with Muffy in a heated discussion.

Under his breath, Clay muttered, "Crime must run deep and true in the Lacroix family," and abruptly strode away.

Since the Mounties didn't react, I figured they hadn't heard Clay's words. My urge to spill my suspicions to Zeke and Dodie grew even stronger.

After awkward goodbyes, the Perkins brothers trudged toward their vehicles until Harrison did an about-face and plowed his way through the crowd to climb onto the porch. He raised his hands for silence. Once everyone had quieted down, his voice boomed out, "Although Luc Lacroix's death appears accidental, I don't want anyone to leave here until I give the go-ahead. We may have more questions."

Once the Mounties departed in a spurt of flying gravel, I had the presence of mind to make one final announcement to the crowd. Taking

Harrison's place on the porch, I assured everyone that Luc's death, although tragic, was accidental, with no evidence of foul play. Except for this evening's hayride, which we would re-schedule for later in the week, the remaining activities would continue as planned—symposium workshops interspersed with fun and friendly dude ranch activities and gourmet meals. Wrapping up, I reminded them the bell would ring at 6:45 p.m. to call everyone into the dining hall for the best dinner of their lives.

The guests drifted away, headed to the bar, the veranda, or their cabins, presumably to gossip about Luc's death.

I moved quickly to block Dodie and Zeke's escape. "We need to talk. My apartment. Now," I ordered.

Chapter 8:
Murder's No Accident

T O ENSURE PRIVACY FOR OUR discussion, I closed the French doors to
my balcony overlooking the pool. With our privacy ensured, I sat in
my La-Z-Boy rocker-slash-recliner, cranked up the footrest, and set the
massage feature to low. The vibration worked its magic on my lumbar area.
Dodie and Zeke watched me from the entryway, their faces etched with
concern. I wiggled deeper into the chair and beckoned them to join me in
the living room.

Dodie crossed the plush carpet to perch gingerly on one of two antique
chairs we'd inherited from Uncle Benny. Zeke assessed the matching chair
and ambled across the room to sink into the white leather sofa. I had
difficulty ignoring him, especially since he stared at me long and hard.

Long and hard. My gaze drifted to his forbidden zone. God help me, I
was one lovesick puppy. Flustered, I switched my attention to Dodie, who
fixed her worried gaze on my face.

"You're flushed," she said. "Drink a glass of water. Sudden death can be
unsettling, especially when our feelings about the deceased are ambivalent."

Relieved my sharp-eyed sister hadn't caught me ogling Zeke's package,
I turned off the massage feature. "I'm okay," I said. "I don't need water, and
I most definitely don't need any sisterly advice."

She gave me a reproachful look. "Fine. You called this meeting.
What's up?"

I hesitated. At Dodie's impatient gesture, I said, "The Mounties called
Luc's death accidental. I'm convinced it was murder. It's up to the three of
us to nail the killer without alerting the guests."

Dodie's forehead crinkled, a sure sign of doubt. "You got any proof?"

"Not a shred, but I know it in my bones."

"This isn't like you," Dodie said. "You always dig up a truckload of information before reaching a decision."

"Happens I agree with Abby," Zeke drawled, his voice re-activating my hormones. He gave me an encouraging nod. "What do your bones tell you?"

Lust was causing my eyes to lose focus, so I looked away in the hope of cooling down. "First," I said, once I regained my ability to talk, "Luc accumulated enemies the way a squirrel collects nuts."

"You're exaggerating," Dodie observed.

"I don't think so. From listening to the guests, I believe someone held a big enough grudge to murder him."

"By the way," Zeke said to me, "thanks for jumping to my defence. When Harrison threatened me with jail time, I thought I'd be sitting behind bars before sundown." I noted his smile didn't reach his eyes.

"No problem. He did it because he's jealous of you. I turned down a date with him. Then he saw us leave line dancing together last week."

Zeke held my gaze. "I'm grateful you were there. I don't know what I would have done if I'd ended up in prison again." I must have looked shocked because he added, "It's not what you think. During my deployment in Afghanistan, the fighting was like nothing I could imagine. Some of us ended up in an Afghan prison facing execution."

I knew he was a veteran, but hadn't realized the extent of the trauma he'd suffered. No wonder his eyes held more secrets than a confessional. The Mounties' threat of a jail cell must have felt like a living nightmare.

Dodie changed the subject. "Assuming Luc was murdered, you must have valid reasons to believe it."

My brain was a minefield of jumbled thoughts. Sometimes I needed to hear myself talk before the facts would cooperate and arrange themselves into tidy patterns. "Okay, so my gut tells me it wasn't all Lancelot's fault." I regarded her warily, anticipating a cool reaction. She didn't disappoint.

"Huh. First your bones, now your gut."

"According to Muffy, the stallion worshipped his trainer. On the circuit, Luc was known as a horse whisperer. That horse would never take him down, at least not without human involvement."

Dodie's huffed-out sigh revealed her impatience. "Harrison said there was no sign of foul play so Muffy's stallion must have killed him."

Heavy silence filled the room.

I needed to make Dodie see the light or she wouldn't help with the investigation. That was when I remembered the most important fact of all.

"While we were up in the main lodge booking facials, I must have left my phone unattended because someone else used it to text Zeke about a fake fire in the back pasture."

"Right. I sent three wranglers to fight the blaze," Zeke said. "That text message removed all potential witnesses from the barn."

"But there was no fire," Dodie said slowly, "so the text was a ruse. Anyone could have found the phone, sent the text, and avoided the barnyard by using the rear door once the barn was empty."

"Not just another pretty face." Zeke smiled in earnest this time. "Luc must have entered through the rear door, too. Otherwise I'd have seen him."

Dodie shook her head and turned to me. "Why didn't you explain this to the Mounties and let them handle the investigation?"

"I did. They chose to ignore it. Granted, it's only circumstantial, but I think it's significant enough to warrant an investigation."

"Did you ever find your phone?" Dodie asked.

I described how I found it with the call log erased and the text deleted. Zeke added, "And I deleted the text at my end."

"So there's no record of a text warning you of a fire," Dodie observed.

"Not unless it's hidden somewhere in the phone," Zeke said, looking dejected. "That means there's nothing that'll stand up in a court of law."

"In that case, we must think outside the box," Dodie said, as good as admitting she agreed Luc was murdered.

I jumped up and gave her a hug to express my gratitude. Her voice was muffled when she said, "It's just as well the Mounties won't be nosing around, hassling guests, threatening to bring them in for questioning. Imagine the horrible reviews we'd receive."

Picturing a string of one-star reviews, I released her. "That would be a disaster. We're in big financial trouble as it is. Imagine what would happen if word leaked out that the RCMP were investigating not only us, but our guests too, as murder suspects—and it *would* leak if the Perkins brothers conducted the investigation."

"Even if no charges were laid, Grizzly Gulch would go under," Dodie said quietly.

I grinned. "We're doing everyone a favor by keeping the investigation in-house."

Zeke nodded. "I reckon we stand a better chance of nailing the killer without riling the guests." Looking me straight in the eye, he lowered his voice. "Better still, I'll get to see you more often."

And therein lay the problem. My attraction to Zeke was growing by leaps and bounds. If I didn't break up with him soon, I was a goner. But with so much happening, the timing was all wrong. I'd deal with my love life later. Much later.

"I'll get us drinks before we discuss suspects," I said. "Beer or wine?"

Five minutes later, I returned with a bag of salt and vinegar chips and three frosty bottles of Kokanee Gold Amber Lager. Once everyone had a beer, I kicked off the discussion. "Any thoughts on our main suspects?" I grabbed a fistful of chips.

Dodie leaned forward. "For now, I propose we focus on people who might have a motive to kill Luc. If nothing pans out, we'll cast our net wider."

I nodded. "Good thinking. Let's rule out the staff. I made sure everyone who works here is bonded."

Dodie's delicate chair released an ominous squeak under an exuberant wiggle. "How about Big John and Sheila Wright? Did you notice his expression when Luc was mean to the twins? He looked like he wanted to rip Luc's heart from his body and stomp on it with work boots."

"It wasn't the Wrights," I said. "They have iron-clad alibis. The whole family was playing volleyball with other guests." I shoved a chip into my mouth and crunched.

"How about we scratch Tess Jenkins as well?" Zeke said. "She's attending the symposium, but doesn't seem to have any connection to Luc."

I noted the way he avoided looking at me as he took a gulp of beer. Yeah, Zeke would want to clear her, I thought sourly. Trying to hide my jealousy, I said, "Let's not be too hasty. We know nothing about her."

"Tess doesn't have a confirmed alibi," Dodie pointed out. "She said she went to her cabin as soon as the tour ended, she'd never seen a lovelier room in all her born days, yadda, yadda, then bent my ear for five minutes gushing about the decor."

"Remember when she tried to give Lancelot a treat?" I said, determined to keep her on the list. "Luc tore a strip off her. She didn't react, but I sensed she was seething." Actually I hadn't sensed anything of the sort, but I didn't trust the woman. I turned to Dodie for support. "What do you think?"

Dodie shrugged. "No normal person would commit murder over a scolding. Then again, Tess may not be normal. The woman's too nice, too meek, and way too complimentary, almost like she's playing a role. I wanted to gag when she gushed over your plaid shirt. No one but you thinks plaid makes a fashion statement."

"You're just jealous. She called me stunning."

"She's right," Zeke said. "But Tess is off the list. Luc was too experienced, too smart to enter Lancelot's stall and turn his back on an unpredictable horse. That means someone must have pushed him inside or dumped him there to make it look like an accident. Luc was solid muscle and real tall, so the killer must be strong. Tess is a little-bitty thing."

Gag me! More like anorexic.

I forced my stiff lips into a semblance of a smile. "Good point. She's off the suspect list." *For now*, I added silently.

Dodie must have sensed my tension, because she jumped in. "Let's discuss Muffy Walton. She's plenty strong enough. I watched her use weights at the gym, and she practically lifted the machine."

"Definitely on the list," I said. "Muffy and Luc were in the same class at university. Maybe she held a grudge of some sort, plus she was his boss. Franklin told her to fire Luc before he returned from his business trip."

"Does she have an alibi?" Zeke asked.

"No," Dodie replied. "She claims she was in her cabin until she heard the sirens."

I considered the possibilities. "Come to think of it, after Muffy and Franklin quarrelled this morning, I didn't see her again until the Mounties arrived. She didn't even join us for the guided tour. I wonder if anyone else saw her." I glanced at Dodie. "What else did you learn about Muffy?"

"She seems worried about her husband's whereabouts," Dodie replied. "She admitted she tried to reach him several times before his flight's departure. Her calls all went to voicemail. Reading between the lines, I'd say they have marriage problems."

"I have more information," I said. "A couple of months ago, I visited Muffy to meet her new racehorses. You'll never guess what I saw." I paused expectantly.

"Stop teasing," Dodie chided. "Just tell us."

I hid a smile at her impatience. "Luc was injecting a drug into Lancelot's fetlock. He claimed it was a mild painkiller. I pretended to believe him. Later I told Muffy what I'd seen, and she was far from happy. She'd never authorized an injection, was worried about doping. What if she caught Luc doing the same thing here? She might have attacked him, especially if there was danger of Franklin finding out."

"Or she might have tried to fire Luc, and he reacted badly," Dodie said. "Maybe she had to defend herself."

"Yep. Muffy's a suspect," Zeke said, acting as facilitator. "Moving right along."

"What about Franklin?" Dodie took a slug of beer. "Abby and I both overheard Franklin order Muffy to fire Luc. He thought Luc was drugging his racehorses. That's a motive for you."

Zeke shook his head. "I doubt Luc is doping the horses. With stricter regulations and new, sophisticated tests, it's too easy to get caught these days." He paused. "But come to think of it, there are always ways to bend the rules. Maybe new drugs can mask other older ones or aren't picked up by any tests."

"So it's possible Luc was a drugger?" Dodie asked, pushing hard.

Zeke huffed out a sigh. "It's possible, but unlikely."

I figured this was a good time for me to step in with a cold dose of common sense. "That's all very well and good, but let me remind you that Franklin's on a business trip halfway around the world."

"He's powerful," Dodie pointed out. "It would be easy for him to hire a hitman."

Yeah, Dodie liked Franklin as the killer. But logic was logic. I said, "If he'd already hired a hitman to kill Luc, I doubt he'd order his wife to fire him. Besides, I got the impression that Luc's reputation for horse drugging was a new discovery for Franklin. Surely it takes more than a few hours on the dark web to hire the perfect hitman."

Dodie released a disappointed groan. "I hate to admit it, but you're right. If Franklin learned Muffy hadn't fired Luc, he might take action on his return, but today's way too soon for that." She glugged down more beer, reached for the bag of chips, and clasped them to her chest as she chowed down.

"What about Veronica Melville?" I asked. "She and Luc certainly knew one another." I nibbled a chip as I thought back to Veronica's peculiar encounter with Luc during check-in. "She and Luc had some sort of relationship at university, but he didn't recognize her when they met at check-in. How is that possible?"

"She must look a whole lot different now," Dodie said, grabbing more chips before handing the bag to me. "Veronica threatened to teach Luc a lesson. When she found out Luc was asleep, she claimed a migraine and hot-footed it away to take a nap too. I bet she went to find him. Now that I think about it, she's probably the foxy sex-kitten who woke him from his nap, teased him, and left him hanging."

I nodded vigorously. "It's a possibility we can't ignore. Let's keep her on the list. Anyone else?"

"Clay Davis." Zeke brushed my hand as he reached into the bag of chips I held.

Dodie frowned. "The cute rancher? I don't see him as a murderer."

"What do we know about him?" Zeke asked.

"He claimed he was enjoying a drink in his room followed by a nap during the time of the murder," Dodie said. "The sirens woke him up."

I leaned back in the chair, gathering my impressions of Clay. Straightening, I said, "During check-in, Clay told us he needed to discuss a business matter with Luc, and took off to find him. But during the tour, he mentioned how Luc had screwed him over on a business deal. When Luc finally showed up in the barn, Clay insisted they go outside for a 'little chat'."

Zeke arched a brow. "And next thing you know, he turns up with a black eye while Luc's dead."

"I wonder what their business matter was," Dodie said slowly.

"I bet it was illegal," I mused.

"Why do you say that?" Zeke asked.

"When Clay overheard Muffy telling the Mounties about Luc's brother being in prison, he commented that crime must run in the family. No one else heard him because there was too much racket, but my hearing's still as sharp as a bat's." I ignored Dodie's snort of derision. "Come to think of it, Clay was probably the last person to see Luc alive."

"So he's on the list," Zeke said. "Anyone else?"

"Only Harmony." I turned to Dodie. "What's her alibi?"

"She went to the kitchen to make sure all her meals were vegan," Dodie said. "Chef Armand confirmed she was there for fifteen minutes. After leaving the kitchen, she claimed she'd wandered over to the goat enclosure, because she loves animals."

After I considering Dodie's words, I said, "I don't buy it. During registration, she mentioned Luc's reputation for horse drugging to win races, and told us she would dearly love to nail his ass. At the start of the guided tour she'd already visited the barn, making Luc angry enough to kick her out. I wonder what happened."

Zeke ran his fingers through his mane of salt-and-pepper hair. "During my argument with Luc this morning, he complained about the carrot-haired crackpot who was out to get him. At the time, I figured it was the booze talking."

I jerked my gaze up to meet Zeke's. "Harmony's a fanatic. Instead of visiting the goats like she said, she may have gone after Luc again."

"Yep. She's another suspect."

Dodie gave a dramatic shudder. "She creeps me out. The woman's unhinged."

"So it appears," Zeke said.

"In that case," I concluded, "our short list is Harmony, Clay, Veronica, and Muffy."

The three of us sat in silence, processing our findings while finishing our beer.

After draining her bottle, Dodie asked, "What's our next step?"

"There's no next step for either of you," Zeke interjected.

His quick reply raised my hackles. "Wrong. Dodie and I will question the suspects, but we'll do it so sneakily they won't know what happened. People don't credit older women with drive, brains, and slick interrogation techniques."

"I don't like it. If either of you gets hurt, or worse, I'll never forgive myself."

"We'll be careful," Dodie assured him. "We both have bear spray."

"Sweet baby Jesus," Zeke muttered. "Please, *please* don't do anything foolish. I mean it. Don't let your guard down with anyone."

"We'll be careful," I assured Zeke, meaning it with all my heart.

With a perfectly straight face, Dodie said, "We wouldn't dream of walking into danger."

I accompanied them to the door. Once Zeke strode away, I said to Dodie, "After you're waxed, plucked, and prettied up for dinner, come right back. We have exactly six days plus this evening to find the killer. We need to strategize."

I intended to make the most of every second, starting with tonight's dinner.

Chapter 9:
Compression Woes

A HALF HOUR LATER, A MORE urgent not to mention mortifying concern displaced my strategy session. "Son-of-a-PEACH!" I hollered. "Buck, buck, buck, buckety buck."

From my prone position on the mossy-soft bedroom carpet, I stared at the rotating ceiling fan, praying Dodie would return soon. Perhaps I shouldn't have pooh-poohed the notion of a panic button.

"The label should say, 'Do not under any circumstance attempt to use this apparatus when alone'," I muttered.

At least Zeke couldn't see me, spread-eagled in the most undignified position imaginable, all waving legs, bulging flesh, and varicose veins. A suitable punishment, I supposed, for outgrowing the outfit I planned to wear tonight.

Feeling as helpless as a pinned spider, I wore nothing but a tummy-taming teddy and Birkenstocks. Compounding my humiliation, the Super-Deluxe Fat Buster Thigh 'n' Butt Toner, which was wedged between my thighs, spread my knees apart to a degree that caused certain ligaments to squeal in agony.

The gizmo, billed as a spring-loaded miracle, was a spring-loaded piece of junk.

A key rattled in the front door, and I breathed a sigh of relief. As soon the door slammed, I yelled, "Dodie? I need help."

"Can't argue with your assessment. Where are you?"

"Bedroom."

Footsteps thumped down the hallway. When the door opened, I turned my head. "This device is defective," I explained from the floor.

The floorboards creaked, and Dodie appeared in my field of vision. After a long moment of silence, she exploded into gales of laughter.

"This is so not funny," I said.

"You should see yourself." Bending at the waist to examine me, she wiped tears of mirth from her cheeks. "Have you tried analyzing the situation?"

"You're a cruel and heartless woman. This sucker's defective." I indicated the Thigh 'n' Butt Toner wedged between my thighs. "I've been using it all month because I've gained a teeny-tiny bit of weight. Between this thing and my tummy taming teddy, I figured I'd be able to squeeze into my favorite outfit without dieting."

"So what happened?"

"I followed instructions to the letter, same as always. First, I placed the foam-covered steel wings between my thighs and unsnapped the easy-loc doo-hickey. The wings sprang apart, same as always. I pressed and released my thighs a couple of times, and then, bam! The wings widened another six inches, then seized up. The sucker's stuck. I swear the spring is stronger than a bear trap. I can't squeeze my legs together to remove it."

"Open wider."

"This is as wide as they go without tearing something." To demonstrate, I raised my legs. In the heat of the moment I forgot the indelicate position revealed far too much cellulite along with my barely concealed private bits.

Dodie cringed and turned her head away. "Your booty's hanging out, and I can practically see your lady playstation."

"This lady playstation hasn't seen any play for over a year, and it's facing another long, dry spell, since dating Zeke's a non-starter. But there's nothing wrong with wanting to distract him from Tess." I warmed to the topic. "She plans to conquer his heart by tending to some other organs. It's not happening on my watch."

"Yes, this approach should do the trick nicely. I'll bring Zeke up, shall I?"

I gave Dodie the stink-eye. "Not funny."

"I hope that thing's not a Super-Deluxe Fat Buster Thigh 'n' Butt Toner."

"Why?"

"The inventor went out of business due to lawsuits over strained groin muscles."

"Great time to find out." I punctuated my indignation with a leg wave.

"Next time I'll let my tummy fly wild and free." I squirmed. "You gonna help me or not?"

"If I must." Dodie squatted in front of me, a hand clamped on each knee. "Let's try closing the gates to paradise first."

"Fine, but don't bruise the merchandise."

As she tried to wrestle both my legs together, a soft grunt escaped her lips. Pain shot down my legs, and I swallowed a scream.

When she let go, I said, "Has anyone ever mentioned you have a soft and gentle touch? You might consider taking up female mud wrestling."

"Been there, done that. It didn't work out so great."

I gave a reluctant snort of laughter. "Can you see what the problem is?"

"The spring won't budge. I gotta warn you. This Thigh 'n' Butt Toner might be here to stay. Better get used to it."

"Wheeling me into the dining hall like this is a terrible idea. Please remove it."

"Thigh closure never was your strong suit. You do better with the outspread."

"Try pulling. Use muscle, and hurry, or I'll never be able to close my legs again."

She braced one foot against the bed for leverage and hauled. Pain exploded. Other than my screech of agony, nothing else happened. Another yank, more powerful this time, and the Super Deluxe Fat Buster Thigh 'n' Butt Toner popped out.

I lay perfectly still, waiting for the pain to subside. Once sensation returned to my toes, I pushed myself into a sitting position and smiled at Dodie. "Thanks. I never thought I'd hear myself say this, but closing my legs feels so, so right."

"Get dressed. You're the one who wanted a strategy session."

Once I was ready, I swept into the living room, prepared for our opening night's dinner. Due to the teddy's compression, my favorite outfit now fit me. Sort of. Okay, maybe the skirt's buttonhole screamed in protest, and maybe the waistband burrowed into my soft flesh, but the top concealed those tiny flaws. I stroked the skirt's rich, satiny fabric. Aquamarine, violet, and emerald swirls splashed the deep plum background, reminding me of my youthful psychedelic days. Pairing the skirt with a poplin blouse in the same deep plum color, gave me a waistline. I felt glamorous, even desirable. Yep, I was prepared to give Tess some stiff competition.

Dodie occupied my recliner. She'd made herself at home in my apartment, opening the sliding doors to let in clean, crisp evening air. I perched gingerly on the living room sofa facing my sister. Sitting or bending posed a challenge, but I didn't care. The result was well worth the discomfort.

"Nice outfit," Dodie said. "Reminds me of a kick-ass acid trip I took in '73."

I eyeballed her black, stretchy mini-dress, which barely covered the essentials. "You're, ah, eye-popping." Boob-popping was a better word, but I bit my tongue.

"Thanks. Men appreciate a woman who's sexy, yet tastefully turned out. This little number has a hidden panel that slenderizes me a whole dress size while elevating the girls. Believe it or not I squeezed all this bounty," Dodie stood and patted her butt, "into a size XXL."

I believed it.

After appraising me, she walked over and unclipped the antique amethyst brooch fastened at my neckline. Setting it aside, she proceeded to undo the top button of my blouse with deft fingers. After gazing at me critically, she unfastened two more. As a final gesture, she turned up the collar, framing my face, neck, and a vast quantity of cleavage, which I feared had seen better days.

"If ya got it, flaunt it," she said.

I re-buttoned one of the buttons and twirled. The teddy had most definitely tamed my tummy.

She nodded. "You'll knock Zeke's socks off." When I went to lower myself again, I made the mistake of wincing. Her eyebrows lifted. "You're still wearing the teddy." She plopped down and frowned at me. "Mark my words, Abby. If you want to enjoy the evening, lose that foundation garment."

"Without the teddy, I can't button my skirt." Leaning forward, I suppressed a pained grunt and got down to business. "We need a strategy for tonight's dinner."

"Leave the vegetables, eat only the good stuff," she said promptly.

"Very funny, but no. Over dinner, we want our suspects to reveal clues that will help us identify the killer."

Dodie's eyes sparkled. "Let's bug their cabins and listen to everything they say."

I closed my eyes and breathed deeply, searching for my happy place. When I looked at her, I put some steel into my voice. "Nope. That's unethical. Guests expect us to respect their privacy."

"Fine," she said in a huffy voice. "It's your turn."

"We get them drunk."

She arched a brow. "Nice, but how? We can't pour wine down their gullets."

"Wine's included with dinner. We simply ask the wait-staff to top up their glasses whenever they drop to the halfway mark."

"Excellent. But it's only a start. Let's see." Dodie closed her eyes, a childhood habit she'd developed whenever serious thinking was required. After a moment, her eyes popped open. "I've got it. I'll seduce Clay and have him fess up during pillow talk."

"Honey, I hate to burst your bubble, but he's two decades younger than you."

"Have you forgotten? He'll be drunk. Also, I can be pretty seductive if I put my mind to it."

"Let's put that one on the back burner for now."

"Fine. Here's an idea that might work even better," Dodie said, an evil grin creasing her face. "Since you like Tess for the killer, I'll convince Zeke to seduce her and coax out a confession during pillow talk."

"Interesting, but no," I said. "Returning to my initial idea, getting the suspects drunk will help, but we need a way to get them to open up."

Deep in thought, we sat in silence. At last, Dodie said, "We need some sort of ceremony to get them talking."

I sprang up and faced Dodie. "You're brilliant. We need a Celebration of Life."

"What's that?"

"Nowadays, lots of families don't do the whole formal, churchy funeral thing. They have a small service, close family only, and a couple of weeks later, they hold a big blast for friends and family of the deceased. It's called a Celebration of Life."

Dodie heaved herself to her feet and grabbed my hands. "Perfect. We'll have a Celebration of Life to commemorate Luc. Naturally, you'll be the spokesperson. Guests will expect our general manager to take charge."

My stomach twisted as my fear of public speaking kicked in. Delivering a speech makes my knees weak, and not in a good way. I preferred to forget my best friend's wedding thirty-five years ago, where I embarrassed myself by throwing up into the punch bowl at the mere thought of delivering a toast to the bride.

"Nope," I said, shaking my head. "No microphone. No speeches. I don't do speeches."

"You do now. Someone died. The GM has to give a speech."

She was right. I had a duty to suck it up for the greater good, both for the guests and for our covert murder investigation. "Okay. How hard can it be? All I have to do is talk. I can talk. Before dinner, I'll mention the Celebration of Life and ask everyone acquainted with Luc to stay. When the time comes, I'll kick it off with a short speech. To loosen tongues, we'll make sure everyone gets good and drunk over dinner."

"Everyone except you. Right?"

Only one teeny-tiny glass to take the edge off . . .

"Of course." I changed the subject. "After dessert, which I believe is blueberry grunt, I intend to—"

Dodie interjected, "You might want to skip dessert. Just sayin'."

I flipped her the finger. "As I was saying, after dessert, I'll kick off the Celebration of Life by inviting everyone who knew Luc to speak a few words about him."

"You sure you're okay to get up and speak?"

"Never been happier." I intended to blow our guests' minds with my eloquence and wit.

"I'll make sure to seat all our suspects along with Zeke, you, and myself at the same table," Dodie said.

"Make sure I'm seated beside Zeke. And let's include Tess to make it an even eight."

Dodie's evil grin stretched from ear to ear. "I like the way your mind works. Even if Zeke doesn't see her as a suspect, we wouldn't want her to feel excluded, would we?"

I laughed. "It'll be perfect."

Chapter 10:
Revelations

WE ARRIVED EARLY. DODIE HURRIED into the dining hall to make sure everything was ready. I, on the other hand, stayed put in the lobby to welcome our guests, who would arrive any minute.

Brimming with nervous energy, I wandered around, swiping at specks of dust, straightening cushions, and snagging a chocolate truffle each time I passed the check-in desk, which was often. Spying a mammoth cut-crystal vase full of red gladioli in a corner, I decided they deserved a more prominent spot on the ornamental table located mid-lobby. Nothing says welcome like fresh-cut flowers, right?

Gripping the hefty vase with both hands, I staggered under its bulk. I was halfway across the reception area when an alarming sensation in the vicinity of my skirt's back closure warned me the tortured zipper had conceded defeat. The waistband tightened around my middle until I thought it would slice me in two. A single straining button was all that preserved my modesty.

I shuffled along faster. My destination was within arm's length when I sensed a faint twang at my waistline as the button parted company with my waistband. Unable to run, I stood frozen in horror as the skirt slithered over my ass, whispered down my legs, and, with a swish of rich fabric, pooled in a psychedelic heap around my ankles. I stepped out of it pronto and maneuvered the vase onto the table.

Holy snot buckets. I was standing in the middle of the lobby wearing nothing but a fancy blouse, strappy sandals, and the fudge-fudgity-McFudging teddy, which had vanished into my most private parts, giving me a killer wedgie. I huffed out a sigh of gratitude that no one else was in sight.

Fighting the undergarment's grip on my privates, I strained downward to rescue the skirt before anyone arrived. Easier said than done. A suit of armor was more flexible than this teddy.

A whisper of cool air against my ass signalled the end of my lucky streak. Goaded by desperation, I executed a deep-knee bend, made possible only by my karate training. Hauling the skirt northward, I pivoted to face the door. For a split second, I closed my eyes in pure humiliation.

I wagered the gorgeous Veronica had never experienced an embarrassing moment in her entire life. She wore a simple little black number, which hugged her body in all the right places, fabulous gold stilettos, and a delicate gold filigree necklace.

I clutched my skirt and waggled the fingers of my other hand at her.

"Abby. How horrible for you," she exclaimed, tap-tapping closer. "Don't worry. It's only me." Her face was bright pink with what I feared was suppressed merriment.

With the teddy sawing away at my lady-parts, I forced myself to pretend skirt droppage was an everyday event. "Veronica. You have no idea how glad I am to see you. As you can see, I've had a slight wardrobe malfunction."

"Going commando tonight are we?" she asked.

Was it my imagination or did her lips twitch with bottled-up laughter? I forced a carefree giggle. "Commando's not my style." I kept a death-grip on my waistband. "I'm wearing a flesh-colored teddy."

"If you say so." She dug into a black-and-gold clutch and rummaged around. "Where is it? Ah, here we go. You should always carry one of these, just in case." She handed me an industrial-sized safety pin.

"Thank you so much." I released one hand to grab the pin and lowered my voice to a confidential whisper. "Woman-to-woman, please don't mention my, um, little misfortune to anyone, okay?"

"I wouldn't dream of it." She glided away and into the dining hall.

The skirt repair job kept me busy for some time. By the time I'd finished, the last of our hungry guests were motoring through the lobby. I let them pass before I worked up the nerve to scuttle in behind them.

On reaching the dining hall, I admired the changes we'd made over the winter. Windows lined two entire walls. Log beams added rustic accents while elegant chandeliers marched down the center of a cathedral ceiling.

No wonder we were in debt up to our eyeballs. I assured myself it was worth the risk. After our symposium, word would spread, and the well-heeled clientèle we needed would flock to Grizzly Gulch.

Guests filled several of the large round tables and six of the smaller ones. White linens draped all the tables, which were set with gleaming cutlery and floral centerpieces. I scanned the room and caught sight of Dodie and Zeke seated with our suspects. Muffy looked as if she'd been crying, but everyone else at the table radiated amusement at my approach. Dodie spread her hands. "Sorry," she mouthed at me.

What the fudge?

My gaze landed on Zeke who was watching me in that special way he had, calm, steady. My pulse somersaulted, then slowed down a whole lot when I realized he was sitting beside Tess. Her barely concealed boobs thrust toward him like a pair of heat-seeking missiles. The only empty seat was between Muffy and Harmony.

Tess, who'd clearly switched seats while Dodie's back was turned, pointed to the vacant spot and yelled, "We saved you a seat, Abby."

Unwilling to call out a guest for spoiling my chance to sit beside Zeke for dinner, I lowered myself into the vacant chair and opened my napkin with a vicious snap.

"I was real sorry to hear about your wardrobe malfunction," Tess said, not bothering to suppress a snicker.

"Thanks so much, hon," I chirped, flicking a malevolent glance at Veronica. She studiously ignored me.

Harmony, a wraparound dress in a drab olive color draped around her bulk, said in a booming voice, "Yeah. I'm impressed. Few women your age have the guts to go commando."

I cast a furtive glance around the room to see if anyone had heard her. Yep. Everyone in the dining hall was staring at me, most in amusement. Several raised a glass in my direction. Dinner was off to a rip-roaring start. Not only had I undergone a humiliating exercise equipment incident, I'd been robbed of my seat next to Zeke and lost my skirt in public. But the kicker was Veronica, a woman I'd liked and trusted. She'd blabbed about my wardrobe malfunction. The whole room knew about my humiliation.

Zeke knew.

I reached for my wine glass and took a slug. It went down so well, I took another.

The discovery that my glass was empty coincided with my recollection that I had to deliver a speech. I gestured to the waiter for refills all around.

After draining my second glass, I had relaxed enough to smile and face my challenges with a can-do attitude. Hey, after surviving a next-to-naked escapade in the lobby, a speech would be easy-peasy.

Feeling mellow, I heaved to my feet. With one hand braced on the table for balance, I leaned across Harmony toward Dodie and said in a stage whisper, "Be a dear, would you? Bring me the wireless microphone from the podium."

"You're tipsy," she hissed. "I thought we discussed the wine situation."

"I would get the mic myself," I said, realizing I might be a tad lubricated, "but my teddy makes it difficult to walk."

"Don't touch another drop." Dodie took off at warp speed.

While she dashed between the tables, I beamed at all the beautiful faces turned in my direction. Raising my now-empty glass, I yelled, "Bottoms up." Everyone in the room obeyed in a most gratifying way. Mindful of Dodie's rebuke, I pretend-glugged and set my glass down.

Clay shouted, "Speaking of bottoms, I understand you're going commando tonight." He gave me a thumbs-up. I gave him a broad grin and signalled the waiters to pour refills all around. At the last second, I had the wits to clap a hand over my glass.

To fill the empty air space, I bantered with the crowd, recounting several anecdotes about growing up with two sisters.

Everyone laughed. Hey, this was fun. I'd never bantered before, and it was exhilarating. Powerful. Addictive.

Dodie, who materialized beside me with the mic, shot me a quelling look and whispered, "You're too drunk to give a speech. Sit down before you fall down."

"It's okay," I whispered back. "I've stopped drinking. I can do the pre-dinner announcement, no problem." While prying the mic from her fingers, I remembered our strategy to loosen the guests' tongues. After beckoning to a server for refills all around, I took a slurp of water and started talking. "Good evening, everyone. Welcome to your first dinner at Grizzly Gulch.

I have information to share with you before we start." Pleased with the way my voice boomed into the room and echoed off the ceiling, I ignored Dodie's scowl and continued. "First off, I will neither confirm nor deny the assertion that I'm going commando tonight." Yeah, maybe a little blitzed after all.

Over the laughter and a couple of wolf whistles, one of the twins yelled, "What's going commando?"

I spoke into the mic, concentrating like crazy on my enunciation. "It means not wearing any underwear, dear."

"Then we go commando all the time," the other twin yelled. "So does Dad."

Hey, this was easy. And fun. I was a born public speaker. I replied, "Well done, boys. Air out your dangly bits every chance you get. In fact that's excellent advice for all males." Glancing at Dodie, I hastened on, "But I digress. In addition to the announcements I made this afternoon after we found the corpse—"

Dodie tugged on my sleeve, whispering, "Ixnay on orpse-cay."

Uh-oh. I recognized the pig-Latin of our childhood. Without missing a beat, I said, "What I meant to say is that in spite of today's terrible tragedy, our workshop schedule remains unchanged. Tomorrow afternoon, everyone is invited to a workshop called *The Challenges of Semen Collection*, followed by a highly stimulating, hands-on semen collection demo."

Dead silence followed my announcement.

Catching Dodie's head-thunk, I clarified my comment. "These events are part of our equine breeding symposium."

A collective sigh of relief rippled through the room, followed by excited chatter. Dollars to donuts tomorrow's demo would have standing room only. Over the din, a twin's voice yelled. "Hey, Mom, what's semen? Is it like maple syrup?"

"Yeah, do you collect it in a bucket?"

For some reason, there were two identical Dodies, both of them glaring at me. Running my words together, I said, "After dessert, which I understand is blueberry grunt—don't you love the name? Blueberry grunt, blueberry grunt, blueberry grunt—" I caught myself and stopped. "You get the picture. In conclusion, after dessert, we're inviting anyone acquainted with Luc Lacroix to stay and share some memories at a Celebration of Life."

I picked up my water glass and lifted it. "To Luc Lacroix."

"To Luc," everyone intoned, and drained their glasses.

The two Dodies, who morphed into one whenever I squinted, lurched to her feet and wrestled the mic from my grasp. Enunciating every word clearly, she addressed the crowd. "Please enjoy your dinner. I hope I can." She switched off the mic and sat to a smattering of polite applause.

I beamed at my sister as I, too, plunked my butt down, wincing as the teddy cut into tender flesh. "That went rather well, yes?"

With disbelief oozing from every pore, she whispered, "Don't even *consider* chairing the Celebration of Life. I'm doing it."

Everyone but Dodie and Tess offered words of praise. Zeke held my gaze, saying, "You gave a memorable performance."

Time sped by, mainly because I managed a power nap between the appetizer and rib-eye steak, medium rare, and another between the steak and blueberry grunt. By the time I'd consumed two cups of coffee, I'd sobered up.

I basked in my success. My banter drew laughter (Dodie's disapproval notwithstanding), dinner was delicious, Zeke more-or-less evaded Tess's clutches, and our suspects were nicely blitzed.

Satisfied that I had primed the pump, so to speak, I stood and clinked my water glass with a spoon. Who needed a mic, anyway? Ignoring Dodie's warning glare, I raised my voice in the sudden silence. "I trust everyone enjoyed Chef Armand's fabulous dinner as much as I did."

I waited for the applause to die and continued, "This is the moment many of us have waited for—the Celebration of Life for Luc Lacroix. I invite everyone who knew him to stay and say a few words about your relationship, how you met him, your memories of him, whatever tickles your fancy." I plopped down again. As far as I was concerned, my job was done. All I had to do was listen and remember what was said.

Most of the guests trooped out of the dining hall, leaving only Luc's acquaintances and a smattering of curiosity seekers in the room. The twins took off to race around the room while everyone else squeezed together around our table.

After a short silence, Clay was the first to stand. "I never actually met Luc in person until today, but I hear he worked magic with the animals he trained."

"Yeah, right. Chemical magic," Harmony muttered under her breath. Raising her voice, she asked, "Why were you so eager to kick Luc's ass? You mentioned something about Luc screwing you over in a business deal."

"A minor misunderstanding. These things happen with emails," Clay said, sitting down and draping his arm across the back of Veronica's chair, letting it rest against her shoulder. Romance appeared to be flourishing.

I made a mental note to learn more about Luc's suspected horse drugging, and to pump Clay for information about the minor misunderstanding he'd mentioned.

I returned to the present when Muffy stood and cleared her throat. "I knew Luc at university," she began. "We were both in the same animal science class." She used her linen napkin to dab her eyes.

I hoped she used waterproof mascara.

"You also dated him," Veronica pointed out, her voice bitter.

Muffy sniffed and shrugged one elegant Versace-draped shoulder. "On-and-off. Luc was gorgeous, always working his bad boy vibe, and don't pretend you didn't notice, Missy. You drooled every time he walked that excellent ass of his into class."

"On-and-off, my sweet patooties," Veronica said. "You guys were inseparable."

Tears streamed down Muffy's face. "I was one of the few people who understood and liked him. After high school, he escaped a horrible home life with an abusive father and alcoholic mother and put himself through university."

Veronica sprang to her feet. "By dealing drugs."

"He vowed he'd never be poor again." Muffy stared at Veronica and used her linen napkin to blow her nose. "He got to you, too."

"What do you mean?"

"You had a huge crush on him. Everyone in class knew fat, frumpy Veronica Melville did all Luc's assignments. It was the only way he managed to graduate."

"I coached him a little, is all," Veronica protested. "I was more than happy to help."

"Uh-huh. You helped him, both in and out of bed. But you didn't understand him. You only thought he was hot."

Veronica flushed a mottled scarlet. Remarkably, she still looked gorgeous. "I owe Luc a debt of gratitude. Look at me." She spun around in a circle, her model's body sleek and limber in its curve-hugging dress. Skimming her hands down her torso, she said, "My appearance is different now, right?"

Unable to contain myself, I blurted, "Luc didn't recognize you at check-in."

Beside me, Muffy whispered, "No wonder. In those days, she had bad teeth, a crooked nose, and a receding chin, plus she carried an excess fifty pounds of flab. My guess is plastic surgery, fat farms, dental implants, liposuction, the works."

It appeared Veronica was a fraud inside and out. No wonder she couldn't be trusted.

Clearly unaware of Muffy's scathing comments, Veronica gave me a condescending smile. "That was part of the plan. At university, I was desperately in love with Luc, and he led me to believe he returned my feelings. Apparently not, because he dumped me as soon as he graduated, saying I was too ugly for his liking. Those words haunted me for years. Thanks to Luc's cruelty, I was motivated to change, not only in appearance, but in savvy. I will never, *ever* let anyone take advantage of me again."

It was obvious Veronica seethed with complex emotions and resentments. Were they strong enough to drive her to murder? Did she go to Luc's cabin to tease him? I caught Dodie's gaze. She gave an imperceptible nod.

At least we were on the same wavelength. I hoped Dodie was taking notes.

At that point, Muffy cleared her throat. "I want to mention how Luc had a magic way with horses. He was the best in the business, so I hired him as my trainer. He takes—took—care of those racehorses as if they were his babies. He loved them, and they loved him back. He was a remarkable man." Muffy sat, leaned her head on her arms, and sobbed.

If I hadn't known how much she loved Franklin, I'd have thought Muffy had the hots for Luc. I reached over and patted her shoulder. We both knew her husband had ordered her to fire Luc because of horse drugging rumors. I needed to follow up on both the horse drugging gossip and Franklin's whereabouts at the time of the murder. Was he really in Saudi Arabia?

I was lost in thought when Harmony jumped to her feet and yelled, "Where there's smoke, there's fire."

Everyone except the twins, who were making pretend-farts against their armpits, stopped talking and settled down to listen. Even Muffy raised her head and dried her eyes. Big John ended the boys' fun by grabbing each by the scruff of his neck and speaking softly. Remarkably, they settled down. I wondered what he'd threatened. Or promised, as the case may be.

"Thank you," Harmony said, frowning around the room. "I met Luc for the first time today when he threw me out of the barn. I did, however, know him by reputation."

She turned to address Muffy. "I hope you realize people in town are talking about how your horses started winning races as soon as you hired Luc." Her voice dripped with bitterness. "Well, here's a newsflash. The magic he used came in pharmaceutical form."

Muffy leaped to her feet again, this time to defend Luc, saying he'd always had a special way with animals, while Harmony yelled about his reputation for horse drugging.

During the ensuing chaos, I mused that drugging was a recurring theme.

Harmony raised it at every possible opportunity. Perhaps there was more than a mere ethical difference of opinion here. What if Luc's horse drugging had harmed Harmony in some way?

The twins' shrill voices interrupted my musing. I turned my head to see the boys advancing on our table and pointing at Tess.

"Look," Wes shrieked, "that lady's showing off her boobies again."

Sure enough, Tess was on her feet and thrusting her boobs at the world.

Coop said, "They sure are big ones, mmpfh—" Big John had clapped a hand over both mouths before hauling them back to their seats.

Ignoring them, Tess beamed at the Wright family. "Aren't you the sweetest little family? Your children are so energetic. I love the way they speak their minds." From the expressions around the room, no one, including the parents, believed her.

Tess chugged her glass of wine before speaking. "The first time I met Luc was today. His horse was upset, so I tried to console him. I always carry glucose tabs to counteract an accidental insulin overdose, but they also do double duty as little treats for Morning Glory, my lovely little mare back home. Luc yelled at me and knocked the box out of my hand." A mammoth sigh inflated her chest so much, her boobage was in danger of popping out. "He actually yelled at me. Can you imagine?"

Absolutely.

"Poor, uptight guy," Tess continued. "No wonder the horse was agitated." With that, she sat and signalled the waiter for a refill.

The remaining speakers weren't suspects, but as a courtesy, they received their air space too. It didn't take long. While the twins tried to give one another wedgies, Big John rushed through his thoughts on Luc, saying he hated to speak ill of the dead, but Luc stepped way over the line when he threatened his sons. After he ran out of steam, Sheila reminisced about Luc's university days. He'd been a practical joker with a high opinion of himself, always surrounded by flocks of women.

Yeah, Luc had been one stand-up dude.

On that note, Dodie decided it was time to wrap up the evening. She stood to remind those who'd stayed behind about the next day's trail ride followed by the semen collection demo.

Tess, who was showing the effects of two bottles of excellent Merlot, gripped Zeke's arm on the way out of the dining room. She giggled as she stumbled against him, making sure her dress gaped to the max.

Zeke disengaged from Tess and faced me. Quietly, he said, "Wait up. I won't be long," before letting Tess suction herself to his arm and drag him away.

My sister grasped my arm and frog-marched me upstairs to my apartment. At the door, I produced my key, and said, "I can't imagine why I was so worried about public speaking. Everybody loved me. I think I have a new calling."

"You're cut off. No more wine, and especially no more speeches for you."

"Nonsense. I'm perfectly sober, and we got plenty of leads from the Celebration of Life."

"True," Dodie admitted, examining my face. "You look like you're fading fast."

"I am."

"Drink lots of water." she advised. "Also take your acid reflux meds and don't forget painkillers for the hangover you so richly deserve."

After she left, I didn't hold out much hope Zeke would arrive. As much as I hated to admit it, fluttery little Tess had out-maneuvered me. My experience with men told me they couldn't be trusted in the face of temptation. And much as I hated to admit it, Tess posed a huge temptation.

If I was wise, I wouldn't wait up for him.

Chapter 11:
Pool Animals

S EEMED I WASN'T WISE AT all. Zeke stood me up in favor of Tess. I'd waited an hour for him to join me before admitting to myself he was a no-show. After performing my bedtime rituals, which took longer with every passing year, I drank a gallon of water to wash down my acid reflux meds and a couple of extra-strength painkillers.

As soon as I snuggled my down-filled duvet up to my chin, a vision of Tess having her wicked way with Zeke popped into my head. To the tune of my monkey-brain's unrelenting chatter, I tried every trick I'd learned to help me fall asleep—drilling my knuckle into the calming acupressure point between my eyebrows, deep breathing (resulting in a nasty hyperventilation episode), visualization (a satisfying blackfly attack on Tess), positive affirmations (I'm ready, willing, and able to take Tess down).

Something must have worked because an unfamiliar noise jolted me from a fitful slumber. According to my clock it was 1:45 a.m. Faint splashing accompanied by not-so-faint bleating filled the night air.

Tossing the covers aside, I hurtled to the sliding glass door, stepped outside, and studied the swimming pool, which was illuminated to a turquoise glow by submerged lighting. Although we always locked the gate after midnight, a late night pool party was underway. Under rising steam, the water surged and frothed with activity.

After running inside to get my glasses, I settled them on my nose and studied the pool. Definitely not people. When a breeze cleared the steam away, I determined that the pool was full of ... animals.

I'd heard of an elk enjoying a soak in a pool up Bragg Creek way, even a black bear with her two cubs escaping the heat in a community pool near

Priddis, but this one would make new history. Larry-the-llama was treading water in the deep end of our brand new heated pool. Eight dwarf goats bobbed around him, bleating their heads off.

This was a deliberate act of sabotage. Without human assistance, there was no way the animals had escaped their pen, trotted to the pool, unlocked the gate, and leaped merrily into the water for a late-night dip.

I shuddered when I imagined the complaints we'd receive. We would need to empty, sanitize, and re-fill the pool before anyone used it again.

I shrugged into a robe, stuffed my feet into flip-flops, and pocketed my glasses and phone. Deciding to take a shortcut by leaving through the kitchen exit onto the back stairs, I snagged my set of master keys from a hook in the pantry. I made sure the lock was engaged before descending. Once my feet hit the ground, I crossed the dew-soaked grass to the pool.

The gate swung open at my touch. Another set of master keys dangled from the lock. I edged inside, staying a safe distance from the pool. The distinctive groan of a distressed llama underscored frantic bleating. Who knew eight goats and one llama could make so much uproar?

I caught a whiff of fresh, ripe manure. The animals had used the pool as a communal toilet. The evidence had sunk to the bottom, forming a dark, cloudy mess. Luckily, any floaters on the surface were pieces of gnawed apple and a couple of carrots. I guessed the perp had used them as bait.

It struck me that adversity had a way of striking while I was in charge. This blow wasn't in the same league as Luc's murder, but still. I'd been asleep while someone had silently coaxed a herd of animals into our pristine swimming pool, transforming it into a smelly latrine.

A shiver of fear rippled through me. What sicko would do this? The deed might be connected to the murder, but I couldn't fathom how.

I pulled out my cell and called Dodie.

After multiple rings, she picked up and yawned into the phone. "Abby? Cheezits. Do you know what time it is?"

"Not important. I'm standing beside the swimming pool. Hustle your buns over."

After a deep sigh, Dodie said, "This had better be good."

"You have no idea."

Next, I got a grip on my emotions and called Zeke, hoping I'd interrupted a crucial moment with Tess.

"Yeah?" he mumbled, sounding groggy, likely in the midst of post-coital bliss.

Something inside me went cold, and I swallowed hard around the lump in my throat before blurting, "It's Abby. There's an emergency. Please meet me at the pool area right away."

"Wait. What—"

I clicked off, flopped onto a lounge chair, and looked up. The crystal clarity of an Alberta night sky never failed to calm me. Breathing in a lungful of crisp air, I marveled at the millions of stars strewn across the black canvas. After a few minutes, my puny emotional hang-ups scarcely mattered in the face of infinity.

Zeke arrived first. He'd pulled on sweats and a black t-shirt with a rampaging bull over the slogan "Got Bull?" on the chest. He oozed sex appeal.

I heaved to my feet. Hopefully, darkness hid the immediate softening of my knees, and surely my heart's quickening thump wasn't audible. "Check it out," I said, gesturing at the animals splashing around in the pool.

Zeke's forehead creased in a deep scowl. He might look as tough as leather on the outside, but he'd walk over burning coals for those he cared about, including helpless animals.

Dodie's arrival curtailed my wistful thoughts. After staring at the incredible scene for a long interval, she said, "Lord love a duck. It's a good job the guest cabins are down in the grove. With luck, no one's noticed the animals. We can't let one single guest get wind of this. What'll we do?"

A goat tried to climb onto Larry's back and failed, splashing down into the water with a terrified bleat.

"We need to get the animals out of the pool and back to their pen," I replied.

Zeke stepped to the edge of the pool. "I'll coax Larry out, and the goats will follow."

He snagged some chunks of apple bobbing within reach. Walking to the shallow end, he held out the apple while speaking softly to the llama. Larry's nostrils quivered, and he surged toward Zeke and climbed out, making a beeline for the fruit. The goats followed Larry, bleating their complaints every inch of the way.

Surrounded by dripping and indignant animals, Zeke said, "I'll take them to their pen and be right back." He held out another piece of apple and started walking. Larry stayed on Zeke's heels, his nose outstretched, and the goats capered behind.

"Wow," Dodie said. "Zeke's better than the pied piper."

Trying to be quiet, we skimmed the pool and dumped the mess into a wheelbarrow kept behind the pool shed. Once we'd cleared out the worst, the water remained cloudy and discolored.

"Now what?" Dodie asked.

Nothing brilliant sprang to mind.

On Zeke's return, he took charge immediately. "First we roll the safety cover over the pool, then I'll turn on the drainage pump. Once the pool's empty, the pool guy will scrub it down and sanitize it. I'll book a pumper truck for the refill."

"Won't the guests notice a foul smell while it's draining?" Dodie asked.

"You did a great job of skimming, so hopefully odor won't be an issue. If necessary, we'll tell everyone the neighboring ranch is mucking out its barns. The backwash hose is long enough to drain into a dry gully leading into the forested area behind us. No one will notice anything's amiss."

While Zeke went to the pump house, I set up a sign saying, "No Swimming Due to Pool Maintenance," in front of the gate.

The pump's hollow thumping preceded Zeke's reappearance. "Drainage will take a couple of days, minimum," he said, removing the keys and locking the gate. Examining them, he said, "Hey, these keys are mine. I wonder how they got here."

"Maybe you lost them and the perp picked them up." I gave an exaggerated yawn. "I'm exhausted. Gotta go to bed." I had no intention of spending more time with Zeke than necessary. It was too unsettling.

In a flash, he was beside me. "Not so fast. I'm not letting either of you wander off alone, especially after midnight. It might be dangerous."

He was right. I had no choice but to let him walk us home. Sensing Dodie wanted to decompress and chat over a nightcap, I had to discourage her from inviting Zeke inside. If he asked to stay, I might not be strong enough to send him away.

The main lodge wasn't far. When we arrived, the lobby was dimly lit. Punching in the code, I rushed inside mumbling, "Thanks for the help. See you both in the morning." I darted for the stairs.

Dodie prevented my escape by grabbing my arm, nearly yanking it from the socket. Turning to Zeke, she said, "Don't mind Abby. She's not at her best. Come on upstairs. I need a nightcap, and Abby has plenty of beer."

"Don't mind if I do," he answered.

Not after standing me up for Tess, you don't.

"I'm afraid not," I said with my sweetest smile. "I have a killer headache."

They ignored my protests and followed me into my apartment.

Chapter 12:
Midnight Resolution

ZEKE DISAPPEARED INTO MY LIVING room. I addressed Dodie's back as she headed for my kitchen. "I've had more than enough to drink for one night." When she didn't respond, I raised my voice. "I'm taking another painkiller and flaking out. You two enjoy your drinks. Lock up when you leave."

"Don't be ridiculous," Dodie said, returning with two Moosehead Lagers and a large glass of something clear and fizzy she'd poured for me. "Have some Perrier. It'll help with the headache."

I accepted the glass and trailed after her into my living room.

Zeke, who'd telescoped his large frame onto my white loveseat, patted the cushion beside him. "Sit. You'll feel better if we talk about it."

I stayed on my feet, unable to look away as he rolled up his sleeves, revealing bronzed and lightly furred forearms. Muscles bunched and corded as he picked up his beer. I suppressed a whimper when his lips closed around the bottle. A large gulp caused his Adam's apple to bob. If he kissed me now, his mouth would be cool, seductive, enticing.

Thankfully, Dodie interrupted my runaway imagination by pulling up a chair and settling herself with a tired grunt. "Who would sabotage our pool?" she asked.

Distracted by lust, I perched on the loveseat's arm. "Anyone." Honesty compelled me to add, "Except Tess."

"How so?" Dodie asked.

"She was with Zeke." I cast an accusing glare at the guilty party, a huge strategic mistake because it revealed my jealousy.

"Tess was under the weather. I walked her to her cabin, but only stuck around long enough to make sure she was okay."

"And how was she? Okay, mediocre, or superlative?" I blurted, then snapped my mouth shut in dismay. Under normal circumstances, I choose my words with care, but this time, my tongue bypassed my brain. "Forget I said that. I'm going to bed." I was too old to play this game.

I prepared to rise but his amused voice stopped me. "Aw, you're jealous. That's sweet."

I shrugged. "Don't be ridiculous." To prove I wasn't the least bit upset, I slugged back a mouthful of fizzy mineral water followed by a larger gulp, which promptly went down the wrong pipe.

The harder I tried to suppress the cough, the more my chest spasmed. Acutely aware of tears streaming down my cheeks and snot leaking from my nose, a particularly attractive touch, I turned away from Zeke while clamping my lips shut against an imminent eruption.

"You okay?" Dodie asked, leaping from her chair and coming around to examine my face, which was probably purple. "You don't look too good. Is there pain in your arm or jaw? Pressure in the middle of your chest?"

Unable to speak, I waved her away.

The explosion was impressive. Fizzy water backwashed up through my sinuses in a burning torrent, coming close to irrigating my frontal lobe before jetting out through my nose in graceful twin arcs.

The blast propelled me into the nearest seat, which was the loveseat Zeke occupied. As I rocketed in for a landing, I caught his startled expression. Hiding my face with both hands, I squinched into the corner, as far away from him as possible.

Angel of Death, please take me now.

How was it that I, a mature woman who would gladly opt to have her eyes poked out with blunt sticks rather than look foolish, had experienced three supremely humiliating moments in under twelve hours?

In the silence following my showstopper, I felt the cushion beside me shift, and sensed Zeke's departure. Yep, I'd scared him off. Just as well. The breakup was cleaner this way. A moment later, a whisper of fabric and the compression of the cushion beside me indicated he'd returned. Taking a sidewise glance, I glimpsed a tanned, sinewy hand holding a wad of tissues in front of my face. I snatched the tissues and buried my face in their softness.

During the mop-up process, which was substantial due to fluids oozing from multiple facial orifices, more tissues appeared. Once the job was done, I raised my head, certain I would see derision written on his face.

His eyes brimmed with compassion and acceptance.

"Things like that happen," he said, trying to comfort me. "During my time in Afghanistan, our entire unit was in the mess hall chowing down on grilled cheese and tomato soup. I'd taken my first mouthful of soup, when an explosion outside caused most everyone to dive under the tables, seeing as how it was a war zone. Except me. See, the shock of the blast made my soup go down the wrong pipe. I sprayed the whole mess tent with tomato soup. Hurt like crazy, like I'd taken a scouring pad to my sinuses. Turned out it was only a truck backfiring. I never lived it down."

"Unnngggh," I replied, trying to sound sophisticated, no mean feat after hosing down the living room and everyone in it—*using my nose*.

"As I was explaining," Zeke continued, as if nothing unusual had happened, "I only stuck around with Tess long enough to walk her to her cabin and make sure she was okay. Turned out she wasn't nearly as drunk as I'd thought."

"Or pretended to be," Dodi noted.

"Exactly," he said. "She got all insulted when I refused to stick around for a drink."

"And whatever else she had in mind," I mumbled under my breath.

Ignoring my interruption, he grasped my hands, damp tissues and all. "Abby, I want you to listen to what I'm going to say." I tried to retreat, but he tightened his grip. "No, don't pull away. Tess holds no attraction for me. I have my eye on someone else, a fascinating and highly intelligent woman." Gazing at me, he shifted slightly, brushing his leg against mine.

My face radiated heat. This must be what a kebab felt like on the grill.

Dodie's question to Zeke broke the tension. "What did you do after you left Tess's cabin?"

I'd never seen a six-foot-three man squirm like a little boy, but Zeke proved it was possible. There was a beat of silence. Avoiding my gaze, he said, "The last thing I meant to do was stand you up, Abby, but truth is I got to thinking Lancelot was depressed over Luc's absence." He looked directly at me. "Horses are capable of simple emotions, even if they don't process them the way we humans do."

As I took in the sight of him, his brow all furrowed at the thought of a grieving horse, my heart kicked hard. "I get it," I said. And I did. If it wasn't for the employee-boss thing, there might be a ray of hope for us.

While looking at me steadily, almost as if I was important, as if I meant something to him, he said "I figured I'd best make a quick visit to the stables to visit Lancelot first. Turned out he was agitated, pacing around his stall and pining for Luc. I hated to leave him alone, so I decided to stick around for a few minutes, at least until he settled."

"It's okay, Zeke. I get it."

But it seemed he had more to get off his chest because words kept pouring out. "I had outstanding bills to pay," he continued, "but first I made sure all the doors were locked. It was only supposed to take five minutes, but I fell asleep at my desk, probably due to all those wine refills over dinner. Next thing I remember is your phone call. I left in such a hurry I didn't think about keys."

"But your keys were in the pool enclosure lock. If you didn't use them and if everything was locked up, how did someone else get hold of them?"

A pained expression crossed Zeke's face. "Before checking on Lancelot, I tossed the keys onto my desk and opened the window to let in fresh air. The desk is under a window. Someone must have reached in and snatched the keys, either when I was with Lancelot or while I was asleep."

Dodie broke the tension with a noisy yawn before standing. "I'm glad you sorted out the mystery. I'm going to bed. At least I don't have far to go." She headed for the front door and let herself out.

A shimmering silence stretched out as I walked to the window, acutely aware of Zeke beside me. We waited there together until the light came on in her apartment next door to mine. Even then, we didn't move.

A quiver of awareness skittered along my nerves. Not just awareness, but bone-deep yearning.

His gaze met mine, heated up, and I reminded myself he was off-limits. Cheezits, this was difficult. I didn't want to announce my policy on dating an employee. For all I knew, he might just up and quit anyway—a disaster I was trying to prevent by refusing to date him.

I chewed my lip.

He wandered over to the loveseat and sat. "Hey, what's wrong? You've been skittish all day." He patted the cushion beside him. "Sit and talk to me."

If I got near him I was a goner, so I moved to the chair facing him. I sat, crossing my legs to show off my ankles, my slimmest part.

"I want you to know I'm not jealous of Tess," I said.

"Good. Because you have no cause for jealousy."

"Tess likes you a lot. You should date her. She seems like a lovely woman."

"There's only one woman I want to date, and it's you." Zeke gave me a searching look. "What are you *really* trying to say?"

I stomped on a surge of longing, and kicked it to the curb. "Okay, you deserve to know." I took a deep breath. "I can't date you. Last week, the thing we did after line dancing, I should never have let that stuff happen."

His smile hit me in the chest like a line drive. "We're too good together to give up without trying. I know you feel it too. Tell me why you're talking such nonsense."

"It's complicated."

"I'm listening."

I scrambled to conjure up a plausible excuse. One that didn't involve an alcoholic and abusive father with commitment issues, compounded by a husband who was so similar, he might have been Daddy's clone.

"My life is out of control," I began. "Besides running Grizzly Gulch and covering for Clara, I have to deal with a murder and sabotage, plus we're overextended financially. I'm afraid there's simply no room in my life for a new relationship."

He fixed those intense, dark eyes on me. "The last thing I want to do is add to your burdens. Tell you what. I'll do everything in my power to help you through all the complications, plus I'm a real good listener. I'm happy to wait until you're ready."

No, no, no. This man was too good to be true. My ex had also been the picture of charm and understanding, at least at the start. Until everything changed. I had to find the strength to push Zeke away. My heart twisted in my chest. Feigning a calmness I was far from feeling, I said, "I'm sorry. Any other woman would count herself the luckiest woman in the world. I'm simply not ready." For emphasis, I added, "It's me, not you."

True, that.

He rolled his eyes. "I'm not buying. You wouldn't have acted the way you did with me last week if you didn't care. We enjoy one another too much, laugh at the same stuff, love the same movies, and would walk a mile in a blizzard for a maple-glazed doughnut or a Montreal smoked meat sandwich. Better still, we both like pineapple, hot banana peppers, and olives on our pizza. Please tell me the truth. I can handle it."

After undergoing years of therapy after my divorce I'd shared my insights with Clara and Dodie, but I'd never revealed the sordid details with anyone else. Zeke deserved the truth, and I didn't know how to begin.

"How 'bout you tell me what the problem is," he suggested. "Sharing can be liberating."

Okay, so he'd given me the opening I needed. My heart cartwheeled, warning me that if I didn't take this leap of trust, I might never be granted another opportunity. Over the roar of blood pounding in my ears, I said, "My problems—and make no mistake, I have huge ones—started at birth. Mom was the perfect homemaker and loving parent. Daddy was charming, charismatic, and handsome. He was also a high-functioning alcoholic, wife-batterer and serial womanizer. The man made manipulation, cheating, and bullying an art-form."

"Sweet baby Jesus." Zeke's voice cracked. "If your daddy so much as laid a finger on you, I'll—"

"You can't touch him now. He's dead." I rushed on before Zeke could ask any more questions. "I always picture Mom wearing long sleeved blouses and high-buttoned necklines, even in the middle of summer."

"To hide the bruises."

The empathy in Zeke's eyes caught me by surprise. "Yeah." To give my hands something to do, I picked at a thread on the sleeve of my robe as I talked. "I felt responsible for my two younger sisters, so I tried to be the perfect daughter. I thought if I could please Daddy, he wouldn't hurt us, at least, not physically. It mostly worked for us kids, but Mom didn't fare so well. At least he waited until he thought we were asleep. I was married when they both died in a car crash because he insisted on driving drunk." I stopped speaking as tears clogged my throat.

"I hope you realize none of it was your fault. You couldn't have stopped him."

"Intellectually, yes. But somehow, my brain forgot to tell my heart," I replied through clogged sinuses, accepting a tissue from Zeke.

Although he hadn't so much as touched me, his calm support gave me the strength to continue. "Elliot Hutton was my managerial accounting professor at the University of Calgary. We re-connected several years after I'd graduated. Like Daddy, Elliot was a high-functioning alcoholic. He hid it well. We fell in love, at least I did. After we got married, he convinced the University of Toronto bigwigs to grant him tenure there. I was so blinded by his charm, I didn't realize he'd done it to isolate me. I gave up my career, family, and friends for him when we moved to Toronto.

"At first, our life together was idyllic. We lived in Forest Hill, the ritziest Toronto area. He showered me with gifts, wined and dined me, yadda, yadda. The changes started gradually, with apologies whenever he hit me. He always made me believe it was my fault while handing me an expensive gift. Before long, I fell into my old habit of trying to please a man so he wouldn't hurt me. After a few months, I felt like a captive in a luxurious and very lonely prison. Any week he didn't punch me was a good week. I welcomed his little jaunts to attend 'academic events', a euphemism he concocted for seducing a student. I let it go on like that for ten years, thinking that if I found the right words, did the right thing, cooked the perfect meal, things would change."

After a long pause, Zeke asked, "Did you and Elliot have any children?"

I shook my head. "He wanted them, but I refused to subject innocent children to the kind of life I'd endured. When I didn't get pregnant right away, I took steps to make sure it never happened." Waves of anger and shame rolled through me at the thought of how much I'd voluntarily relinquished.

"How did you escape?"

I frowned as I examined his face, but detected no judgement, only compassion. "My parents died in the car crash I mentioned, but Elliot refused to let me attend their funeral. Dodie, who had her suspicions, didn't buy his excuse that I had pneumonia. She flew to Toronto. When she saw what was happening, she pulled me out of there while he was teaching a class, or, more likely, at the Royal York Hotel banging his student-du-jour. I left with whatever I managed to cram into two suitcases. Fortunately, he was more than happy to divorce me in order to acquire the newer model he'd impregnated, proving he could, indeed, produce progeny." At this admission, my mouth was so dry, my tongue stuck to the roof of my mouth. I reached for my Perrier and took a careful sip.

"Elliot's a monster," Zeke said at last, his voice a low growl. "He should be behind bars."

"Yeah, about that. With Dodie and Clara's support, I took him to court for spousal abuse. It was a scandal in the academic world, but he was found to be innocent. Lack of evidence. I'd been a fool, never reporting him, never taking photographs." I took another sip of Perrier before wrapping up my confession. "I haven't dated anyone since Elliot."

His eyebrow shot up in response.

"I'm not sure I'm ready for dating. It's been a long climb and many years of therapy to find myself," I said defensively. "My sisters and I have teamed up to run a resort, I take karate lessons, I love line dancing, and I have friends. It's enough for now."

"I get it. You're afraid you might lose yourself again, but it needn't be like that. Neither of us is getting any younger." He ran his fingers through his hair. "Don't you think you've waited long enough?"

I couldn't think of an answer. We both sat there in silence. Convinced I'd scared him off, I took pity and gave him an easy out. Feigning a yawn, I said, "Now you know I'm an emotional basket case. You deserve someone better. We should end it … us. Now. Before things get out of hand."

He released a deep sigh. "Abby, I'm already in too deep to step away, and I suspect it's the same for you." His voice was low and sexy, a soft prairie drawl. "We'll keep it platonic for now, but you won't get rid of me so easily." He reached across and placed his hand over mine. "Take whatever time you need. All I ask is that you be yourself."

My heart caught. His touch was warm and comforting, and made me want to move closer. "Does that mean we're still friends?" I asked.

"Besties." He shrugged and grinned. "Isn't that what they call it nowadays? From now on, you're calling the shots, at least, romantically. The next move is up to you." He stood and dropped a kiss on my forehead. "I'll see myself to the door. Be sure to lock up behind me."

As his footsteps faded, my heart did a crazy happy dance in my chest. Even knowing my baggage, Zeke wasn't giving up on me. Instead, he he'd handed me total control along with permission to be myself.

Ah, but who, exactly, was I?

Excitement built in my chest. I needed to get acquainted with the real me, to define my likes and dislikes, my hopes and dreams, my strengths and weaknesses, my priorities and beliefs. In other words, I needed to meet the real Abby Foster and shake hands with her (metaphorically speaking) before I would have enough courage to make the move both Zeke and I longed for.

The good news was that I'd already discovered a small, and hitherto hidden facet of the real me without realizing it. Although the thought of making a speech had scared me spitless, I'd gone for it and connected with the audience. Next time, though, I would do it without the benefit of a half-liter of wine under my belt.

I would continue my journey of self-discovery tomorrow. Hey, better late than never. And in the meantime, Zeke had offered me the driver's seat.

I wondered what kind of adventures lay in store for me.

Chapter 13:
Something's Missing

A T THE UNGODLY HOUR OF 6:30 the next morning, I was showered, dressed, and ready to conquer whatever I encountered.

In spite of the pool closure, the day ahead was loaded with guest activities—a choice of morning trail ride or a visit to nearby Banff for a sightseeing tour, followed by the afternoon semen collection workshop and demo, starring Muffy and Zeke, who'd volunteered to help in light of Luc's demise. And for those guests who preferred something else, there was goat yoga, hiking, fly fishing, archery, board games, horseshoes, tennis, even pickleball. Pickleball was my idea, seeing as how it's the fastest-growing racquet sport in North America, suitable for all ages.

I, on the other hand, looked forward to spending quality time with my figures and spreadsheets, which I'd abandoned for several days. I would take another kick at finding ways to reduce our expenses while increasing revenue, heady fun for an accountant.

Since Vancouver was an hour behind us, time-wise, I waited until 8:00 to call Clara. Turned out, Wendy had broken bones including wrist, two ribs, and her left femur, also concussion, sprains, and multiple scrapes. I made an executive decision not to worry Clara by mentioning Luc's murder and the fact that someone had encouraged our goats and Larry to swim in our pool. There was nothing she could do to help.

Five minutes later, Dodie and I strolled toward the main lodge. I breathed in the scent of warm earth. The May sun was so unseasonably warm, the Alberta sky so big and blue, the puffy clouds so white and perky, that I hummed under my breath. In spite of the presence of a murderer and saboteur, the knowledge that Zeke cared about me enough to let me call the shots had left me elated.

"I have a good feeling about today," I announced to Dodie, flinging my arms into the air as we neared the main lodge. "I'm convinced we'll have a breakthrough with finding the killer."

Dodie's gaze was dubious. "You don't sound like a woman who dumped the man who might be Mr. Right."

"I tried, but Zeke wouldn't hear of it. I told him my whole story, the good, the bad, and the ugly. We decided to keep it platonic. For now."

"He's letting you take it at your own speed? Oh, my."

"I know. Remarkable isn't it? He told me I was in the driver's seat."

We walked several steps in silence, then Dodie said, "I assume you're joining the trail ride this morning."

I stood stock still and frowned at her. "What part of, 'Horses terrify me,' did you not understand?"

She took my arm and hauled me along on legs that had turned rubbery. "For some reason, horses like you. This is your chance to overcome your fear." She paused and added slyly, "Besides, it'll give you a chance to grill our suspects without raising suspicion."

She had a point. If I was serious about discovering the real me, I wouldn't learn anything new about myself by hiding in my office. I needed to embrace the challenges life threw at me, including horses, not flee from them.

I unglued my tongue from the roof of my mouth. "Okay, okay. I'll join the trail ride. Finding the killer is my top priority. This will be an adventure. Spreadsheets can wait."

Thankfully, the crunch of approaching footsteps distracted Dodie from grilling me about my newfound attitude. If she knew, she would take credit for sowing the seeds of my illumination. Which she totally had. We both turned to find Zeke striding toward us.

"I understand why you're going the distance with this guy," Dodie whispered.

My breath caught in my throat as I took in the long, easy lope, the lean, sinewy muscle, and the aura of kindness he radiated. He stopped so close I inhaled the clean scent of soap, shampoo, and fresh air.

"Hi," I croaked, grinning like an idiot and hoping he couldn't tell I was as tongue-tied as a teenaged girl. He looked delicious in well-worn jeans, a black shirt, and tooled leather cowboy boots.

"Morning Zeke," Dodie said.

He tipped his black hat, revealing a worried expression instead of the warm gaze I'd anticipated. "Morning, ladies. I'm afraid I have more bad news."

"What now?" I asked with trepidation.

"The barn door was unlocked when I got up this morning. Lancelot's gone."

"Say, what?" I asked, feeling color drain from my face as I processed the implications. The entire symposium was designed around Lancelot, the star of the semen collection demo.

"He isn't in his stall."

"Maybe Muffy took him for a ride," Dodie suggested.

Zeke shook his head. "She knows better than to ride Lancelot."

"But how did this happen?" I asked.

I felt the weight of those intense dark eyes on my face as he said, "My theory is whoever stole my keys last night also unlocked the barn and released Lancelot, maybe even before putting the animals in the pool." He squeezed his eyes shut, his mouth compressed. Then he looked at me. "It likely happened during my snooze. When your call came in, everything was quiet in the stable. I didn't give Lancelot a second thought. I assumed he'd quieted down. Now that I think about it, he was likely gone."

"It's not your fault," I said.

"I should have checked on him again. All the horses are my responsibility. After leaving your apartment, I went straight to bed without making sure the doors were locked, with Lancelot safe in his stall."

"Stop blaming yourself," I said. "Someone's out to cause trouble. I wonder why."

"Maybe it's all tied to the murder," Dodie suggested.

Zeke shrugged. "I intend to find out. I've already sent the wranglers out to search for Lancelot, and I'll contact all the neighboring ranches. If we don't find the horse, there'll be no demo this afternoon. I'll break the news to Muffy."

Relief washed over me. I was off the hook with the unpleasant task of informing Muffy her six-figure racehorse was AWOL. I relaxed until I remembered it was my responsibility as GM to suck it up and tell her the bad news.

"No," I said. "You have enough on your plate. I'll be the one to tell Muffy about the missing horse. It'll be tricky if guests are within earshot, though, so I'll have to choose my time carefully."

Zeke's shoulders relaxed as if shedding a weight. "Thanks. Muffy was so relieved when I promised to fill in for Luc during the demo because Lancelot trusts me. I hate to be the one to disappoint her."

"Go ahead," Dodie urged me. "I'm heading in for an early breakfast. After that, I'll spend the morning in your office. That way, I'll be near the lobby in case anyone needs help."

"Keep your bear spray handy," I advised. "There's a killer on the loose."

"To be doubly safe, I'll post a wrangler in the lobby," Zeke answered. "Don't worry, he'll be unobtrusive."

Dodie disappeared up the path to the main lodge while I accompanied Zeke poolside to check the drainage situation. He'd barely opened the gate when a muffled giggle announced the twins' arrival. A moment later Wes and Coop bounced up to me. They wore bathing suits and carried towels, goggles, and water noodles.

The sight distracted me from the pleasant view of Zeke's butt as he bent down to pull at a corner of the pool's safety cover. The twins darted by me, headed for the pool.

"Sorry, boys," I said, grabbing their tee-shirts and halting their headlong rush. "The pool's off-limits." I pulled them outside the enclosure and kicked the gate shut before releasing my grip.

"Awwww," Coop said. "No fair. We wanna go swimming."

"Yeah. It's the only fun we're gonna have all day," Wes said. "Mom and Dad won't let us go on the trail ride because they're afraid we'll get hurt."

"No, dummy. They're afraid we'll hurt the horses."

"I think it's because they're hungover and don't want to go riding with us. They had lots of drinks last night." Wes hit me with a piteous gaze. "They're making us go fishing. They said a wrangler would take us to a good spot."

I tried to hide my sympathy over the poor kids having indifferent parents. "Sorry, boys. The sign says the pool is closed for maintenance."

"What's wrong with the pool?" Coop demanded. "Will you fix it?"

"Last night we discovered the water was too dirty to be safe, so we have to drain it and re-fill it with clean water. The pool should be ready in three days, and then you can go swimming again, but your parents have to go with you."

"But we got up early to swim."

I wasn't up for an argument so I settled on bribery. "If you change out of your bathing suits, there's a special breakfast for you in the dining hall."

"Special how?" Wes asked.

I mentally reviewed the buffet's contents. "Pancakes with both chocolate and blueberry sauce."

"Maple syrup and whipped cream too?"

At my nod, the twins cheered and dashed down the path toward their cabin.

I was considering how to break the news of Lancelot's disappearance to Muffy, when Zeke returned and reported the pool was draining well, and would take less time than he'd originally thought.

I wished him luck with finding the stallion and announced I would join him on the trail ride. His astonishment told me he was aware of my horse phobia.

"In that case," he said, "I know just the horse for you. He's a sweetheart."

As he strode away, I absolutely did not watch his ass. Okay, maybe I did. A little. Hey, I was old, not dead.

Chapter 14:
Remember the Alamo

MY WALK TO THE STABLES gave me time to rationalize why I hadn't informed Muffy of Lancelot's disappearance. As wary as a Canada goose being stalked by a grizzly, I'd made an executive decision to postpone disclosure. With her marriage troubles and Luc's death, Muffy had enough to contend with. If we were lucky, someone would find Lancelot before the demo. As Mom used to say, why borrow trouble?

Braking before I reached the barnyard, I shaded my eyes and adjusted my sunglasses. My favorite white cowgirl hat with its faux diamonds studding the brim dangled against my back. Why risk hat-hair when I might change my mind about riding?

Stop, I told myself. *That's Old Abby's negative thought pattern. New Abby looks forward to a new and exciting experience—a trail ride.* I crammed the hat onto my head and slowly approached two horses tethered to a hitching rail.

The animals stood quietly while a wrangler adjusted their saddles. The largest horse swiveled its head toward me.

Recognizing Alamo, I halted and forced myself not to panic. What was I thinking, placing my life in jeopardy merely to get in touch with myself? There were plenty of other opportunities to learn who I was without getting trampled under slashing hooves.

After a moment of terror, I got a grip on my emotions. The gelding was far too placid to do any trampling.

Alamo shifted while the wrangler reached under his barrel underbelly to tighten the cinch, a vital item standing between the rider and sudden death. I took a tentative step forward. And sucked in a breath when the wrangler peered over the saddle.

"Zeke," I said, feeling my knees weaken. "I didn't recognize you."

"Hey, gorgeous." His smile wrapped me in a blaze of white heat. "I was starting to wonder if you'd ditched the trail ride."

"Never." To demonstrate confidence, I moved closer, injecting a swagger into my step. The presence of horse droppings made me bob and weave, detracting from my can-do attitude. Stopping before I reached Alamo, I gazed around the barnyard. "Where is everyone? Did they all chicken out?"

"They're behind the barn with their horses. You're the last to arrive." He studied my face. "Hey, there's no need to be nervous. Come and meet Alamo."

"We've already met, thanks. We're good."

Too good.

At the sound of my voice, Alamo turned his head and gave a welcoming nicker. His bulging eyes lit up. I held my breath and waited for more to happen.

Sure enough, out it came and a-swingin' it went.

"He seems to like you," Zeke observed.

My face heated up. "Why does he do that?" I demanded. "Make that hornball put his thing away. It's embarrassing."

Zeke's bark of laughter shattered the morning stillness. Once he recovered, he said, "Boys will be boys, even geldings. Seems Alamo's taken a shine to you."

"It must be my organic body-wash. It's all-natural, made from green tea, oatmeal, and honey, with a touch of apple blossom."

Zeke leaned down and sniffed my neck, nuzzling a little. "Delicious."

"Behave." But my insides gave a funny little tremor. Fighting the urge to fling myself into his arms, I pulled away. "Let's get this show on the road."

"Have you ever ridden before?"

"Once. It didn't end well." I outlined my horrible experience, which had resulted in a broken arm.

"It'll be different this time. Let's get you mounted."

"Correct me if I'm wrong," I said, wishing with all my heart the horse would retract his pride and joy, "but didn't everyone at the Alamo die?"

"This Alamo's real gentle," Zeke assured me. "I chose him specially for you."

I pretended his really great smile didn't affect me. "I thought we were friends. You expect me to ride this ... this ... monster? Surely you have something …" I hesitated, wanting to say, "less scary," or "less studdish," but substituted, "smaller."

"Alamo's perfect for you." He led the horse to a mounting block beside the fence. "Up you go." When I didn't budge, his grin broadened. "Don't tell me you're chicken."

That got me moving. I adjusted my hat to a jaunty angle. With the help of the mounting block, much undignified straining, and an embarrassing quantity of muscle on Zeke's part, I found myself on board Alamo, my legs spread to the max. It was a miracle my straining ligaments and tendons didn't squeal out loud.

"Yowza," I muttered. "I'm relying on you to scrape my remains off the trail."

"You'll be fine."

Reins clutched in both hands, I said through gritted teeth, "Yeah, peachy."

Throwing up was out of the question. So was flinging my arms in a death grip around Alamo's neck. I assured myself I'd get the hang of this horseback-riding thing before long. How hard could it be?

As if reading my mind, Alamo shook his head and started moving. Fudge nuggets. Where were the brakes on this sucker? Stifling a shriek, I used both hands to grip his mane as we ambled along the fence where grass grew long and green.

The motion stopped. I tugged on the reins.

Alamo merely tossed his pride about and eyeballed me, as if to say, "Seriously?" before lowering his head to rip out a clump of grass.

"Pull his head up," Zeke advised. "Show him who's boss."

I pulled like crazy and replied, "Alamo knows who's boss. Hint, it's not me."

The sound of equine chomping freaked me out, especially when Alamo raised his head and whickered, spraying the area with green drool.

Zeke mounted a magnificent chestnut mare called Reba, and they trotted a short distance, then stopped. Was he waiting for me to join him, or what?

Only one way to find out. Bravely, I tapped my heels against Alamo's side.

The horse gave me a quizzical stare I interpreted as, "In your dreams." The sound of belly-thwapping was unmistakeable.

With a laugh in his voice, Zeke said, "I think you're turning him on. Kick harder."

I intensified my heel-digs.

With an alarming clink of metal, Alamo shook his head and exhaled, producing a vibrating sound. My noble steed proved he had a gift for standing. Also thwapping.

I leaned down and hissed into his left ear, "Put your thing away. Move."

The beat of more hooves grew louder and stopped behind us. With an effort, I swiveled in the saddle to see who'd joined us. Perched on a golden Palomino, Tess offered a dazzling smile, a smile so straight and white it was scary. She was perfectly relaxed in the saddle. I wanted to smack her. Alamo, the traitor, nickered a welcome.

Leaning over her horse's neck, Tess cooed, "Good golly, Sunbeam. Your boyfriend sure is happy to see you today, eh?"

Relief washed over me. This show of equine friendship provided cover for Alamo's studdish behaviour. Remembering I was supposed to bond with the guests, I chirped, "Hey, Tess. Looking good this morning."

Yeah, she did look good. Too good for my liking. She'd applied makeup, hidden her hair beneath a cowboy hat, and painted skin-tight jeans onto her scrawny legs.

When our gazes collided, Tess's smile became a tad less blinding. "Why, thank you, hon. Those jeans are very slimming." She glanced meaningfully at my closest thigh, which was as hefty as both of hers combined.

A smart-assed retort hovered on the tip of my tongue, begging for release. Catching myself, I beamed a dazzling smile at her. "Why, thank you, hon. Aren't you an angel to say so. I'm so happy you're able to join us for the trail ride."

"I'm exhausted after last night, but I wouldn't miss a chance to ride, especially with an expert like Zeke." A flick of her crop had Sunbeam trotting toward him. She leaned in to touch Zeke's arm while batting mile-long eyelashes.

Who glued on fake eyelashes for a trail ride?

I answered my own question. A woman on the make, that's who. I reminded myself that Tess was indulging in wishful thinking. It seemed I needed work on my self-esteem a tad. Nothing had happened between them, and nothing would.

Zeke maneuvered his horse a few steps away from Tess's horse and turned to me. "Here comes everyone else."

I recognized some, but not all, of the riders bearing down on us. A smattering of guests chatted among themselves as they approached, but I focused my attention on our main suspects—Harmony, Clay, Veronica, and Muffy.

Zeke addressed the group. "Remember to stick together. That way, if a predator's nearby, it'll hear us coming and clear out." He nudged Reba with his heels and set off at a brisk walk, while Muffy, who appeared unusually subdued, positioned herself at the rear to make sure no one strayed from the trail.

The morning was glorious, unseasonably warm with a light, flirty breeze. Birds cooed and chirped and warbled in the speckled shadows overhead. It was the kind of day that boosted my spirits and made me feel as if anything was possible—including trampling Tess into the dust. Not because I was jealous, no siree. Because she raised my hackles.

No, no, no. I reframed my thinking. Tess was a challenge I could surmount in order to become an improved, *kinder* person.

Zeke on Reba led the pack, accompanied by Tess on Sunbeam. I bounced along behind them, eating their dust, too busy concentrating on staying in the saddle to notice much else. Harmony, Veronica, and Clay were somewhere behind me, but I couldn't imagine juggling any interviews with, say, keeping myself on board.

I forced myself to ignore Zeke's occasional rumble of laughter and focused on the sound of hooves thudding on the soft ground, the rustle of poplar branches, and the occasional bird trill. The delicious scent of spruce and pine filled my nostrils. Gradually, my death-grip on Alamo's mane loosened.

Harmony, who rode a white horse called Snowflake, pulled alongside me and said, "Gorgeous day, isn't it? Mind if I join you?"

My pulse quickened. Here was my chance to interrogate a potential killer. "Please do," I replied, wondering how to broach the topic of Luc and horse drugging. To break the ice, I started with a subject I knew she would pounce on. "So you're an animal rights activist, right? How satisfying."

"Yeah, especially when combined with environmental impact." Harmony launched into a lecture on how wolves actually help restore the environment by reducing the deer and elk population, which destroy the vegetation, resulting in soil erosion and landslides. She didn't pause for breath, so I remained silent. Sooner or later, she'd run out of steam, and I could get down to business.

Once we left the shady pine forest, ligaments and tendons I hadn't known existed made their presence known. I felt as if I was doing splits. On the bright side, my legs would benefit from the stretch. Hey, it had been a long, dry spell of non-action. Biggie Bart, my favorite sex toy, didn't count.

Harmony continued her diatribe. To distract myself from the building agony, I was plotting dire revenge on Tess for scoring the prize position beside Zeke, when a horsefly the size of a sparrow landed on my right leg. Undeterred by denim, it used its knife-like mouthparts to take a chunk out of my thigh. I swatted it and flicked the corpse away. Turning my head to see why Harmony had broken off in mid-sentence, I encountered her horrified stare.

"Filthy murderess," she hissed at me, pursing her lips into that familiar puckered "O" configuration.

Not as filthy as the rotten fly, was my first thought. My second was, *I've blown my chance to ingratiate myself with Harmony.*

One glance at her face yielded seriously bad news. Harmony's complexion, normally milky-pale, was purple with rage, an interesting combo when combined with carroty hair. Knowledge of my mistake nearly unseated me. Fortunately, I retained enough presence of mind to grab a handful of Alamo's mane.

"I apologize," I said, trying to project remorse. "Reflex action. The fly was a biter."

Harmony's cheeks returned to a healthier hue. "Oops. I'm the one who owes you the apology. I get carried away over the sanctity of life, even of a lowly fly. Everyone tells me I'm over-sensitive."

Too bad Harmony didn't apply the same sensitivity to her fellow humans. Digging deep into my dwindling store of patience, I chirped, "No problem."

She launched into a long-winded rant about horse racing.

Since she'd broached the topic I most wanted to discuss, I encouraged her by saying, "Are there problems?"

She sucked in a deep breath. "Horse racing is totally corrupt. You'll never believe the tricks they pull to ensure a winner."

"I bet you know them all."

Harmony nodded. "Yep. I sure do." She spoke so fast, she tripped over her words while describing the use of sub-zero liquid nitrogen to kill pain in a horse's legs, and moved on to the administration of diuretics before a race to cause weight loss and enhance the horse's performance. She detailed drugs that masked other drugs and many more tricks including jolting the poor animal with concealed shocking devices. Pluck a duck. You couldn't make this stuff up. Harmony was a walking, talking encyclopedia on enhancing a horse's racing performance.

Desperate to steer the conversation toward more relevant topics, I laid it on thick. "You're so knowledgeable, Harmony. When we met yesterday, you hinted about having a special reason to book a week at Grizzly Gulch. I sensed there was an underlying purpose that was more important than a mere symposium or class reunion."

"You're too perceptive." She lowered her voice. "Can you keep a secret?"

I made a point of unobtrusively crossing my fingers. "Absolutely."

"The reunion's my cover for a secret mission. The symposium's a bonus."

"No kidding! How exciting." I was, in fact, so excited I loosened my grip and nearly slid off Alamo. Recovering my balance, I tightened my thighs and leaned closer to Harmony. "Maybe I can help if you explain what's happening." Noting her hesitation, I added, "But only if you feel comfortable. I believe two heads are better than one."

She chewed her lip and said, "Okay. But you can't tell anyone."

"Wouldn't dream of it," I lied, more convinced than ever she was a crackpot, fanatic, and possibly a murderess.

After darting a furtive glance over her shoulder, Harmony nudged her horse closer to Alamo, and spoke. "Muffy, Luc, and I, along with some of the rest, go way back to university. When I received the invitation, I signed up even though I dreaded seeing everyone again. Everyone in the class viewed me as a freak." She slanted me a hopeful glance, as if seeking absolution.

"People often misunderstand individualists like you," I said.

Harmony grinned at me. "You do understand."

"Yeah. But why bother with people you dislike?"

After a long silence during which I kicked myself for pushing too hard, Harmony said, "When I recognized Muffy and Luc's names on the invitation, I did some research."

"What did you learn?" I held my breath, hoping I hadn't scared her off. I needn't have worried. Harmony was on a roll.

"When Muffy bought Lancelot, she also hired Luc Lacroix as her head trainer. Before long, her horses started winning an unusual number of races. Coincidence? I think not, so I signed up for the symposium."

"Why? You detest these people."

"That brings me to why I'm here," she said. "But you probably won't believe me."

Concealing my excitement behind a conspiratorial smile, I said, "Try me."

"It's a long story."

"It'll take my mind off my own problem." I scowled at Tess eagerly chatting with Zeke, now several horse-lengths ahead.

"Okay. As you know, I'm a PETA volunteer. I want a full-time position, but they won't hire me because of my record, so I need to prove I'm qualified. You'd think my previous assignment would speak for itself, but apparently jail time's a turnoff."

"Oh, dear. What happened?" I struggled to keep my expression sympathetic.

"Three years ago, I was instrumental in sniffing out a horse drugger named Luc Lacroix. I stalked the creep, caught him injecting a racehorse, and beat the stuffing out of him. Once he was unconscious, I duct-taped his arms together and dragged him into the police station."

"Well, pluck a duck," I said in a faint voice.

"No kidding," Harmony said in an aggrieved tone. "Luc was charged with administering performance-enhancing drugs to horses, but there wasn't enough evidence to convict him. I, on the other hand, was convicted with aggravated assault and received a six-month sentence behind bars. I tried explaining everything to PETA, but they wouldn't listen to reason."

"Convictions can be deceiving," I said weakly. "You were motivated by kindness to animals."

"I knew you'd understand." Harmony flashed a smile. "So after I was released, I received Muffy's invitation to the symposium at the same time I learned the racing community suspected her horses were winning because Luc was drugging them. This was another chance to take him down."

While I wondered if "take down" meant "kill," she continued, "It's too bad Luc got himself trampled to death my first night here. I figured it was all over for me with PETA until I realized there was still hope. If I can prove Muffy and Franklin approved of Luc's drugging scam, PETA might still hire me."

I took a moment to absorb the bombshell. Muffy adored her horses. Then again, if the racing community learned she'd hired a drugger, the couple's reputations would suffer. Remembering Franklin's divorce threat, I realized he might end their marriage. That was a strong murder motive.

As for Franklin, we'd ruled him out because he was visiting a glittering office tower somewhere in the Middle East.

Concerned about Harmony's fanaticism, I led with, "Have you ever considered you shouldn't get involved in a potentially dangerous situation?"

"I thought you understood. Horses are my top priority."

Her zeal bordered on lunacy. I took another stab at convincing her to lay off. "I get it. But you may be playing with fire. Let me call the authorities, hon."

"And let the Mounties take all the credit? Are you kidding?"

I shifted in the saddle, trying unsuccessfully to find a more comfortable position. "If you're right about Muffy and Franklin, you'll be placing yourself in grave danger."

Harmony's broad grin unsettled me. "I can handle myself. Besides pepper spray, I carry a handgun," she patted her jacket, which was bulky enough to hide an assault weapon or two, "and there's a shotgun back in my cabin."

Wondering if she was actually packing heat or merely bragging, I decided to warn Zeke on our return. To distract her, I changed the subject. "I hope I'll see you at the semen collection demo this afternoon."

Her eyes shot daggers at me. "Wouldn't miss it for the world," she snapped.

Uh-oh. I took a long, hard look at her face. I recognized disapproval when I saw it. Seemed I'd touched another nerve. "Did I say something wrong?"

"I can't believe you're making a poor, helpless animal perform a very private act in front of a crowd of busybodies."

"There's nothing voyeuristic about it, Harmony. This is an educational event."

"Is there no end to cruelty in the world?" she wailed. Digging her heels into Snowflake's ribs, she galloped away, splashing through a puddle. Over her shoulder, she yelled, "You'll see me at the demo."

Fudge nuggets. I'd upset a guest. Wanting to placate Harmony, I dug my heels into Alamo's side. He merely plodded forward until he reached the middle of the puddle, where he stopped, as if debating his next move.

"Don't you *dare*," I muttered, guessing he intended to indulge in a nice mud bath. If that happened, I might find myself trapped under a one-ton monster.

The water reached his hocks. He circled, the splashes soaking my jeans.

"Giddy up, or I'll tell Zeke to sell you to the glue factory." I flapped the reins while drumming my heels into his sides.

Alamo tilted his body to one side and pawed the water. He was going down.

Gripping the saddle horn, I gazed ahead in alarm. Everyone in front, including Harmony, had disappeared around a bend. Twisting in the saddle, I realized the others had lagged behind. Panic was not an option, especially with Tess ready to point out any rookie mistakes I made. Reaching down, I patted Alamo's neck. "Nice horsy. I was joking about the glue factory. We both know you like me."

But all evidence of Alamo's liking had vanished. His tail swished against my leg.

"Help!" I hollered desperately.

He swiveled his head, glanced at me, and splashed deeper into the puddle.

Pounding hooves gave me hope. Releasing a scream that nearly pierced my own eardrums, I yelled, "He's going down and taking me with him!"

I'd extricated my feet from the stirrups and managed to swivel both legs to one side, prepared to jump, when Zeke thundered toward me at full gallop. His horse stopped on a dime beside the puddle.

"Hold tight," he yelled, steering Reba into the puddle until they were beside us.

He hooked one arm around my middle, dragging me off Alamo and plastering me against his side. The man must do some serious workouts because I'm no featherweight. Once the puddle was safely behind us, he deposited me on dry land before hopping down and wrapping his arms around me.

Splashdown occurred while I clung to Zeke. Oblivious of his saddle, Alamo collapsed into the puddle and rolled on his back, squirming in the muck, kicking his legs in ecstasy, and uttering satisfied nickers.

He was still in the throes when Zeke's warm breath tickled my ear. "You might have been crushed," he said, his face wreathed in concern. For me.

I shivered in the most delicious way. For once, I made no smart-ass comment, probably because of severe dry mouth. To hide my weakness, I burrowed my nose into his chest, inhaling an intoxicating combination of soap and clean man.

My triumph was brief. Tess's appearance on Sunbeam, closely followed by Harmony on Snowflake, destroyed the moment. Harmony cast one long, accusatory glance at me and arrowed into the puddle where Alamo cavorted.

Straightening my hat, which, remarkably, had stayed put, I shifted my attention to Tess. I gauged her mood as pissed.

"Well played," Tess said softly to me.

I had a hard time believing she thought I was devious enough to orchestrate what might easily have had a disastrous ending, at least for me. It spoke volumes about her ethics. And indicated she felt threatened, which made her dangerous.

Ignoring Tess, Zeke loosened his grip on me and said, "I'm an idiot, Abby. Alamo loves water. I should have guessed what he'd do. He might have crushed you."

"It's not your fault," I assured him.

The rest of the riders had caught up with us. They asked questions, which I wasn't up to answering, so Zeke gave a brief explanation. Adding to the confusion, Harmony appeared again, this time leading Alamo by the reins. "Here he is, safe and sound, and gentle as a kitten." She patted his neck, which dripped mud. "Thank goodness he wasn't hurt."

Tess's cool voice sliced through the air. "Can we please get this show on the road? It's nearly lunchtime."

"Sure thing." Zeke's deadpan expression indicated that Tess had one less fan in the world. "Abby will ride with me."

Harmony jumped right in. "I'll be happy to lead Alamo to the ranch."

She switched to a sugary voice as she stroked the horse's muzzle. "You're such a good boy. Poor Abby doesn't know how to handle you, does she, baby?"

And so it was settled. Zeke loaded me in front of him, and I found myself leaning against a most excellent chest. Everyone else fell in behind.

We didn't talk much. Euphoria at his closeness acted as an anaesthetic for the first mile. Slowly, however, growing distress replaced my contentment. Mild discomfort morphed into throbbing pain before blasting white-hot agony into some highly sensitive areas—knees, hips, butt, and, most especially, my lady-parts. I swallowed a whimper. Horses would ruin all possibility of a love life for me—assuming I ever got lucky again.

Before I could obsess about Zeke's reaction, I placed my mouth close to his ear and spoke my truth. "This is the last time I'm getting on a horse's back. I know how important horses are to you, but riding isn't for me." I snapped my mouth shut. For the first time in my life, I'd refused to mold myself into somebody I wasn't, simply to please a man. In the past I would have signed up for riding lessons.

Zeke twisted his neck to answer. "I think our relationship can survive your lack of riding skills."

Holy cruller. He'd accepted my decision without a fuss. His reaction astounded me so much I barely noticed our arrival at the stable until he dismounted.

"Your turn," he said. "I'll help you down."

Fudge nuggets, the ground was a long way down. Not wanting to look like a total idiot, I gripped the saddle horn, stood in the stirrups, and swung one leg over Alamo's ass. Feeling Zeke's hands close around my waist, I forced myself to let go and execute a long leap of trust. With his support, I landed as gracefully as a ballerina. Well, almost.

Once I recovered my balance, I turned around to whisper, "We need to talk. I learned a lot from Harmony during the ride. How about my place after the demo?"

He nodded before turning to help an overweight businessman dismount.

I'd planned to wait over at the fence for him to finish, but a phone blasting out *Ghost Riders in the Sky* halted me. Recognizing Muffy's ringtone, I strained to hear her end of the conversation. No such luck. She'd dismounted and moved away.

After a few seconds of muffled dialog, Muffy ended the call and addressed me. "Sorry. Gotta run back to my ranch for a few minutes. I'll return in time for the demo."

I swore I heard a note of anxiety in her voice.

Chapter 15: Performance Anxiety

FOUR WRANGLERS MOVED IN TO take care of the trail horses. I talked to guests while waiting for Zeke to help the remaining riders dismount. Predictably, Tess was the last one down. I figured she'd plotted her timing to catch him alone.

After Zeke exchanged a few words with the wranglers, he returned to me and took my hand. I beamed a brilliant smile at Tess. "Nice riding with you today, hon. See you later. Don't forget the demo this afternoon." After giving her an extra-cheery wave, I felt the weight of her gaze drilling into my back as Zeke and I headed off to debrief with Dodie in my apartment.

Zeke and I had barely set foot on the path to the main lodge when a young wrangler hailed him. We stopped and waited for him to catch up with us.

"What's up?" Zeke asked.

Sweat dripped off the tip of the wrangler's nose. Gasping for breath, he said, "Lancelot's back. I ran all the way here to tell you the good news."

Relief coursed through my veins. We could proceed with the demo.

Zeke let out a wild, "Yee-haw." With no apparent effort, he lifted me off my feet and swung me around in a circle.

Once he put me down, I managed, "How? When? Who?"

"Lancelot spent last night and this morning at the Baxter farm," the wrangler explained. "We brought him home in the horse van and put him out in the meadow to recuperate."

"Recuperate?" I squawked, my voice an octave higher than normal. "Is he hurt? Sick? What?"

The wrangler shot Zeke a pleading glance. "Uh, not exactly. It's just … well … let's say he's been a real busy boy."

"It's okay, Abby," Zeke said in a reassuring voice. "Whatever it is, we'll deal with it." He turned to the wrangler. "What happened?"

"Lancelot mounted three mares that were in estrus. Baxter's doing a happy dance because he reckons a winning racehorse knocked them up."

"Seriously?" I said, processing the implications of the news.

A sharp voice behind us said, "I sincerely doubt Lancelot knocked up any mares."

I whirled around. "Clay. I didn't know you were there. Why the doubts? Lancelot has a proven track record as a sire."

"That's not what I heard," Clay said. "Wish I could stop to chat, but I'm on my way to meet Veronica for lunch. Don't worry, I won't tell anyone your stallion was missing." He tramped away.

"Much appreciated," Zeke shouted at Clay's back.

Yeah, right. Like he wouldn't spill the beans to Veronica, inventor of the commando lie. I had to find a way to convince Clay to zip his lip, but how? I had an inspiration and went for it. "Clay," I called. When he turned around, I ignored Zeke's frown and said, "Don't tell a soul. That means Veronica, too. If word leaks out, we'll know who talked, and it won't be pretty." I paused before taking a risk that might backfire. "We know your secret."

Clay's eyes narrowed. "How did you find out?"

"Not important. Suffice it to say, we know."

Once Clay disappeared, Zeke gave me a quizzical look. "That sounded a whole lot like blackmail. Gonna tell me what it's all about?"

"Clay would have told Veronica, and she's a blabbermouth," I murmured. "She'd broadcast the news to everyone in Alberta, so I bluffed, okay? But now we know Clay has a secret. I think it's safe to say we can rely on him not to talk."

A discrete cough alerted us of the wrangler's presence. He was still hanging around and looking uneasy. Zeke asked him, "Is there anything else we should know about Lancelot?"

The kid removed his hat, swiped his forehead, and jammed it back on his head before replying, "Lancelot's asleep on his feet. Literally. Our boy's worn out."

Noting Zeke's stunned expression, I said, "Thanks. You did great."

The wrangler looked relieved and headed for the barn.

"Good God," Zeke muttered. "What if Lancelot can't, uh, perform? The demo could be a disaster. Maybe we should postpone it until he recovers. I'd better call Muffy." He pulled out his phone.

I shook my head. "We can't postpone. How would we explain it without telling the truth. No, this demo is a huge drawing card. Everyone, including staff, guests, even the local vet, signed up to watch."

Zeke's dark eyes reflected misgivings at the wisdom of my decision, but he shoved his phone in his pocket. "Okay. But we'll have to find a way to deal with Lancelot."

"And I have to make sure Muffy returns in time for the demo. Lancelot's return changes everything." I reached for my phone and called her landline. After six rings, a male voice answered with a curt, "Yes?"

I nearly dropped the phone in surprise. After a long pause, I said, "Franklin?"

"How can I help you?"

"I … uh … I was trying to reach Muffy. Never mind, I'll talk to her later. Bye." Heart pounding with excitement, I clicked off. Noting Zeke's quizzical expression, I said, "That was Franklin. Either he returned early, or he never left in the first place."

"We'll have to discuss Franklin later. I'd best get down to the barn to help the boys set up the stage and bleachers for the demo."

I nodded. "What'll you do about Lancelot?"

Zeke shrugged. "Let him sleep as long as possible. Make sure we have a mare in estrus nearby in case he needs extra incentive. Feed him an aphrodisiac."

"I didn't know there were any horse aphrodisiacs."

"There aren't. Unless you count certain vet-approved stimulants … or your organic body-wash."

My spidey senses tingled. "Bring on the stimulants. I am *not* going anywhere near Lancelot."

He laughed and gave me a brief hug before walking away, leaving me uneasy that perhaps Zeke viewed me as a secret weapon to get Lancelot in the mood.

I grabbed a sandwich for lunch and dashed off to scarf it down in my apartment. My premonition of being strong-armed into participating in the semen-collection demo gnawed at my gut. I refused to bow out as a spectator. All I needed was a good hiding spot where Zeke wouldn't find me and rope me in to helping with the demo. But where?

After finishing my smoked salmon with capers and cream cheese on a bagel, I reached a decision. Hiding in plain sight was a strategy, right?

Delaying my arrival at the demo until I was sure the paddock was overflowing with people, I crept along the pathway, stopping to admire tulips poking green leaves out of the soil. At the same time I scanned the area for Zeke.

The sun, which was intense during the morning trail ride, slid behind a cloud, a reminder that springtime weather in the foothills could change in an instant. Thank goodness for my hat and woolly sweater. Clara had knitted the sweater as my Christmas gift when she was ten. Good job she was a loose knitter, because it now fit perfectly. A few woolly loops poked out. That was okay with me. They didn't show.

Inhaling a deep breath of fresh air holding the rich promise of new growth, I edged into the shade of spruce trees guarding the pathway. I peeked around the final curve before the paddock where the demo would be held.

The site was incredible. Zeke and his crew had transformed the paddock into a mini-auditorium. A raised stage surrounded by a maze of audiovisual wires and loudspeakers faced a set of collapsible bleachers. Beside the stage, Zeke was engaged in conversation with Muffy.

The bleachers were crammed with people, all talking to one another. Clearly the topic appealed to a broad audience. Dodie had found a seat on the topmost bench, front and center, and was yucking it up with Chef Armand. There was nothing like semen collection to unite a crowd.

A pretty little mare stood tethered to a post in the shade. I assumed she was the mare in heat Zeke had mentioned, a secret weapon to entice Lancelot into a romantic mood. The stud himself was nowhere in sight, likely zonked out, recovering from his fun time at the Baxter farm.

Slipping behind the bleachers, I hugged the shadows until I reached a perfect hiding spot beneath the benches and clutched a support post. Every muscle in my body screamed in pain from the trail ride. I tortured myself by sinking gingerly into a kneeling position before plopping my butt on the ground.

"That looks painful," Dodie's voice said.

"Not at all," I lied, looking up and around a substantial rump to discover my sister grinning down at me from an upper bench. "It's part of my daily yoga program."

"In a pig's eye," she scoffed. "Guess who's heading this way."

I knew without asking but peeked anyway. Zeke was rapidly closing in on my hiding spot, every inch a man on a mission.

"You can't hide there all afternoon," he said, standing over me.

Refusing to look at him, I muttered, "Watch me. It's nice and private down here." Wishing for an invisibility cloak, I glanced up. "How did you find me?"

"Your hat. The bling is dazzling. I need you to sit with me on the stage."

"Why?" I asked cautiously.

"Call it insurance."

Yeah, my premonition was spot on. "Not happening."

He extended a hand. "Please? This demo may fail without you, and I know how important it is, not only for Grizzly Gulch, but for you, Dodie and Clara as well."

Not fair. He'd played the family card. Reluctantly, I gripped his hand and allowed him to tug me upright. As I clambered to my feet, I suppressed a groan at the twinges in my right knee. Served me right for climbing onto a horse. Zeke was seeing the real me, perhaps for the first time. Too bad if he didn't like it. I was too old for this nonsense.

The clamor started with a low hum of conversation, which progressed to louder exclamations, followed by loud, "Yee-haws," and excited applause. My skin crawled as I realized everyone in the audience was standing.

I wasn't sure I wanted to know what was happening.

Chapter 16:
Hands-On Experience

A S WE WALKED TOWARD THE stage, Zeke said, "Muffy will be too busy explaining every step of the process to the audience to do anything else. I need you to help with the AV."

I was about to assure him I knew next-to-nothing about audiovisual equipment, when Lancelot, led by a wrangler, made a bedraggled entrance. His eyes at half-mast, the horse was groggy from a post-coital nap. I swore I detected a satisfied grin on the long, hairy face.

As we sank onto two folding chairs beside the stage, I leaned closer to Zeke. "What's the protocol here? Do I offer Lancelot a cigarette, or congratulate him on his stamina?"

"Not funny," Zeke said over a stifled laugh.

Harmony's voice rose from the bleachers. "What happened? That horse looks half-dead."

I hid my irritation and shouted, "Don't worry about Lancelot. He may be a slow starter, but he's strong in the finish."

Muffy interrupted the exchange by tapping the microphone to attract audience attention. If she was worried, it didn't show. Good job I hadn't told her of Lancelot's disappearance. After everyone stopped talking, she introduced the event. A description of the semen collection process followed, during which I warned Zeke in an undertone that audiovisual wasn't my area of expertise and suggested he find another technician.

He wrinkled his forehead and stared at me. After a beat, his confusion disappeared, replaced by amusement. In a choked voice, he explained, "In this context, AV means 'artificial vagina'."

It's a good thing I was seated. Although he kept talking, the words, *artificial vagina*, rang in my ears, obliterating everything else.

His nudge cut through my panic. "Earth to Planet Abby. Did you hear me? This model's size and weight make the AV convenient to handle, while providing rigidity and good heat retention properties. If all goes well, Lancelot will ejaculate into it. All you have to do is position the AV and hold it steady."

I stared in horror at the object he held. It was a large, tubular device, a good three feet long, boasting two handles and a latex hood.

"No way," I said, heaving to my feet with escape in mind.

Zeke had the nerve to grab my arm and yank me back down. "Guests have paid good money for this demo. It was the major selling point for this symposium. The audience expects a performance."

I folded my arms. "I don't give a hairy rat's ankle about their expectations."

"If you say so. But I need an assistant. Luckily, Tess was kind enough to volunteer as an assistant." He scanned the bleachers and waved.

"Not fair."

"She's my second choice, but you leave me no alternative," he said, adding a smile to the wave.

I huffed out a long-suffering sigh. "Fine. I'll do it."

At Muffy's cue, I trailed after Zeke, up the ramp, and onto the stage. To a roar of applause, he positioned me at one end of a single-legged vaulting horse. Wondering why athletic equipment had ended up on the stage, I stroked the fleecy cover someone had wrapped around the midsection. Nice. Bunny-soft.

Muffy's voice speaking into the mic drew my attention. "You'll notice Abby is standing at the head of a dummy mare called a 'breeding phantom.' The phantom is a stand-in for a live mare during semen collection. The fleece cover she's stroking is for the stallion's comfort."

I yanked my hand away, and a wave of laughter erupted from the audience.

While Muffy described the phantom's use, I scanned the audience. Noticing Harmony's scowling face, my determination grew. I intended to give the most educational performance in my repertoire. With my brightest smile, I indicated the end where the head would be, that is if the thing actually had a head, followed by a hand-sweep over the fleece-encased leather haunch, which, according to Muffy, was sturdy enough to support a rutting stallion. Goodie! As a grand finale, I made a graceful gesture at the approximate location of its non-existent lady-parts. It wasn't as hard as I'd thought because I fantasized about being Vanna White to Zeke's Pat Sajak.

The crowd erupted, with everyone except Harmony and Tess cheering me on and hollering for an encore. To sweeten the moment, I caught Tess digging through her purse, a handy way to avoid applauding my performance.

Oh, yeah, I could grow to enjoy being center stage. Perhaps I should take acting lessons.

Audience silence jolted me down to earth. At the slow clip-clop of hooves, I turned my head and followed Lancelot's painfully slow progress as the wrangler hauled him up the ramp and onto the stage. There was no kicking of hooves, no snapping of teeth, in fact, no complaint whatsoever from the near-comatose racehorse.

I whispered to Zeke, "I thought you said you'd give him a stimulant."

"I did," he murmured, "You should have seen him before."

To be on the safe side, I retreated several feet—okay make that yards—while Zeke positioned Lancelot behind the phantom.

Muffy's amplified voice explained, "The first step in semen collection is to ensure the stallion is aroused. That should be easy because Lancelot has used the phantom many times and associates it with pleasure."

Zeke winked at me. "Time to get the ball rolling, so to speak," he whispered, tugging Lancelot closer to his fake lady-love.

The ball refused to roll.

"Nothing's happening," Clay yelled from the bleachers. "That horse is a dud."

Veronica chimed in, "You weren't kidding when you said he was a slow starter."

I wanted to holler, "It's a miracle he's still standing after mounting three mares this morning," but restrained myself. His escapade would remain our little secret.

"This is animal cruelty," a voice boomed from the bleachers. "I'm reporting this horrible exploitation to PETA."

I scanned the stands. Sure enough, Harmony, her face fiery red, had leaped to her feet and was waving a fist. If she wasn't careful, she might blow an artery.

I would have jumped in, but Muffy was faster, offering an explanation I hoped everyone, particularly Harmony, would buy. "Sorry folks. Lancelot's pining for Luc. But don't worry. We have another trick up our sleeves," she paused to smile in Harmony's direction, "one I'm certain will perk him up."

After a hushed consultation, Zeke left the stage and returned leading the mare.

With professional poise, Muffy addressed the audience. "Meet Diamond Girl. She's what we call a 'tease mare', meaning a mare in estrus. A fertile mare is irresistible to any stallion worth his salt."

"Shame," Harmony shouted. "You should be ashamed of yourselves."

Someone who sounded suspiciously like Chef Armand thundered. "*Merde.* If you don't sit the arse on the bench, woman, I won't give you a single butter tart tonight."

Harmony sat.

Ignoring the outbursts from the stands, Zeke positioned Diamond Girl beside Lancelot. The stallion's eyes glazed over before closing slowly. His breathing deepened, and his lower jaw hung open. Any moment now, he'd begin snoring.

Clay's voice rang out. "I guess you can't claim that your stallion's a stud."

Over the smattering of laughter, Tess shouted, "The teaser mare isn't working any better than the phantom. You need someone who knows how to handle his problem. I've helped many studs reach the finish line."

Since she appeared ready to jump onto the stage (and Zeke), I had no alternative. Tess was not stealing my opportunity to discover more about myself. Tiptoeing toward Lancelot, I stretched out my hand.

A murmur rippled through the audience.

After a couple of false starts, I stroked the soft, velvety muzzle. Lancelot's nostrils twitched. Ever-so-slowly he opened his eyes. I shuddered as his moist nose nudged my neck and he inhaled deeply, blowing out with a loud, purring sound. He liked my organic body wash. He liked me. There was nothing to fear.

Taking a peek at Lancelot's undercarriage, I gawked at his emerging man-tackle. "Bingo!" I shouted to the audience. "We have liftoff."

"Hoo-eee. That horse has got hisself some kickstand," someone shouted.

"Yeah. With a pony-poker like that, you should re-name him *Porn Star*."

"How about *Humpasaurus Rex*?" I responded, grinning at my own wit.

The applause was deafening.

I glanced at Harmony. Her expression was thunderous, but Chef Armand's presence appeared to keep her in check.

Once everything quieted down, things happened quickly. With Muffy describing the process, Zeke and I washed our hands in a bucket of sudsy water, dried off, and gloved up. After showing me how to position the AV just so, Zeke used a sponge to lather up Lancelot's glory while Muffy explained how contamination was a no-no. The final step was to line up the stallion behind the phantom so he could mount it in a controlled fashion, nice and straight. My job was to slide the appropriate appendage into the AV.

Lancelot obliged by jumping the phantom and shoving his nose into my neck. After a couple of deep inhalations, he began pumping air. I did my best to angle the AV the way Zeke had shown me, but it was awkward, plus I'd underestimated the force of a stallion's thrusting power. Time after time, Lancelot missed the mark.

Flustered by hot horse breath on my neck, I forced myself to grab the goodies with a gloved hand and attempted to slide Mr. Winkie into the receptacle.

Big mistake.

Lancelot made a rogue thrust, knocking the AV aside. To my horror, I felt his pride and joy slip up my woolly sleeve.

My shriek had the legs to travel all the way to Calgary. "Get it out!" I bellowed at Zeke, who was doubled over with laughter.

The crowd's reaction was deafening. Tess's shrill giggle and Harmony's powerful booing rose above all the rest as I danced around, trying to hold onto the AV with one hand and remove Lancelot's equipment with the other.

The stallion, clearly approaching the grand finale, ignored my fumbling as he doubled down on his efforts.

Zeke stepped in and had a go at Operation Removal. After a couple of strokes, he stopped laughing. "He's caught up in something inside your sweater."

"It's a strand of wool. Ease it away gently."

"Sweet baby Jesus, it's like a spider's web up there. I'll have to break the strand."

"Don't you dare. It'll unravel. Clara knitted that sweater for me."

"What do you suggest?"

"Wait for the out-thrust and unsnag his junk."

Using both hands and considerable muscle, he fumbled around inside the sleeve to make some critical adjustments. Without missing a beat, Lancelot exited the sweater and entered the AV. Another major thrust nearly tore the receptacle from my hands, but I held on for dear life. The horse's tail flagged several times, signaling culmination, and he slumped over the phantom, front legs dangling, chest heaving.

I took the opportunity to disengage the AV from Lancelot. Striding to the front of the stage, I waved the AV in the air, taking care not to dump the contents over my hair, and yelled, "We have a winner."

As Zeke assisted Lancelot with the dismount, applause morphed into a standing ovation, with much stomping, hooting, and hollering. Everyone went wild, with two notable exceptions. Tess and Harmony remained seated. Tess was rummaging in her purse again, and Harmony's stony gaze promised me a world of hurt.

A chill skittering down my spine, I looked away. It dawned on me that I'd made one, perhaps two, mortal enemies. When I looked again, Harmony was on her feet, exchanging comments with Veronica as if nothing had happened, and Tess was smiling at our local veterinarian.

"Hey, stop waving the AV around before you drop it," Muffy shouted, removing it from my grip.

"Sorry," I muttered, wondering if I'd imagined the hatred in Harmony's eyes.

Muffy reached into the AV and extracted the collection cup. After sealing it with a lid, she placed it inside a blue container. While she worked, she explained to the crowd that the semen must be refrigerated immediately, processed as quickly as possible, then placed in liquid nitrogen to keep it viable during longer term storage.

Tess piped up. "How will you process the semen?"

"Good question," Muffy said. "First, I'll conduct an evaluation, a mere formality with Lancelot, as he has super-sperm."

From the stands, Clay asked, "How can you be sure?"

"He's sired dozens of foals." She gave him a quelling look. "As I was saying, once I determine everything is within normal ranges and values, I divide the semen up into five-millimeter straws, place them in a storage container of liquid nitrogen. With Lancelot's high sperm count, five straws always does the trick. We get anywhere from 100 to 150 straws from one collection, translating into twenty to thirty of what we call breeding doses."

I studied Clay, who wore a thoughtful expression.

Zeke wrapped his arms around me and hugged me hard. Any curiosity about Clay's attitude faded as I returned the hug with enthusiasm, enjoying the sensation of lean muscle pressed against every inch of me.

"Well done, Abby," he said. "You're an amazing woman, and that's a fact."

A warm feeling enveloped me. I'd overcome my fear, not to mention aversion, and helped jerk off a horse. Another first. "Thanks," I whispered. "It wasn't as gross as I'd thought. Matter of fact, it wasn't gross at all, simply another horse breeding duty."

"I'm so proud of you." His arms tightened around my shoulders, and I nestled my head against his chest.

A soft whicker broke the moment. Lancelot had dredged up enough strength to raise his head and stare longingly at me.

Zeke grinned at me. "I believe you made a new friend today."

I nodded. Amazing how my fear of horses had vanished. Lancelot deserved a medal for delivering his fourth, and most important, touchdown of the day.

Unafraid, I stepped toward the horse and laced my arms around his glossy neck while letting him nuzzle to his heart's content. It didn't matter if horse-drool dampened my hair. I stroked Lancelot's flank while idly scanning the crowd and trying to gauge the success of the demo. I sagged with relief at the audience's reaction. Everyone appeared happy and excited, especially Muffy, who was carrying the blue container and walking out the gate accompanied by a wrangler, presumably to guard the semen.

I glanced up at Zeke in time to catch his quick frown. "What's wrong?" I asked.

"Nothing, I guess, so long as she starts processing the semen right away. Otherwise, the blue container must be immersed in liquid nitrogen to keep it viable. We hauled several tanks of the stuff into the outbuilding. I can't imagine why she wants to do the processing here instead of at her ranch."

"Stop worrying," I advised. "I imagine she wants to be here to field questions, maybe make some sales."

Zeke's face was impassive, but I could tell he was worried. He said, "I pointed out that the tack room would be a more secure location than the outbuilding to process the semen, but she laughed at me. According to Muffy, the padlock we bought is made of hardened steel and perfectly secure. Also, too many people come and go in the barn, increasing the danger of contamination. The task shouldn't take long. When she finishes, she plans to immerse the straws in liquid nitrogen and take them to her ranch right away to hold them in a secure area until she finds buyers."

"In that case, we have to trust her judgement. Lancelot's her horse, so his semen is her responsibility."

He nodded. "I promised I'd get the teaser mare back to her owner as soon as the demo was over. I'd better run. See you later." With a light brush of his thumb against my cheek, he was gone, leaving me quivering with anticipation.

As the crowd exited the stands, everybody, with the notable exception of Harmony, who glowered at me as she shoved past, congratulated me on my impressive performance. Even Tess assured me that good golly, she couldn't have done a better job of it herself.

I was wading through the crowd toward the gate when Harmony gripped my arm and marched me aside. It was pointless to resist. The woman was massive. Once we were clear, she let go. I planted my feet and faced her, forced to crane my neck.

"What you did was inexcusable," she hissed, steam practically shooting from her ears, "You exploited a poor, helpless animal against his will, invaded his privacy, and manipulated him into giving up a part of himself."

I fisted my hands on my hips and let loose. "Helpless? I don't think so. In case you hadn't noticed, Lancelot is a master at expressing his displeasure, but I didn't hear a peep out of him during the demo. As for privacy, you saw for yourself the lad's motto is, 'If ya got it, flaunt it'. So if you ask me, he had a blast giving up that part of himself."

She drew herself up to her full height. "You had no business doing what you did." She stomped away, leaving me wondering if I should warn Dodie and Muffy about Harmony. In the end, I let her go, hoping she would simmer down.

As I turned to leave, I caught sight of Muffy walking out the gate with one of Zeke's wranglers. She was talking on the phone and gesturing. As she put her phone away, I assumed they would both head for the outbuilding. After exchanging a few words with the wrangler, she handed him the blue container before turning onto the path to the parking lot while he continued along the trail to the outbuilding. There was no doubt in my mind Muffy was heading home to Franklin.

Curiouser and curiouser.

Chapter 17:
Everything Went Black

FOR THE NEXT HOUR, I pitched in to help with the cleanup while Zeke returned the teaser mare to her owner, Dodie called Clara, and Muffy did whatever she did. Every muscle in my body ached and several joints throbbed in tandem. Even my hair hurt, yet I was smiling. With a sense of satisfaction, I leaned against a rail fence to examine the paddock, now returned to its former state.

Although I yearned for a hot bath followed by a pre-dinner nap, there was one last chore I wanted to address—make certain the wrangler had refrigerated the semen we'd worked so hard to collect and locked the outbuilding. I'd bet a month's salary that Muffy was too engulfed in personal problems to worry about semen processing today.

I hurried along the narrow dirt path toward the outbuilding Muffy had converted into a mini-laboratory. I halted at the sight of the open door and relaxed. I'd misjudged her. She must have returned and was inside processing the semen after all. This was a good time to catch her alone and pump her for information about Franklin's unexpected and, so far, undisclosed presence at home.

Voices inside made me pause. Neither sounded like Muffy. I reached into my pocket for the bear spray I carried. Taking a firm grip on my weapon of choice, I crept forward, peeked inside, and ducked away, thinking furiously.

Clay and Tess stood nose-to-nose, arguing in low voices. I strained to hear what they were saying, but was unable to catch the gist of their disagreement.

Keeping my hand inside my pocket, I stepped inside. "May I help you?"

The pair sprang apart and stared at me.

I swung my gaze to the stainless steel lab table. Assorted equipment including beakers, pipettes, even a microscope sat there. I assumed Muffy had instructed the wrangler to put the semen in the refrigerator. Had he forgotten to lock up when he left? I made a mental note to talk to Zeke about it.

Aware that Clay and Tess were staring at me, I went to the fridge and opened it. The blue container sat on the middle shelf. Using one hand, I unlatched the lid and peeked inside. The collection cup sat there with its seal intact. I closed the lid while suppressing a sigh of relief. It appeared that no one had tampered with the semen. As stealthily as possible, I removed my other hand from my pocket, but hooked my thumb inside it. Just in case.

Clay spoke first. "I was taking a walk when I noticed the open door. Figuring it was Muffy, I checked inside and guess what I found. Tess here, standing in front of the open refrigerator. I'm sure she planned to pop the blue container into her monster purse and slip away."

Tess laid a hand on my arm and appealed to me. "This is all a terrible mistake, Abby. The door was open when I arrived." She stopped talking and wrung her hands. "I assumed Muffy was inside processing the sample. I wanted to ask her some questions."

"Like what?" Clay demanded.

Tess's big, blue eyes swam with unshed tears. "Please don't yell at me. I want to breed my precious mare, Morning Glory. Money's a little tight, but she deserves the very best. I'm willing to make sacrifices. All I wanted was to ask Muffy if we could work out a deal that would let me buy some semen. I'd opened the refrigerator to make sure the blue container was safe, and was digging into my purse for my phone to call her when Clay barged in and scared the living daylights out of me." A tear trickled down her cheek.

Tess's distress appeared genuine. That, or she'd missed her calling. Another tear joined the first, and I relented, saying, "I'll be happy to pass your message on to Muffy."

"Oh, thank you. Thank you so much." Tess gripped my hand in both of hers. "I can't begin to tell you how much your understanding means."

This was too much closeness for me. I doubted the news that Zeke had committed himself to me would gladden her heart. Extricating my hand, I made a suitable response. "You must be worn out with all the excitement, hon. I know I am." I glanced at my watch. "Look at the time. I want to talk with Clay in private for a few minutes, so there's no need for you to stay. Happy Hour kicked off fifteen minutes ago, and our bartender makes a mean Appletini."

Tess took the hint. "Sounds good. Maybe I'll see you there?"

"I'll try," I lied, walking her to the door, mainly to verify she headed in the right direction.

Once Tess disappeared, I closed the door and faced Clay. "Okay, your story had better be good."

"I thought Muffy was here," he insisted. "I wanted to talk to her."

"You know what I think? I think you both saw Muffy leave after the demo and decided to have a go at stealing the semen. Tess got here first."

Clay's face turned a dull brick red. "That's not true. I'm not a thief. I only wanted to talk to her."

Letting it drop for now, I crossed my arms and gazed steadily at him. "I know there was a problem between you and Luc."

"You have a vivid imagination." Clay's smile didn't quite reach his eyes.

"During registration, you mentioned a business matter you needed to discuss with Luc."

"It was nothing. I wanted to follow up on an email he'd misinterpreted."

"Uh-huh. And before the guided tour started, I overheard you tell the group that Luc screwed you over in a business deal. And at the end of the tour, you were in Luc's face, insisting you needed to talk to him. When he refused, you threatened him. I didn't see you again until after Luc's death. By the way, that's a real impressive shiner you have."

"Hey, if you're implying I was involved in his death, you're wrong." Clay's voice cracked with alarm. "We had a simple misunderstanding, is all. I set him straight."

I folded my arms across my chest and went with the bluff I'd started before the demo. "I made some phone calls," I lied. "It was easy to learn about your 'simple misunderstanding'. I would be furious with Luc, too. Why don't you tell me your side of the story before Zeke arrives? He'll be here any minute now." I'd thrown Zeke's name into the conversation because I'd finally clued in to the fact that I was alone in a secluded outbuilding with a potential killer. As unobtrusively as possible, I slid my hand into my pocket to grip my bear spray.

Clay didn't appear to notice. He ran his fingers through his hair, which was a nice salt with plenty of pepper, and gave a resigned sigh. "Fine. Let's sit down." He indicated a pair of metal lab stools flanking the table.

Once seated across from one another, I stared at him in silence, the way my favorite TV cop did when she wanted someone to talk.

Clay cleared his throat and obliged. "I didn't like Luc. After university ended, I hoped I'd never see him again."

"But you did," I prompted.

Clay nodded. "A year ago. He contacted me, claimed he was doing business on behalf of his terminally ill boss. All proceeds of any business deals he made, less his tiny cut of course, would pay for his boss' experimental cancer treatment. I should have known better than to believe his story, but he was convincing. Long story short, I purchased ten doses of semen from a winning stallion called Lancelot."

"I assume this was before Muffy owned the horse."

"Yeah. But even then, Luc was Lancelot's trainer. So after inseminating my ten mares, I jumped the gun and started bragging about my entry into the world of horse racing and how I would soon be rolling in money."

The picture was growing clearer. I spoke with certainty. "Too bad for you it was a hoax."

Clay propped his arms on the table. "Right. There were no foals. Zero out of ten mares. Either the donor stallion was infertile, or I'd been scammed. Instead of owning several foals destined to become winning racehorses, I became the laughing stock of the racing community. My AI experiment became the joke that refused to die. My nickname is 'Shoots Blanks'."

I bit the inside of my cheek to prevent my amusement from showing. "That must be humiliating."

"Ya think?" he asked, his voice dripping with sarcasm. "Then, as if my situation wasn't bad enough, Luc disappeared around the same time as rumors about his horse drugging surfaced. I heard he'd been charged and released. A year later, I received Muffy's invitation, noticed Luc's name as a presenter, and here I am. Turns out Lancelot's former owner, who, by the way, was perfectly healthy, sold the horse to her, and Luc had sweet-talked her into hiring him as the trainer."

"So you signed up for the symposium to confront Luc."

"Yeah. He'd scammed me. I wanted him to give me what I'd paid for, and then, I planned to destroy his career."

"What about your bruises?"

"After the barn tour, I took Luc aside to confront him about selling me dud semen. We fought. He was winning, so I pulled my gun on him. It would have been easy to kill him then and there, but I didn't. He was worth more to me alive than dead."

"How so?" I asked. Hoping Clay wasn't armed at this moment, I edged my hand closer to my pocket.

"He admitted the semen he'd sold me was a scam, and promised to provide all I needed, this time from Lancelot."

"From today's demo," I guessed.

"Yeah. Delivery was scheduled for this evening, after Muffy had processed the stuff. Mainly, I wanted revenge, not the semen, although that would've been a nice perk. See, I always liked Muffy, thought she was too good for a jerk like Luc. I intended to prevent him from ruining her reputation, so I played along."

"What was your big plan to ruin his career?" I asked, genuinely curious.

"I was gonna tape our conversation when he turned over the semen." Clay flashed his phone. "It was supposed to be a setup that would put him away for a long, long time."

"Then why are you here now?"

"Believe it or not, I tried to chat with Muffy after the demo, but she said she had to go home for a few minutes. Several minutes later, I saw Tess booting it in this direction. Putting two and two together, I figured she was up to something, so I followed her."

I'd nailed it. Clay was here to steal the semen. But I didn't want to press him too hard. Instead, I asked, "What did you want to say to Muffy."

After a longish pause, during which I sensed his brain spinning madly, he said, "I wanted to tell her about Luc's scam and ask if she could see a way to making a deal with me for some of Lancelot's semen."

I didn't push my luck by expressing my skepticism. Instead, I picked up a glass pipette and fiddled with it. "I want to believe you, I really do. But Luc's dead, and you're likely the last person to see him alive."

"Hey, I had nothing to do with his death." He paused, drilling me with a penetrating gaze. "Anyway, I thought his death was an accident. Has anything changed?"

"Not at all. We're merely tying up loose ends."

"You were lying to me all along about knowing my secret."

I replaced the pipette, folded my hands in front of me, and worked up a defiant glare. "Yes."

Clay's eyes hardened and a muscle in his cheek flickered. He stood and aimed a savage kick at his stool. It toppled with a metallic clatter.

All the saliva in my mouth dried up.

In a grating voice, he said, "I don't like being tricked. Next time you lie to someone, you might not be so lucky. So unless you have more questions, I have to get changed for dinner in time to pick up Veronica." He didn't wait for my answer before striding outside and disappearing from my line of sight.

I slumped against the table, my heart thudding in my chest. The certainty that I'd pushed him too hard made me shiver. I had an uneasy feeling I'd better watch my back.

Once Clay's footsteps disappeared, I sat perfectly still inside the outbuilding for several minutes, waiting for my pulse to stop racing and my legs to regain enough strength to support me. After several minutes, I headed for the door. A warm bath with my name on it sang a seductive song. The debriefing with Dodie and Zeke would have to wait until I felt more like myself.

Stepping outside, I realized the door wasn't self-locking. The only way to lock up was with a padlock. There were hooks on the doorframe, but no padlock.

Someone, likely Clay or Tess, must have cut the padlock, and I needed to find it. There would be forensic evidence like fingerprints or DNA.

I eyed the bushes and long grasses surrounding the outbuilding. The glint of metal at the base of a nasty-looking thorn bush a few feet from the outbuilding gave me hope. Much as I wanted to leave immediately, I had a responsibility to retrieve the padlock. This would take only a few seconds.

I dropped onto my hands and knees and wormed my way forward. The exercise was trickier than I'd estimated. Sweat was dripping down my brow when I finally managed to grasp the padlock. I was backing out when a nearby rustle alerted me to company.

I tried to move faster, but the bush had other plans.

As I struggled to disentangle both arms of my woolly sweater from the bush, a shiver of panic trickled down my spine. I'd been so intent on finding evidence, I'd forgotten I might be in danger.

In my defence, this was my ranch, with friends, family, and employees nearby.

"Who's there?" I yelled over the pounding of my heart while groping for my bear spray. Unfortunately, my snagged sweater made it impossible to reach my weapon.

The silence freaked me out. Small hairs on my arms prickled as I imagined someone standing behind me. I ripped at the bush until my hands bled.

My sweater sprang loose to the simultaneous sound of a dry branch cracking.

"Run," my brain shrieked. But at my age, rising was an effort at the best of times, never mind after a long trail ride. Balancing on both hands, I raised my ass in the air, and awkwardly pushed myself upright.

That was as far as I got.

White-hot pain exploded in my skull. I staggered and managed to sink to my knees. My last thought before my vision clouded and everything went black was, "*Why had I been so stupid?*"

Chapter 18:
Everyone Has a Motive

Neil Diamond's voice penetrated the dark fog holding me hostage. I hovered on the edge of consciousness, smiling as he serenaded me with *Cracklin' Rosie*, then opened my eyes a slit. Two anxious faces swam into view. Based on Zeke's unshaven chin and Dodie's exhausted expression, I assumed they'd been at my bedside for a long time. At least I wasn't in the hospital. That was a good sign, right?

I squeezed my eyes shut against the memory of terror and dazzling pain followed by fragments of an ambulance ride, then nothing. I had a feeling I was forgetting something, but it was difficult to think with someone taking a hammer to my head.

Dodie's voice said, "Good. She's awake. Her eyelids are twitching."

A large, warm hand gripped mine. "The doctor says you're okay, Abby." Zeke's breath tickled my cheek. "There was no concussion, only a huge bump and a nasty case of shock. We let you sleep all night, but the drugs must have worn off by now. It's time for you to tell us what happened."

I tried floating back into the welcoming darkness, but the strains of *Hotel California* dragged me from dreamland. Knowing my weakness for classic rock, I assumed Dodie had fired up my iPod. Opening my eyes, I mumbled, "What time is it?"

"Morning," Dodie announced. "The doctor said light food only for the next twenty-four hours, so I brought you juice and dry toast."

"That's not worth waking up for." I closed my eyes and rolled over.

Zeke's voice pierced my nice, comfy cocoon. "You could have been killed. It's time to give up this murder investigation and call in the Mounties."

That caught my attention. I opened my eyes and suppressed a whimper of pain as I squinted at Zeke, then Dodie. They were seated, one on either side of me. "Give up?" I squawked. "Over my cold, dead body. We're not giving up now, and we're not calling in any Mounties because of my little mishap, which, come to think of it, most likely had nothing to do with Luc's death." I gazed at Zeke defiantly.

"Holy flaming hell," he growled. "At this rate, it *will* be over your cold, dead body. This little 'mishap', as you call it, was attempted murder. We wanted to notify the RCMP last night, but you flipped out. Convince me we did the right thing."

My eye roll triggered a fresh burst of pain. When it passed, I went for a more reasonable tone. "There's no point calling in the Perkins brothers. They're useless. We agreed to conduct our own investigation, and that's what I intend to do, with or without you. I'd prefer to do it with you. We're too close to give up now." I struggled to sit up.

Dodie pinned my shoulders to the bed. "No sudden moves."

If I'd known she would go all Florence Nightingale on me, I'd have brought on my A-game sooner. "Stop bruising the merchandise," I ordered, using all my strength to peel away one of her hands. "You been working out, or what?"

Dodie ignored my feeble attempt at humor and said, "Believe me when I say I will sit on you all day, if necessary, to keep you in bed. You're lucky to be alive. If the dead branch used to clobber you hadn't broken on connection with your hard skull, you'd be stretched out beside Luc in the morgue right now instead of lying in your own bed."

I rolled my eyes. "It's not serious, Dodie. You heard Zeke. There's no sign of concussion." But my sister was right. Once again, I experienced a niggling feeling that I was forgetting something. "How did you find me?" I asked.

Zeke clasped my hand. "Veronica called it in. Seems she went for a walk after the demo and stumbled upon you lying in the bushes beside the outbuilding. She thought you were dead." He took a shaky breath. "So did I."

"Guess it takes more than a little whack on the head to kill me," I said. Since lying flat on my back put me at a disadvantage, I asked to be helped upright. Dodie frowned her disapproval but plumped my pillows while Zeke propped me into a sitting position. I stole a look at his face, catching him scowling at me.

Not good. I busied my hands smoothing the covers.

"Why were you alone in a remote outbuilding when you knew there was a killer on the loose?" he asked. His surprisingly calm voice only served to underscore his agitation. "What were you thinking, Abby?"

Filling the silence, Michael Jackson's high-pitched squall launched into *The Love You Save*. Dodie turned down the sound, no doubt in order to hear every syllable of my lame explanation.

Truth be told, I hadn't been thinking. I cast my mind back to the end of the demo. I'd been elated, exhilarated, and bursting with pride over my accomplishment. Trying to analyze my motives (or lack thereof) for my solo stroll, I hesitated a beat, then admitted, "With all the excitement of the demo, I'd actually forgotten about Luc's death." I averted my gaze, unable to face the concern and disapproval I was certain filled their eyes. "I was operating on automatic pilot, taking care of things around the ranch, chatting, joking. Everything felt normal. I was concerned about the semen and I needed a walk, so I decided to check the outbuilding. I can't believe I was so idiotic."

Zeke reached over and turned off the iPod altogether. The silence was deafening. "I get it," he said at last, his voice gentle. "But please don't do that again. I doubt my heart or my sanity could take it."

"Same goes," Dodie said.

"Thanks, guys," I said, relief washing over me. And in that moment, I recalled what had slipped my mind. "I think I interrupted a robbery," I blurted. "Is the insulated container still in the outbuilding?"

"No. It's missing," Zeke admitted. "How did you know?"

"Gut feeling. One of them must have stolen it."

"Holy flaming hell. There was more than one? Who was there?"

"Tess and Clay."

"Wasn't Muffy there?" Dodie asked. "I thought she was processing the semen."

"After the demo I saw her heading for the parking lot in a big hurry. I suspect she went home, but I digress. More on that later. Truth be told, I believe Clay and Tess, independent of one another, noticed Muffy's departure and jumped on the chance to steal the semen."

"It's odd that Muffy left the semen unattended," Zeke said. "I think you'd better start at the beginning and tell us what happened."

Taking a deep, calming breath, I described everything that occurred after I started out on my fateful walk, and ending with the attack.

A throbbing silence greeted my revelations.

Yeah, my actions didn't exactly showcase me as the brightest bulb in the string. No wonder they were upset. To cover my embarrassment, I babbled on. "Here's my thinking. Tess came prepared to steal the semen. Do you know she carries both a bolt cutter and hacksaw in her purse? I believe she cut the padlock. On hearing Clay's approach, it would be easy to toss the lock into the bushes and dart inside to lie about finding the door open."

"But you said Tess left first," Dodie prompted.

I nodded. "She left before I did. Clay, too. But either one could have hidden outside and waited for me to leave. Trouble was, I stuck around. How could I leave when I saw the padlock lying in the bushes? I had to salvage it in case it held evidence. And yeah, it was a dumb move. I made it easy for someone to attack me."

"Either of them could have done it. They both had a motive to steal the semen," Dodie said. "Clay thought he deserved it because he'd already paid for it. Tess wanted it for her mare, but couldn't afford it. The container holds twenty to thirty breeding doses. After using one to inseminate Morning Glory, the rest would be worth a small fortune."

"It would still be difficult," Zeke said, defending Tess. "Even if Morning Glory's colts turned out to be good runners, she wouldn't dare register Lancelot as the sire. The colts would only be valuable if they won enough races. And it would be dangerous to sell the rest of the semen. She'd have to go the black market route."

"Don't rule Tess out again." Dodie warned. "That's still plenty of motive."

Encouraged by my sister's support, I blurted out the logical conclusion. "And if I was out of the picture, she would have access to an entire batch of free semen—and Zeke's too." My face grew hotter than a blast furnace. Had I really said that?

Yep. It appeared I had. Zeke's eyes danced with suppressed amusement.

"Sorry," I mumbled. "Residual jealousy. That didn't come out right."

"Sure it did," Dodie said, grinning at Zeke. "Tess has the hots for you. No, don't try to deny it. It's another motive for the attack on Abby."

Apparently not feeling compelled to speak, Zeke rose from his chair and strolled over to my sliding door. Opening it, he peered outside, likely coming to terms with the fact that innocent, fluffy little Tess with her endless prattle and big boobs might well be a ruthless thief—or worse.

"Would someone please turn on my iPod again," I said, seeking music to cut the awkward silence.

Dodie obliged, and the Rolling Stones started up with *Satisfaction*.

He ambled back to sit on the edge of my bed, facing me. "You're both right. Tess is a suspect. I guess I didn't want to believe it." He angled his head in concession and silent apology.

Gripped by warm fuzzies, I nodded to indicate my equally silent understanding.

Dodie broke the moment by asking me, "Could Clay have done this to you?"

I shifted my legs to give Zeke more room. "I suppose so," I said, hyper-aware of his proximity, "but I doubt it. Clay admitted he had a gun. We were alone in the outbuilding. He could easily have overpowered me there."

"He probably assumed you would leave, just like a normal person," Zeke said in a reasonable tone. "After that he could steal the semen, no fuss, no muss, no risk."

My warm fuzzies vanished. "Normal is highly overrated."

"What about Veronica?" he asked. "Could she have done it?"

"You said she's the one who found me. Are you sure it was mere coincidence her stroll took her to the outbuilding where the semen was stored?"

"She and Clay could be in cahoots." Dodie bounced with excitement, but stopped when her chair gave a dangerous creak. "I sat beside her during the demo. Long story short, she described how, after Luc dumped her, she invested all her energy and a large trust fund into changing her appearance. She'd planned to make Luc fall in love with her new, gorgeous self before dumping him. At least she had the insight to admit she'd wasted a decade obsessing about revenge. Now that he's dead, her life has opened up in so many new directions, she doesn't know where to start."

"Maybe she started by stealing Lancelot's semen," I suggested.

"You sure you two aren't inventing suspects?" Zeke asked.

"Think about it," I said. "Veronica and Clay are inseparable. What if they cooperated to steal the semen and share the profits? Or maybe she acted on her own, figuring she deserved compensation for the years she spent obsessing over Luc. Either way, it's entirely possible she hit me, stole the semen, and hid it for pickup as soon as the coast was clear."

"Then why would she phone reception about finding you out cold?" Zeke asked.

I thought that over. "Remorse, maybe? Most people own a conscience."

"Sweet baby Jesus. I hope neither of you conjures up another suspect," Zeke muttered.

"Now that you mention it," I said, "Harmony's another suspect."

"I'm almost afraid to ask, but why Harmony?"

To Neil Young's wail about a horse with no name, I described my unsettling interaction with her after the demo, ending with, "She's convinced we took advantage of a poor, exhausted stallion, calling it animal abuse. She sure sounded capable of hitting me and stealing the semen as punishment for violating Lancelot's privacy, or maybe she planned to sell it for money to bribe PETA to hire her."

After Neil's final *La, la, la-la-la-la* faded away, Dodie said, "Yep. Sounds to me we've got a whole whack of viable suspects."

Gazing into my eyes, Zeke stroked my hair away from my forehead. "Abby, I won't rest until I get whoever hurt you."

At his touch, my heart kicked hard. My bladder kicked harder. Suppressing a desire to leap into his arms, I said, "I need to tend to the call of nature. It looks like another beautiful day, so let's move to the balcony."

Zeke nodded, and helped me swing my legs over the side. Once I was on my feet, he supported me as far as the ensuite door, which I promptly closed in his face. Once I'd finished what I needed to do, including a quick splash of water, a struggle with my hair, and a teeny-tiny dab of makeup, I made my way to the balcony.

Zeke's eyes telegraphed his approval. You gotta love a man who notices.

Once I was settled on the chaise lounge, Dodie tucked a blanket over me. My juice and dry toast sat on a small round table within easy reach.

Feeling pampered and cared for, I turned my face into a light breeze, which lifted my hair and cleared out any remaining cobwebs. I breathed deeply, savoring the scent of fresh pine trees. "Ah, that's better," I said. "My brain's functioning again. I believe we were discussing the suspect list for my attack. Let's move on to Luc's killer. I bet there's a lot of overlap."

Dodie jumped right in. "Perhaps we were too quick to rule out Tess as a suspect in Luc's murder."

"You mean I was too quick," Zeke pointed out. After a long pause, he conceded, "Much as I hate to admit it, you might be right."

This was no time for an I-told-you-so moment. Dodie's broad grin held more than enough smugness for both of us.

"Glad you're finally on board," she said. "Although Tess has no apparent motive to kill Luc, I suspect she's more than capable of murder to get what she wants."

"That's right," I said. "All we have to do is figure out what that might be. She's definitely dangerous and warrants investigation."

"Agreed," Zeke said.

"What about Clay," Dodie asked.

"Definitely a candidate," I replied. "We have only his word he didn't kill Luc. Clay had the means, motive, and opportunity for the killing, especially if his fight with Luc got out of hand. Plus, his reaction on figuring out I was bluffing about knowing his secret proves he has the disposition. Revenge murders happen all the time."

Dodie nodded her agreement. "Then there's Veronica. I don't believe she had anything to do with Luc's murder. She intended to get her revenge in other ways."

"True, but what if Luc rejected her advances?" I said. "Imagine how that would have gone down. If Veronica was angry enough, she could have taken him by surprise."

Zeke, flashed a smile at me. "That clever and devious mind of yours never fails to impress me."

Ridiculously happy, I smiled back. It was so easy to enjoy this man.

"Now let's look at Harmony," I said. "I haven't had a chance to tell you, but the reunion gave her cover for a covert mission to take Luc down."

"Shut the front door," Dodie exclaimed.

"You should've heard her during the trail ride and after the demo. She's nuts." I related everything I'd learned from Harmony during the trail ride, including how her first takedown of Luc had backfired and she'd ended up behind bars instead. I finished with, "PETA washed its hands of her, but Muffy's invitation provided a second chance to nail Luc for horse drugging, thus proving her dedication to protecting animals."

"But killing Luc wouldn't have helped her cause," Dodie pointed out. "Harmony needed him alive so she could take him down."

"True. But what if Luc resisted capture and things got out of hand? Harmony's big enough and strong enough to kill a man. Want to know the kicker?" I didn't wait for an answer, but rushed on. "She's now focussing on Muffy and Franklin. Harmony believes that if she provides the RCMP with proof that the Waltons knew Luc was drugging their racehorses, PETA will hire her in a flash."

Zeke snagged a piece of my dry toast and chewed thoughtfully. "If you're right that Harmony's set her sights on Muffy and Franklin, she may well be the next victim instead of a suspect."

"Oh, dear. I never considered that," I admitted.

"At least we don't have to worry about Franklin," Dodie said. "He's overseas."

"No he's not," I replied, appalled that I'd forgotten to tell her. "He answered the phone when I called Muffy's ranch yesterday. I imagine he's been at home all along."

Dodie, who gazed at me accusingly, said, "And you didn't think to mention that teeny-tiny piece of information to me?"

"I know, I know," I wailed. "I didn't have a chance, what with semen collection demos and nearly getting myself killed. Forgive me?"

I must have looked worried, because Dodie replied immediately, "Of course I do. I wasn't thinking straight. Strange Muffy didn't mention it, though. It appears she wants to hide the fact that he didn't go on his business trip."

"Likely because it makes him look guilty," I said.

"Maybe he is," Dodie said. "What if his business contacts heard the rumors circulating about his wife's horses winning races due to drugging? They'd believe he was involved, too. If you ask me, that gives him one kick-ass motive for murder."

"Muffy, too," I said. "We heard Franklin as good as admit he'd divorce her in a heartbeat if he thought Luc posed a threat to his business dealings. I suspect she would stop at nothing, even murder, to protect her marriage."

"Possibly. It's obvious something's been bothering Muffy ever since Franklin ordered her to fire Luc. Here's another possibility." I paused to gather my thoughts. "What if she tried to fire him and he took offense?"

Zeke who'd been sitting quietly and listening to the discussion while watching a pair of ravens soaring overhead, ran his fingers through his hair, fluffing it up in the most adorable way. "No wonder Muffy left the semen unattended. I imagine she had bigger fish to fry. That means we've got six suspects and five days to solve everything before the guests check out." He looked at me, his eyes clouded with doubt. "That's not much time. Think we can pull this off without the Mounties?"

"Definitely," I assured him with more confidence than I felt.

Dodie backed me up with, "There's no doubt in my mind that between the three of us, we'll find the guilty party," she paused, "or parties."

Since Zeke looked unconvinced, I changed the subject. "What's our approach?"

There was a long-suffering sigh before Zeke said, "I can't fight you both, so I suggest we go at it the same way you eat an elephant." At my quirked eyebrow, he clarified with, "One bite at a time."

Dodie's eyes filled with approval. "Nice. So who will be our first bite?"

"I suggest we start with Tess." Zeke examined my face, as if deciphering my reaction. "As you both pointed out so tactfully, she likes me. I'll ask her out on a date. If she accepts, I'll have a chance to pump her for information."

Although I recognized the wisdom of his suggestion, I didn't like it. "Oh, she'll accept all right," I said, attempting to project serenity.

"As long as the only pumping you do is for information," Dodie said.

He slid Dodie a long, withering look. "The only woman I'm interested in is right here." His gaze softened as he studied my face.

The light brush of his fingers on my arm was disturbingly electric. My pulse gave a crazy jump as I held his gaze. Certain he was minimizing Tess's psychotic tendencies, I touched his arm. "Be careful around Tess, Zeke. There's something wrong with her, something broken. I don't trust her."

He chuckled. "She's half my size. I'm an ex-Special Forces officer." He reached for my orange juice and handed it to me with a flourish.

Yeah, the macho gene was alive, well, and thriving. "The woman's twisted," I warned. "Don't underestimate her capabilities, is all I'm saying," I sipped my juice and let the sweet, cold liquid slide down my throat.

"Okay, children," Dodie said, interrupting our squabble. She turned to Zeke. "What sort of date were you thinking?"

Zeke scratched his head, looking perplexed. "I'm not sure. I want to keep it public, but I doubt line-dancing's her thing."

Against my better judgement, I suggested, "Invite her to the campfire tonight."

As if agreeing with me, *Light my Fire* started up on my iPod.

His brows slammed together. "It's supposed to be cool tonight. I draw the line at sharing a blanket with Tess. Other than toasting marshmallows and singing *Kumbaya*, what do you suggest I do with her at a campfire?"

"Chat her up." I finished the juice and handed it back.

"As opposed to feel her up." Dodie snickered at her wit. So did I, but I concealed it with a cough.

Zeke manfully ignored the lewd comment. "I'm not into chit-chat with Tess. Got some suggestions?"

It went without saying I had suggestions. "First off, don't ask her if she tried to kill me. She'll deny it. Be oblique. Ask questions. Act interested. Start with her mare, work your way up to her family, especially ex-husbands, her financial situation, that kind of thing. Try to learn her feelings about Luc."

Dodie added, "And keep your hands to yourself."

Zeke grinned. "Abby has nothing to worry about, and that's a fact."

The warmth started low inside me, expanded, and blossomed into my heart. To divert my sister's attention, I pointed out, "That still leaves five suspects."

"I'll tackle Veronica, Clay, and Harmony today," Dodie volunteered. "I'll be all casual-like, asking questions to assess their guilt. At the very least, I'll get a good reading on whether or not anyone's lying."

My throat tightened with apprehension, but admittedly, I was in no shape to help her today. At my age, a blow to the head was more debilitating than I would ever have believed. "Don't do what I did," I said by way of advice. "Be sure to talk to them within sight of witnesses. One of them may also be Luc's murderer."

"Oh, man," Dodie said, reaching for a slice of my toast and waving the pointy end at Zeke. "She's into her bossy mode. Watch out."

The sun felt so heavenly, I ignored the dig and suggested to Dodie, "How be you and I double-team Muffy tomorrow, try get an answer about Franklin's whereabouts?"

Dodie nodded her agreement. "The three of us can meet and share our findings afterward." To celebrate, she crunched down on the toast. After swallowing, she made a face. "Ack. That's horrible. Toast was invented as a vehicle for butter and honey."

The doorbell rang, giving Dodie an excuse to ditch the remaining toast. "Who can that be?" I asked, struggling to rise.

She made sure I stayed seated by pressing down on my shoulders. "Probably your real breakfast. Chef Armand was worried about you. He claimed dry toast wasn't enough, insisted on sending you a decent breakfast, one worthy of his skills." She went to the front door, returning with a tray, which she set on the side table. "It's not as light as the doctor recommended, so go easy."

The light breeze wafted the scent of bacon toward me. My mouth watered. "Bless you, my child. Everything's better with bacon."

"I'll keep Abby company while she eats," Zeke offered.

"Oh, no you won't," Dodie said hastily, much to my disappointment. "She needs peace and quiet. You and I will go down to breakfast, where you will sweet-talk Tess into a date for the campfire."

Once they left, I removed the plate covers. Unfolding the napkin provided by Chef Armand, I popped the tip of a buttery croissant into my mouth and contemplated the best way to convince Zeke he needed to take steps to protect himself around Tess.

I drew a blank.

But before I'd finished my lightly scrambled eggs, I'd come up with the next best thing—a way for me to lend a helping hand.

If Zeke finds out, he'll go ballistic, my inner critic warned.

I shrugged off my concern. Even an ex-Special Forces officer needed backup when deliberately blind to danger, right? I intended to be there for him tonight, albeit undetectable. If all went well, and I sincerely hoped it would, he'd never find out.

After devouring every scrap of breakfast, I wobbled back to bed, pulled the duvet up to my chin, and closed my eyes for a long nap. I needed recovery time before tonight's mission.

Chapter 19:
Backup Support

Later that day, Dodie informed me Zeke had scored a date with Tess for tonight. Not sure whether to be worried or excited, I passed the rest of the day flip-flopping between both, interspersed with eating, reading, and snoozing. Between naps, I dug out dark clothes for my nighttime mission and hid them in my closet.

I was enjoying a cup of tea in my kitchen when a key turned in the front door. A moment later, Dodie entered without knocking. "I was afraid you might be asleep. I have news about our suspects," she announced, plunking down on the stool opposite me.

"That was fast work." I poured another cup of tea and handed it to her.

"I know," she said, grinning as she dumped in three teaspoons of sugar and stirred. "I've ruled out Harmony as a suspect in your attack." She slurped her tea, prolonging the drama.

"I'll bite," I said, humoring her. "What did she say to convince you?"

"Apparently, she was agitated after the demo because you were rude. She needed a stiff drink, so she went to the bar instead of her cabin." Dodie dabbed her lips with a paper napkin. "What did you say to her?"

"I was not rude to her. I merely shot down each of her absurd accusations. Nicely, I might add." I repeated my words to Harmony.

"It worked, because she asked me to tell you she wants to apologize," Dodie informed me. "Anyway, the bartender corroborated her story. Apparently they chatted the rest of the afternoon while she consumed six Molson Canadians with no ill effect. She was contemplating a seventh when the dinner bell rang."

"That's some power-drinking. What time did she arrive?"

"No idea," Dodie said, looking crestfallen. "I didn't think to ask."

"So she could have followed me to the outbuilding, waited until I was alone, then attacked me. There would have still been plenty of time for Harmony to hit the bar before dinner. Plus, she's not off the hook yet for Luc's death."

Dodie sighed. "I'd better warn Zeke."

"Right. What about Clay and Veronica?"

"Veronica got all coy, and admitted she spent the rest of the afternoon with Clay."

"In bed?" I asked.

"Yep. When I cornered Clay, he wasn't shy about admitting it."

I took a sip of tea. "So essentially, they're providing one another's alibis."

"That's what it boils down to. But I believe them. They had that freshly minted horniness about them."

"Horny doesn't mean innocent."

"I still think Tess did it." Dodie took another sip of tea.

"Yeah. Me, too." We finished our tea in companionable silence, then Dodie left, telling me to get some sleep.

My nap was longer than I'd intended. I jolted awake to find my sister shaking my arm like a terrier, presumably to make sure I was still alive. What if the campfire was over?

I squinted at my bedside clock. Nearly ten-thirty. I'd come close to missing my window of opportunity to help Zeke. My first thought was I had to get this show on the road. My second was I had to lose Dodie first.

To let her know I wasn't dead or unconscious, I uttered a sleepy grunt and rolled over, feigning sleep. Hopefully, my sister would take the hint and leave.

No such luck. After a couple of beers at the campfire, Dodie had morphed into Chatty Cathy. Perched on my bed, she rattled on, telling me Zeke's big date had gone better than we could have imagined. Although the singalong had drowned out most of the lovebirds' conversation, she'd sat close enough to catch Tess insisting they go to his place because her cabin was a mess. They'd left together, even though the songsters were belting out *American Pie*, which went on forever. Since the song had been Dodie's request, she'd felt obliged to stay until it ended.

All sorts of alarm bells clanged in my brain. I had to leave. I yawned, claiming exhaustion, and closed my eyes. By keeping my breathing deep and rhythmic, I must have convinced Dodie I'd drifted off, because five minutes later, she tip-toed out.

I waited until my front door clicked shut before hopping out of bed. Assuring myself it was eagerness, not fear, that made my hands tremble, I donned a black outfit—windbreaker, yoga pants, socks, even black sneakers. A ski mask would have been nice, but I made do with a black headscarf, tucking in every strand of my hair. At the last minute, I remembered to grab my keys, bear spray, and cell phone, shoving them in my pocket, before hurrying toward Zeke's quarters.

The frosty night air, a contrast to the daytime warmth, made me glad I'd worn a windbreaker. I felt like a teenager again, sneaking out of the house to meet the boyfriend who'd insisted we see each other on a weeknight, regardless of parental rules—an event which ended in a three-week grounding and the loss of my first love to a cheerleader with perky boobs and more tolerant parents.

Ten minutes later, I reached the barn. Everything was dark and quiet. It occurred to me a murderer always returned to the scene of the crime, but I refused to let fear derail my mission. I was here to ensure Zeke's safety.

Gripping my bear spray, I tested the double front doors. Locked.

I placed my ear against the heavy wood and listened. Everything was silent, without so much as a neigh or shuffle of hooves in the straw.

I edged around to the far side of the building, where Zeke's apartment was located. I was *not* there to prevent Tess from having her merry way with him. Nope. I was there to make sure she didn't maim, mutilate, or kill him.

Channeling my inner ninja, I sprinted as far as his living room window. From there, I slunk forward, approaching the darkened bedroom window, which I happened to know he kept open at night, but of course, he wouldn't be there. I told myself he'd probably insisted on walking Tess home.

Who was I kidding? Although I was here to provide backup, albeit clandestine, I also wanted proof I could, indeed, trust him. Wouldn't every woman feel the same way?

It wouldn't hurt to peek. On the off-chance he needed help.

He'd left the curtains open. Before I chickened out, I peered into his bedroom. There was enough ambient light to reveal his bed, which was made up with knife-edge precision, a habit learned during his military career.

Zeke's place was empty. They must have gone to Tess's cabin.

My knees weakened with the force of my relief. Why had I jumped to the worst possible conclusion? I'd come a whisker away from blowing it. I was smart enough to realize the only way to learn if Zeke was trustworthy was, well, to trust him. Zeke was nothing like my daddy or ex-husband. Not even close.

I dropped to the ground and leaned against the wall, my heart thumping heavily. I sat there for a while before pushing myself awkwardly to my feet and continued along the rear wall, intending to return home. Passing the back door, I twisted the handle, fully expecting it to be locked. To my astonishment, it turned easily. Either Zeke had forgotten to lock up, or the lock had been picked. I pushed the door open.

The interior was pitch black.

The back of my neck prickled. Why were the lights off?

Rejecting the use of my phone's flashlight feature, which would broadcast my presence, I followed a hunch and retreated a step to run a hand around the doorframe. As with the outbuilding, a set of heavy padlock hoops was present, the padlock missing.

I tried phoning Zeke, but it went straight to voicemail.

Where was he? What if Tess had struck again?

I'd no sooner decided to be sensible and leave, when a horse's enraged scream accompanied by the banging of hooves halted me in my tracks.

Lancelot.

With my instincts screaming at me to flee, I gripped my bear spray with both hands and stepped silently inside, closing the door behind me. The air, heavy with the pungency of leather, pine shavings, liniment, and the unmistakeable odor of horse, not entirely unpleasant, filled my nostrils. I ignored Lancelot's commotion and focused on my surroundings.

I was standing in the tack room. A thin partition separated me from the agitated horse. Something or someone was making him real unhappy.

A thousand and one excellent reasons to turn tail and run galloped around my brain, complementing the jittery cha-cha dancing in my chest. But what if I was right? What if Tess had overpowered Zeke and he needed my help? With her, anything was possible. She probably had a gun.

Maintaining a firm grip on the canister, I edged into the main corridor with its double row of stalls. The windows let in enough light for me to pick my way. Guided by Lancelot's restless movements, I stumbled toward his stall, when the thud of hooves hitting wood combined with a frantic neigh signalled distress.

A soft sound behind me caused all the small hairs on my arms to stand at attention. I fumbled for my phone with my free hand.

At that moment, Lancelot's door crashed open, pushed from the inside. The metal grill hit me hard as someone flew out, head-butting me aside. Before I recovered, a powerful fist hammered into my solar plexus. Agony shot through my body and I was unable to breathe, either in or out. I found myself flung through the air to land inside Lancelot's stall, where I managed to resume breathing. The door slammed with terrifying finality. I had enough wits left to be thankful a thick layer of straw had cushioned my fall.

A soft nicker was the only sound to break the silence. I nearly let out a shriek when a wet nose nudged my neck. Lancelot appeared to remember me.

Uttering tiny whimpers, I scrabbled my trembling hands through the straw, hunting for the phone, which I'd dropped upon making a landing. I encountered what felt like a candy, and shoved it into my pocket to prevent Lancelot from eating it. Once I found my phone, I clicked on the flashlight app and let out an undignified screech. I'd ended up between four long horse legs. And one equally long stiffie.

Yeah, he remembered me all right.

The stallion lowered his head to nudge my shoulder. Slowly, I crawled into the corner and pushed to my feet. The creak of the stall door opening halted my flight to freedom. As I squinted into the darkness, a tall, dark shadow materialized in the doorway. I came close to losing my dinner until the shadow moved forward with the loose-limbed grace I recognized.

"Zeke," I managed through chattering teeth. "We c-can't keep meeting like this."

Darkness made it impossible to read his expression.

"In case you've forgotten, this is a murder scene, and the killer is still at large. What in God's name are you doing inside the stall of an unpredictable stallion in the middle of the night?" His voice was controlled, telegraphing strong emotion, but he remembered to break off a chunk of carrot and toss it to Lancelot.

The horse turned his attention to the snack while Zeke helped me up.

"It's not like I went into the stall voluntarily," I said. "Someone pushed me."

"Who?" his voice reminded me of rough gravel.

I shook my head. "It was too dark to see. But the person was incredibly strong."

For a man of few words, Zeke was sure able to run his mouth off when riled. He read me the riot act while hustling me out of the stall, though I noticed he positioned his body to shield me from Lancelot, who was blissfully munching something that appeared chewy, definitely not a carrot.

Once in the corridor, he flipped a switch. I looked around for my attacker, but whoever it was had disappeared.

The faint light revealed the harsh angles of Zeke's face as he towered over me with narrowed eyes. "You were doing a stakeout, weren't you?"

"Um. Not exactly." I suspected learning I was here to protect him from Tess wouldn't sit too well either.

"I'm listening." Frustration rolled off him in waves.

I bristled at his tone. "In my defence, Lancelot likes me. Second … " I rummaged in my pocket for my canister and pointed it at him. "I'm armed, motivated, and dangerous—"

His movement, so swift I didn't see it coming, knocked my weapon to the ground.

"Ouch. Did you really need to do that?" I rubbed my wrist.

"Sorry. Reflex." He stooped to pick up my canister and handed it to me. "Lesson one—never point a weapon at someone unless you're prepared to use it."

Glad the dim lighting camouflaged my flush of shame, I muttered, "Lesson learned. Next time I point it at you, I'll be sure to use it."

"Lesson two—I need to be able to trust my woman."

My woman.

"I was worried you had underestimated Tess."

"And you figured an ex-Special Forces officer needed help from a woman armed with only bear spray?"

My heart flip-flopped in my chest. "Well, put that way—"

"I'm not finished. The only reason I'm not walking away from you right now is because I understand how, based on your background, you might find it difficult to trust me with Tess. But I need to know I can trust you, too."

"You're right. I am so sorry. I promise you can trust me. I won't go behind your back again. I was only—"

In the blink of an eye, I found myself wrapped in Zeke's arms. Shocked to discover he was trembling, I strained to catch his words.

"You nearly died. Lancelot would have trampled anyone else. I don't know whether to wring your neck or kiss you."

"Door number two, please." I melted into him.

Obligingly, he wrapped his arms around me and kissed me. It was a long, thorough kiss, stealing most of my breath and all of my ability to concentrate. When we finally broke apart, my breathing was choppy. Between gasps, I tried to speak. "Let me explain why—"

"Not here, not now. You'll get your chance later."

Dodie's voice sliced the darkness. "And it had better be good."

We sprang apart. I recovered first. "Dodie. What are you doing here?"

"I went to bed right after I checked in on you, but I couldn't sleep. You seemed antsy, like you wanted to get rid of me, so I decided to make sure you weren't out doing something real dumb."

"Yeah, about that—"

"I returned to your apartment. When I realized you'd snuck out, I didn't know what to think. Maybe you were with Zeke or tracking Tess, or maybe lying dead somewhere, so I headed for Zeke's place and ended up here."

Dodie's voice was calm, conversational. Bad sign. It meant she was furious. Generally speaking, Dodie bent over backwards to avoid entering what she called "a place of anger," which she claimed resulted in loss of personal power to another person.

Zeke took control of the situation. "It sounds as if we all need a stiff drink. I know I do. If you two play nice together, I'll share my booze and also what I learned about Tess."

Chapter 20:
Explanations & Revelations

SINCE THE PADLOCK WAS MISSING, Zeke used his key to lock the barn's back door. The three of us walked to his quarters. No one spoke a word.

With Dodie ahead of me, we silently followed Zeke into his apartment. Everything in his living room was exactly the way I remembered—cozy and lived-in with exposed wooden beams, butter-cream stucco walls, and arched doorways. Matching arched windows framed the star-studded sky. Braided rugs softened natural brick floors.

Zeke disappeared into the kitchen while Dodie and I perched at opposite ends of an overstuffed sofa—her doing, not mine. She picked up the *Big Sky Equine News* and flipped through it, rustling the pages. The only other sound was the clink of ice cubes from the kitchen. I gazed moodily at a framed photograph on the end table beside me. A much younger Zeke sat behind the wheel of a military truck in what appeared to be a bleak desert. Four grinning soldiers hung out the windows, waving at the camera.

I looked up when Zeke returned carrying three old-fashioned glasses full of dark liquid. "Crown Royal, rocks," he announced, placing a brimming glass of prime Canadian whisky in front of each of us.

He disappeared again and returned with the bottle, which he plunked down on the coffee table before lowering himself into a leather recliner. "This may require refills all around."

Uh-oh.

Dodie slammed down the magazine. "I seldom touch the stuff, but in this case, I'll make an exception." She grabbed her glass and chugged.

Zeke followed suit and poured them both refills before nodding at me.

"Seems you've had an eventful evening. How 'bout you fill us in on what in tarnation you thought you were doing?"

"Yes, please do," Dodie agreed. "Make it good, because I didn't sign up for this."

A wave of remorse washed over me. I'd been so focused on telling myself I was keeping Zeke safe from Tess, that I'd lost perspective about how my actions might affect the people closest to me.

I stared out the window rather than face two pairs of accusing eyes. Addressing the window, I pretended I was alone in the room. "I blew it. I was so sure Zeke was ignoring, or at least minimizing, my warning about Tess, I decided he needed someone to guard his back in case it went wrong." Even as I said it, I realized how idiotic I sounded, so I turned to face them. "I planned to stay out of sight unless Tess …I don't know, pulled out a gun on you," I finished lamely.

"You? Backup for an ex-Special Services officer?" Dodie punctuated her disbelief by draining the contents of her second glass.

Zeke reached across me and re-filled her glass. She nodded her thanks.

Nothing I'd done this evening made sense anymore, even to me. Unless I looked at it differently. "Okay, so maybe I'm a tad insecure," I admitted, looking straight at Zeke. "I know you assured me I have nothing to worry about, but Tess had made it clear she intended to seduce you." I glanced at him. His mouth didn't even twitch, so I took a gulp of rye to bolster my courage. It burned a path clear down to my stomach, but I was able to look him in the eye and say, "I know she comes across as all sweet and sugary, but she'll stop at nothing to get what she wants. And what she wants is you."

"Sweet baby Jesus," he muttered.

"I can't believe you were so idiotic," Dodie said. "Whatever happened to the common sense you pride yourself on having?"

I took another slug of my drink. Not daring to look at either of them, I stared into the golden contents of my glass. "Okay, so it wasn't my finest hour. I should have trusted Zeke, and I did … do, but Tess isn't normal, and he didn't seem to realize the danger she poses." I raised my pleading gaze to Dodie. Finding nothing but skepticism, I soldiered on. "I'm so sorry. I didn't mean to worry you. Either of you."

"I would have helped if you'd asked, you know," Dodie chided.

To my horror, a tear trickled down my cheek. A moment later, her arms were around me. "I should kick your ass," she said, "but you're doing such a great job of it yourself, I guess I can cut you some slack."

Dodie and I had a moment. Once I'd mopped my face with a slightly used tissue from my pocket, Dodie said, "Who pushed you into Lancelot's stall?"

I cut a glance at Zeke to see how he was taking my confession, but his shuttered expression was hard to read. I turned back to my sister. "I have a theory. A murderer always returns to the scene of the crime to make sure there's no incriminating evidence, right? Maybe that's what happened tonight. Luc's killer wouldn't expect company in the barn late at night."

Dodie's exasperated sigh indicated she wasn't buying. Zeke, on the other hand, merely sipped his drink.

I squirmed farther into my corner of the sofa. "Okay, here's something more concrete. I was thrown, not pushed. So whoever it was had to be strong. Right? And the person was inside Lancelot's stall when I arrived. Why? No one in their right mind would go near that horse unless there was something important in there, or they were hiding in the last place anyone would expect."

In the face of the resounding lack of response, I glugged down another mouthful and went for the gusto. "I'm certain the same person was behind both attacks on me, which implies the semen theft, too."

Zeke drained his glass and placed it on the coffee table. "Why do you say that?"

"The padlock on the barn's rear door was missing. Both my attacks involved a missing padlock, most likely cut by a hacksaw, like the one I saw in Tess's purse during check-in." I shrugged at Zeke's surprise. "She had the purse with her in the outbuilding."

"But tonight's attack and Luc's death both required unusual strength," Dodie interjected "You said your attacker lifted you off your feet and threw you into Lancelot's stall, and you're not a small woman."

Zeke wisely said nothing.

"Harmony would be strong enough," I suggested, avoiding any mention of Tess. "Or Clay. Either of them could have done it."

"But Tess?" Zeke said. "She wouldn't be strong enough to lift you." At my sharp inhalation, his eyes locked on mine, and he made a rueful grimace. "I only meant she's so tiny, a strong wind would blow her away. No offense intended."

"None taken," I lied. "By any chance, did Tess snort cocaine this evening?" I asked, deliberately planting the seed.

One eyebrow shot up. "Yep. She offered me coke, and I don't mean the drinking kind, which I refused, but she snorted a line or two." He paused. "I see what you're getting at. Drugs could account for her strength."

Satisfied I'd conveyed my message, I said, "I rest my case."

When Zeke hesitated, I was certain he was still angry in spite of the kiss we'd shared in the barn. I'd driven him away. I opened my mouth to tell him he was off the hook, but the force of his gaze halted my words.

He said, "I think Abby may have a point."

I sagged into the cushions with relief. "How so?"

He settled deeper into his chair and crossed one long leg over his other knee. "I reckon it's best to take it from the top and start with my date. Tess was real happy to join me at the campfire. I'm pretty sure she'd been drinking, or was on drugs, maybe both, because she was all over me."

"I bet she was." Okay, I was being snarky, but the words popped out.

He laughed. "I didn't ask for it. In fact, it was downright embarrassing."

"You left the campfire early," Dodie prompted.

"Again, not my doing. Seems campfire songs and ghost stories bore the stuffing out of Tess, and yeah, before you ask, she wanted to come to my quarters, but I insisted on walking her to her cabin, even went inside for a drink. That's when she snorted the cocaine."

I was so caught up in Zeke's story I blurted, "I bet that loosened her up. What did you learn?"

"Turns out she's a divorcée with one daughter, also divorced, who, according to Tess, has given her two of the smartest and most beautiful granddaughters in the whole wide world. Took me over ten minutes to change the subject. Turns out Tess and her daughter are estranged, and those granddaughters are off-limits. She started crying at one point, told me she was trying to heal the rift."

"Did you believe her?"

Zeke shrugged. "Maybe. Then again, it might have been the coke talking."

"What happened next?"

"Here's where it gets interesting. She got more and more riled up, then turned real antsy for no apparent reason and kicked me out."

He sounded so bewildered, I snickered. "The first time's always the hardest."

He gave me a dark look. "This was different. Something set her off. She told me she'd remembered there was something she needed to take care of right now, and to get my ass out of her cabin."

"Weird. Did you leave?"

"As fast as humanly possible, but once outside, I hid and watched her leave. She had her purse slung over her shoulder. I figured she was returning to the campfire, and decided I would have enough time to conduct a search. So I returned and used my master key to unlock her cabin."

"I'm surrounded by lunatics." Dodie whacked a hand against her forehead. "Why on earth would you do that?"

"I wanted to know if she'd stolen the semen from the outbuilding. I hunted high and low, found bondage equipment, even a leather harness thing, but no insulated container. If she took it, she hid it somewhere else, so I locked up."

In my excitement, I nearly jumped off the sofa. "What if Tess remembered she'd hidden the insulated container in Lancelot's stall and decided to rescue it before someone else found it?"

"That would mean Lancelot would have to cooperate, and that's highly unlikely, don't you think?"

Deflated, I sank back into the corner. Lancelot would never let Tess into his stall.

He held my gaze. "But it was a good idea. Now, where was I? Yeah, I locked her cabin and decided I'd best go to the barn to check up on Lancelot before returning to tell you about my date. The back door to the barn was open, so I slipped inside and waited in the tack room to listen, figure out what was happening. I heard someone moving around in the corridor, opening a stall door. I was about to make my move, nail the intruder in the act, when another person entered the barn and snuck past me." He looked at me. "I recognized you right away. Real bad timing on your part."

I sat in silence as his words sank in. "I thought I heard someone else but I wasn't sure. You let my attacker—and the more I think about it, the more I'm sure it was Tess—escape to save me," I whispered around the knot in my chest.

"Guess that about covers it."

I hid my face in my hands and groaned. "I really blew it this time, didn't I?"

"Not really. In fact, it's just as well I didn't show my hand. She doesn't know we're onto her, and we need more proof. So far, everything we have is circumstantial. A decent lawyer would make mincemeat of us."

I raised my head. "But she attacked me tonight, I know it. Boy, if I ever get my hands on her—"

"You'll do nothing." Dodie's voice was sharp, urgent. "We don't know for sure if Tess is guilty. If so, she's one extremely dangerous woman." Dodie grinned at me for the first time this evening. "You'll be happy to hear I have some pertinent information of my own."

I tried to quell my impatience, failed dismally. "Cough it up. Don't keep us in suspense."

"When I was out searching for you, a car left the parking lot. At the time, I didn't give it much thought, but who would leave Grizzly Gulch at midnight? There's nothing to do, nowhere to go at that time of night. I bet it was Tess."

I turned to Zeke. "The timing's right. You said she took her purse. She'd have her keys in it. I bet she found a way to keep Lancelot from attacking her and retrieved the insulated container from his stall where she'd hidden it, maybe under a pile of straw." Excitement fizzed through me. "I wonder where she took it."

We kicked the notion around for another ten minutes, deciding that although Tess was our prime suspect for the semen theft and two attacks on me, we couldn't pinpoint a reason for her to murder Luc.

"There's no smoking gun," Zeke reminded us. "We need proof before we notify the police, and by police, I don't mean the Perkins brothers. Once we have proof, we'll take it to the RCMP Headquarters in Calgary."

"Agreed," Dodie said. "It might help if we knew someone who could coax Tess to open up."

Simultaneously, Dodie and I swung our gazes toward Zeke.

"Don't even *think* it," Zeke said, rising from his chair. "No."

"You can't fight us both." Dodie linked arms with me.

"She's right," I said. "Much as it pains me to say this, you need another date with Tess, this time to learn where she went, and also if she had a motive to kill Luc."

Zeke's shoulders slumped and he let out a heartfelt sigh. "You won't give up until I agree, will you?"

"No," we chorused.

"Fine. One more date with Tess," he conceded, eyeing me sternly. "But this time, I want you trust me to take care of myself."

Cheezits, but this healthy relationship thing was harder than I'd imagined.

Chapter 21:
Tension in the Kitchen

EKE'S DATE WITH TESS DIDN'T happen, at least not on day three of the symposium. Word was, she was holed up in her cabin all day with a migraine. My day passed without incident, mainly because Dodie barred all visitors, even Zeke, from my apartment. I welcomed the enforced isolation. Seemed I wasn't as young as I thought I was. Two attacks in two days had knocked the stuffing out of me.

While I coddled myself, sleeping the morning away and curling up with a romance novel all afternoon, our guests immersed themselves in archery, more trail rides, mountain biking, and a nature walk. According to Dodie, a large crowd attended Muffy's workshop, *The Pregnant Mare*. Goat yoga was also a huge hit, as was the lasso lesson, especially with Wes and Coop, who each managed to lasso a goat (*not* part of the lesson). An informative naturalist delivered a presentation after a cookout.

True to her word, Dodie had talked to Veronica, Clay, and Harmony. No one revealed anything new. We were no closer to finding my attacker or Luc's killer.

I pampered myself with a solitary dinner in my apartment and hit the sack early.

By the morning of Day Four, I was my normal self and raring to go. I needed to squash rumors about my fragile mental state, no doubt started by Tess. But more to the point, I was dying to learn about Zeke's dating situation.

To prove I was in good shape, I sashayed into the dining hall and treated myself to the Hearty Cowpoke Breakfast. Once I'd savored every delicious, calorific bite, I injected extra chirpiness into my delivery of the morning announcements, which included the imminent refill of the swimming pool.

Satisfied my performance had demonstrated stability, I slipped outside to collar Zeke. I found him inside the pool enclosure, his Stetson tipped back and his sleeves rolled up to reveal sinewy arms. And oh boy, howdy, that cowboy was smokin' hot. He and the pool supervisor were involved in a deep discussion.

While tamping down my lustful thoughts, I waved at Zeke.

He wrapped up his conversation with gratifying speed and loped over to greet me. "You look great," he murmured, surprising me by leaning down to nuzzle my neck.

My breath caught in my throat. "We shouldn't do this in public. Tess might see us." I glanced around to see if anyone had noticed.

"Don't remind me," he said, stepping away, making me wish I'd yanked him closer.

"I heard last night's date didn't happen. Are there any updates?" I asked, hoping my voice was suitably casual.

"Tess grabbed me this morning on the way to breakfast. Literally. Like a python. Took all my strength to fight her off."

I forced my fist-clenching muscles to relax. "Glad you survived the encounter."

He gave me a wary glance. "I did, but barely. She was apologetic about ditching me during our first date, but avoided explaining why. She suggested we have an after-dinner drink at her place tonight and pick up where we left off."

Thanks to the appearance of Wes and Coop, my opinion of Tess was curtailed.

"I told you the pool was clean again," Wes told Coop, trying to squeeze past us. "Let's go swimming."

Zeke nabbed each twin by the arm. "Maybe later, boys. The pool's not ready yet. Go play somewhere else."

"Awwww," Coop said. "No fair."

"Life's not fair," I muttered under my breath as we sent them packing. I checked the time and turned to Zeke, hoping I appeared relaxed about his imminent date. "I should mingle with guests, maybe see if Muffy needs my help with the morning workshop. Dodie played events manager all day yesterday, so I have to focus on guest relations instead of murder and mayhem for a change. I'll see you later."

As I turned and fled, his voice followed me. "You have nothing to worry about, you know."

Time passed quickly. I answered questions, tried to hit the archery target, joined three other guests for a pickleball lesson, and generally enjoyed myself. In fact, I had so much fun, I didn't open a single spreadsheet, balance a single budget, or talk to a single bank. I was enjoying the brief respite from stress way too much to risk spoiling it.

Two hours later, I was in the lobby discussing the workshop schedule with a guest when a commotion outside made me jump to my feet and rush to open the door.

Tess stood there, gripping a squirming twin in each hand and glaring at Sheila. "If you don't discipline them, I will, and it won't be pretty." Her face was a mask of rage.

"Ow. Mom. She's hurting me," Coop yelled, while Wes released a high-pitched screech that put Michael Jackson to shame.

Sheila's lips twisted into a snarl. "Release. My. Boys."

Tess's eyes widened at Sheila's mama-bear intensity.

I rushed outside but hung back, reluctant to get too near what promised to be a ferocious catfight. "Ladies, let's not get carried away, eh?" I suggested.

The twins took advantage of the diversion by twisting and wriggling, until Coop landed a kick on Tess's shin. She loosened her grip with a shriek, and the twins darted away, taking refuge behind their mother.

Tess inched closer to Sheila. "Keep those little thieves out of my cabin." Her soft voice was more chilling than her shouting.

"My sons don't steal."

"I caught them rummaging through my purse."

I mentally ran through a couple of karate moves and was about to intervene, when Wes piped up, "We were only hunting for those candies."

Candies? I dug into my pocket and fingered the tablet I'd picked up in Lancelot's stall. It looked like one of Tess's glucose tabs. But what did that prove?

Coop corroborated Wes' story. "Yeah, Zeke told us to find something else to do, so we decided to feed the goats. But we were afraid to ask the chef for carrots because he's scary."

Right. Because he'd already caught the boys setting fire to the kitchen steps.

Wes indicated Tess. "We remembered this lady tried to feed Lancelot those candies she carries in her purse."

"If horses like candies, we figured goats would, too," Coop supplied.

Wes picked up the thread. "She didn't answer the door, but we looked in the window and her purse was on the floor. The door was unlocked, so we went inside. We didn't think she'd mind because she used to be nice."

Sheila took over, stepping forward until she was in Tess's face. "Listen up. If you so much as lay a finger on my sons again, I will tear your arm off and beat you with the soggy end." She hustled her sons away.

As they departed, I called out, "Wes. Coop."

They turned and waved at me.

I waved back. "Go ask Chef Armand for some carrots to feed the goats. Tell him I said it was okay."

Tess stood perfectly still, then spun away in the opposite direction.

I was standing beside the horseshoe pit fantasizing about lunch when my phone rang. I checked the caller id. Chef Armand. Since I wanted to visit the swimming pool (and Zeke) before lunchtime, I debated whether or not to answer. Our head chef was a bit of a drama queen. On the other hand, keeping him happy mattered.

I answered. Big mistake.

He was inarticulate with anger. Eventually I deciphered the gist of it. There was big trouble in the kitchen, and I was implicated.

Muttering several forbidden curse words that nice women never utter, I hustled my buns over to the kitchen's back door. Chef Armand flung open the door and met me outside. His white chef's outfit contrasted nicely with his face, which was scarlet with a touch of purple. I couldn't tell whether his colorful complexion was the result of heat, exertion, or displeasure.

He brandished a spatula under my nose. "This is all your fault. The woman told me you sent those brats here to get *les carrottes*."

Yeah, displeasure it was. My spidey senses rose to attention. I tried to peer inside but failed.

Chef Armand blocked the doorway, yelling, "The kitchen, she is off-limits to … to … *les bestioles*."

A crash of dishes and a feminine shriek alerted me to trouble. Taking advantage of Chef Armand's distraction, I ducked under his arm, nimbly avoiding the spatula. I dashed through the pantry, the agitated chef dancing with rage at my side.

"You seem a little out of sorts, Chef. What can I do to help?" I asked.

"They destroy my kitchen. Listen." He made a sweeping gesture.

Muted bleating grew in volume when a sous-chef crashed through the kitchen's swinging doors. As soon as he saw me, he said, "Please, Ma'am. You gotta get the critters outta the kitchen." He held the door open. "The guest, too."

I froze in the doorway, absorbing the scene. Silhouetted against the window was Larry the llama, who was demolishing a romaine heart, his large teeth sawing away in a crazy sideways motion. His eyes were at half-mast in gastronomic bliss. Surrounding Larry, eight goats grazed at what they clearly viewed as a buffet of delicacies. Lettuce, cherry tomatoes, celery, and radishes, which had somehow ended up on the floor, disappeared into greedy mouths.

But the kicker was Tess. She stood in the middle of the kitchen, swatting a tea towel at a dwarf goat with a carrot dangling from its mouth. Glaring at me, she said, "I hope you're happy with the damage you caused, encouraging the twins to get carrots to feed the goats." Picking up a large bunch of celery, she brandished it at me.

I ignored Tess and turned to Chef Armand. "What happened? And why is she in the kitchen?" I indicated Tess.

"The twins arrived, wanting carrots for the goats. I sent them away. Not long after, this woman, she arrives with the whole herd of goats, Larry too."

"I was trying to clean up the mess Abby caused." Tess waved the celery at me. "Those two little hellions were in the pen, teasing the goats. When they saw me coming for them, they were smart enough to run, but too dumb to close the gate. The flock escaped before I was able to stop them. I followed them to do as much damage control as possible."

Tess was so busy blaming the twins, she took no notice of Larry, who'd polished off another three romaine hearts and was now focused on the celery bunch she waved at me.

I managed to keep a straight face when Larry sauntered up from behind and snaked his head over Tess's shoulder. He snatched the celery from her grip and started crunching, leaking green drool into her hair.

Tess responded with frantic hand-flapping.

Larry's ears went back, and he aimed his damp nose at the irritating human.

Tess obliged by stamping her feet and yelling louder. Clearly she didn't realize both actions were signs of aggression to a llama.

By now, Larry's ears lay flat against his neck. I knew what was coming. I could have called out a warning. Maybe I should have. It would have been the kind thing to do. But I wasn't feeling the warm fuzzies for a woman I was convinced had tried to kill me, not once, but twice. So I held my breath as Larry thrust his head up and down a couple times, then angled it upward one last time before lowering it toward Tess. He stretched his neck as far as possible without dislocating any vertebrae and let fly.

The foul-smelling spray caught her square in the face.

Her scream intensified to a sonic shriek as green-flecked spit dribbled down her chin and onto her cleavage, staining the pristine white blouse.

Larry and eight goats milled around the kitchen in a state of panic, knocking over tables and jostling one another. Amid a clatter of broken dishes and mingled howls from Chef Armand and our pastry chef, a server grabbed a broom and shooed the animals outside.

Amid the chaos, Tess slipped away along with the animals, but not before I noted her expression morph into a sly smile.

When the dust settled, Chef Armand threw up his hands and announced, "This is the last straw. I resign."

I flinched, picturing Dodie's reaction on learning the best chef in the province had quit. I pulled Chef Armand aside to settle him down. It took all my negotiating skills, a great deal of flattery, and two extra vacation days, and in the end I made him an offer he couldn't refuse—I would set him up with my line-dancing friend, a cute accountant with a vast love of food and a huge crush on him.

Once he returned to the kitchen to finalize lunch, I was eager to describe the latest drama to Dodie over coq au vin, a delicious marriage of chicken, baby onions, and red wine. After that, we planned to ambush Muffy before her next seminar kicked off. It was time for a discussion about Franklin's current whereabouts.

Chapter 22:
The Crazy Cow

DURING DESSERT, I WAS TOO busy informing Dodie about the kitchen critters to notice the dining hall was emptying out. "It's a blessing Larry didn't reach these pies," I said, savoring the final bite of sweet-tart creaminess. Key lime pie was one of Chef Armand's specialties.

Dodie drained her coffee cup and set it down with a clink. "Tess made sure to publicize what she called the kitchen crisis by running around covered with smelly llama-spit and blabbing to everyone within earshot about how the twins released barn animals into the kitchen, which they proceeded to trash. She claimed you stood there laughing while the llama attacked her."

I smiled at the memory. "That last part might be true. How did the guests react?"

"The general consensus was that Tess probably irritated poor Larry and deserved what she got."

"That's exactly what happened," I said, stirring cream into my coffee. "Come to think of it, I don't believe for a second Wes and Coop released those animals."

"Who did?"

"Tess," I replied.

"Aw, come on."

"No, listen. I swear she was happy about the damage the animals did—in spite of the fact that Larry spat in her face. It made us look careless, even incompetent."

"She certainly tried to bad-mouth us. But it backfired. Everyone laughed. All it did was make her look vindictive."

"Good. Because when I walked past the Wrights' cabin to clean up for lunch, Wes and Coop were inside, crying. I heard them tell their parents they hadn't gone near the goats because they'd had nothing to feed them. Chef Armand was mean and wouldn't give them the carrots they asked for."

"I don't see what good that does," Dodie said.

"Tess overheard me tell the twins to ask Chef Armand for carrots. She likely assumed that's exactly what happened, and everyone would think the twins had let the animals loose. But Chef Armand refused to hand over carrots. At the time, I assumed the twins had managed to grab some on the sly, but now I believe they were telling the truth. They told their parents they played shuffleboard after he kicked them out."

"That should be easy to confirm," Dodie said, standing. "Let's wander over to the courts and ask around."

I finished my train of thought as we walked. "So if they didn't let the goats out, that leaves Tess. Let's go prove the boys' innocence."

We joined a cluster of guests at the shuffleboard court.

There was no need to dig for the answer. One of them confirmed that the twins had, indeed, played shuffleboard. In fact, they'd hogged the court until asked to leave.

The boys had told the truth. As I suspected. Tess was lying.

"I'd better let Zeke know about this before his date," I told Dodie, reaching for my phone. "Then we'd best hustle our butts over to the conference center to catch Muffy before guests start arriving for her workshop on sperm injection."

Ten minutes later, Dodie and I arrived at the main conference room to find Muffy inside, talking on her cell. She glanced up, spoke softly into the phone, and ended the call. We entered, locking the door behind us to ensure privacy.

"Hi," she said, smiling. "As you can see, I'm ready for the afternoon workshop. I'm surprised so many guests are interested in the topic. This whole symposium exceeds any expectations I had."

A carafe of iced water surrounded by six glasses sat in the middle of each table. Someone had set out pads and pens at each place. It looked as if Muffy anticipated an excellent turnout.

"Actually, we're not here about the workshop," Dodie said.

"We're here to talk about Franklin," I clarified. "We know he didn't leave the country."

Muffy paled and sank into the nearest chair. Thick carpet muffled our footsteps as we made our way to the table she'd chosen. We took the chairs flanking hers.

"How did you find out?" she asked at last.

I explained about the phone call I'd made to the house and how I'd hung up on Franklin when he answered.

"I would have told you, but you were convinced Luc had been murdered," Muffy said, glancing at each of us in turn.

We must have shown our surprise, because she said, "I heard you both talking to Zeke on your balcony after Luc's death. If I'd told you Franklin hadn't left on his business trip after all, I was afraid you would see him as the prime suspect."

Since she was right, I said, "Would you mind telling us what happened? Start with what you did after you left the check-in area that first day."

She picked up a pen and played with it. Several seconds went by before she dropped the pen and started talking. "After Franklin left me standing in the lobby, I went to my cabin to figure out what to do. I tried to reach him on his cell, but he'd turned it off. I was pouring myself a stiff drink when a neighbor called to tell me a taxi had dropped my husband off at home around lunchtime, and how ten minutes later, an attractive woman joined him. I suspected he was having an affair, so I rushed home to confront them." Muffy fell silent as she clasped her hands together, but not quickly enough. I'd noticed their trembling.

You gotta love a nosy neighbor. I wondered if Franklin's business trip been cancelled, or if it was a lie to cover an affair.

"Cheezits," I said, unable to restrain myself. "You must have been frantic. What happened next?"

Muffy poured herself a glass of water from the carafe and took a sip. "I raced home, entered the house quietly, and heard voices. They were in Franklin's office, not the bedroom, which was a relief. After pulling myself together, I stood in the corridor and listened outside the door. They were discussing an oil project. I called out to announce my presence and entered to find them studying a clutter of papers, maps, and charts."

"That all sounds very innocent," Dodie said.

"It was. I pretended to be surprised and pleased to see Franklin while giving them my cover story—that I'd left a printout for my workshop on pregnant mares at home. Turned out the woman was a colleague on the same Saudi project, which had been cancelled along with their business trip. Franklin said he'd decided he'd get more work done at home than at the office, especially since I would be busy at the symposium. There would be more room to spread everything out and he could eat all the takeout he wanted. Since his colleague and her husband live nearby, he suggested she join him to work on developing a business case for re-activating the project."

Dodie crossed her legs and looked thoughtful. "Why did he turn his phone off?"

Muffy took another sip of water. "He always does that when he's working. Says he can't concentrate if it's on."

"Wow," I said, "You must have been relieved. How did Franklin react?"

Muffy gave me a wan smile and picked up the pen again. "He took me aside and asked if I'd fired Luc yet, only this time, he was different—respectful, even kind, not the tyrant you saw in the lobby. He apologized for the way he'd acted, and explained how worried he'd been. If Luc was arrested again, everyone would assume we condoned, even asked him to drug our horses so they would win races. We'd be blamed too, possibly prosecuted. The consequences would be disastrous for our reputation in the racing industry and on so many other levels—social, family, career, you name it." She picked up the pen. "It appeared our marriage was back on track. I promised to fire Luc right away."

The only sound in the room was the scribble of Muffy's pen on the pad as she doodled. I glanced over and saw that she'd written Franklin's name over and over, surrounding it with hearts and curliqueues.

"Did you fire him?" I asked.

She stopped scribbling, but didn't look up. "I never got the chance. When I arrived back at Grizzly Gulch, the Mounties were pulling in." She put the pen down and studied the doodles she'd made on the pad.

Dodie jumped in with, "Did you go home again after the demo?"

Muffy raised her gaze. "Yes. Franklin called to let me know he was taking the afternoon off work, and wanted me to join him. I forgot everything else, including the semen I'd promised to process." She swung her gaze to

171

me. "I am so sorry, Abby. If I'd been in the outbuilding, no one would have attacked you."

"It wasn't your fault. I'm delighted that everything's coming together for you on the home front."

After we said our good byes, Dodie and I left Muffy sitting in the conference room. Maybe it was my imagination, but I thought she looked sad.

"Did you believe her?" Dodie asked.

"Sure. Why not?" I replied.

"I don't," Dodie said flatly. "She should have been walking on air if her marriage was on the mend. I didn't see a trace of happiness."

"Maybe he really was having an affair. Remind me to follow up on that."

As we walked through the main lobby into the sunshine, Dodie asked, "What are you doing this afternoon? I thought maybe we could tackle Clay together. I didn't have much luck with him this morning."

"Fudge, fudgity fudge," I said. "I nearly forgot again. I have an appointment out at The Crazy Cow Guest Ranch this afternoon. I'm lucky the owner phoned to confirm. I'd like you to join me."

"Sure thing. Did you figure out what it's about?"

"We're meeting to discuss how the two ranches could work together to boost our businesses."

"Sounds like fun. Let's go."

Ten minutes later, I'd called The Crazy Cow to inform the owner we were on our way and to get directions. We drove through the small town of Rainbow Point, turned left at the main intersection, and followed the secondary road to Moose Corner, where we veered onto a gravel track flanked by grassland.

"We'll be there in fifteen minutes," Dodie said. "Got any ideas on how we could work together with another dude ranch?"

I maneuvered around a pothole. "Let's see. Apparently The Crazy Cow is an old-time working cattle ranch offering cattle drive vacations. Grizzly Gulch is more upscale, so we're not in direct competition."

"That's a good thing," Dodie said.

"Yeah," I said, getting excited. "What about including an activity from one another in the guest packages?"

"Or a meal. Grizzly Gulch has Chef Armand, and I bet The Crazy Cow offers real deal cowboy fare under the stars."

I was getting into the swing of it. "How about cross-promotion?"

We were still tossing around suggestions when a long laneway lined by a rail fence appeared. We turned in, driving beneath an ornamental entry sign announcing, "Welcome to The Crazy Cow," and parked beside the main lodge, which was fronted by a white porch. The front door flew open to reveal a slim woman wearing faded Levis and a Calgary Stampeders sweatshirt. Dark brown hair curled around a pretty face.

"Hi, I'm Sherrie," she said with a welcoming smile as we piled out, "and you must be Abby and Dodie. Come on inside." Still chatting, she led us into a sitting area filled with books. "I've got coffee and chocolate chip cookies waiting for you."

Dodie sank into an easy chair, while I selected one corner of the matching chintz sofa, Sherrie placed a plateful of cookies on a coffee table in front of us.

After several minutes of chatter about the weather (always a hot topic for Albertans), a new restaurant opening in Bragg Creek, and a recent bear attack on Mount Norquay, I studied Sherrie's face. "You look familiar," I announced. "Have we met somewhere?"

"I was thinking the same thing," Dodie agreed. "Do you ever get in to Rainbow Point or Bragg Creek?"

Sherrie shook her head. "Not really. We get most of our supplies delivered to the ranch. Moose Corner's fine for small stuff, but if we need to do major shopping, we drive up to Calgary."

"This feeling that I know you is driving me nuts," I said. "Maybe we met through your husband."

"I doubt it. I bought The Crazy Cow after Jim and I got divorced."

"Maybe through a mutual acquaintance." I launched into a recital of friends and acquaintances, starting with members of the Hale and Hearty Karate League and moving along to fellow line dancers, neighbors, and townsfolk.

All Sherrie did was shake her head. When I ran out of steam, she said, "I have an idea." She rose and disappeared from the room, returning immediately with a framed photograph, which she placed on the coffee table in front of us. "Do you see anyone familiar in this photo? Jim took this picture shortly before we split up." She resumed her seat on a rocking chair.

I reached into my purse for my reading glasses while Dodie picked up the photo and held it at arm's length to study the small group of people. One was Sherrie. She was kneeling, her arms around two little girls, who snuggled into her. A man and a slightly older woman stood behind them. The woman smiled into the camera.

Dodie was the one who nailed it. "Good grief. Is that Tess?"

"Where?" I asked.

"I told you to get stronger glasses. Look at the older woman standing behind Sherrie and the girls."

Sherrie nodded. "The older woman's my mother."

I narrowed my eyes into a squint and focused on the woman in the background, then let my gaze sweep Sherrie's face. "Of course. You're the spitting image of your mom. The hair threw me off."

"She highlights it now. Says it makes her look years younger."

"Why did you think we would recognize your mother?" I asked.

"I had a hunch. She lives up Edmonton way, but she told me she was in the vicinity, staying at another guest ranch for a horse breeding workshop." Sherrie frowned. "Now that I think about it, she probably signed up to spy on the competition."

Oh, she was doing a lot more than spying. I refrained from mentioning we believed Tess tried to kill me twice, undoubtedly stole a small fortune worth of horse semen, liberated a menagerie in both our pool and our kitchen, and had most likely killed our trainer.

"She's a guest at Grizzly Gulch," I explained with remarkable self-restraint. "If you don't mind my asking, has she visited you recently?"

After a long silence, Sherrie said, "I won't allow her anywhere near my daughters until she can prove she's clean and undergoing therapy. She knows she's not welcome here, but she visited us late last night, anyway. Her pounding and yelling woke all of us out of a sound sleep. The girls were terrified. Mom was clearly stoned."

"What did she want?" Dodie asked, after we exchanged a meaningful glance.

"Claimed she wanted to deliver a gift as her way of making amends."

Goosebumps popped out on my arms. "What sort of gift?"

"It was an insulated container with a blue flask containing a lidded cup inside it. Sort of a container within a container within a container."

So Tess had tried to preserve the semen, likely with liquid nitrogen Muffy had stored in the outbuilding. I examined Sherrie's hands for burn marks, but found none. Clearly the preserving liquid had evaporated. "What was inside the lidded cup?" I asked.

"Mom was delusional. She claimed it was full of semen from a winning racehorse. She'd purchased it thinking I should breed racehorses and leave the hospitality business altogether. I gather she believes Grizzly Gulch is too much competition for The Crazy Cow, but I don't look at it that way."

"Me, neither. By the way, what did you do with the contents of the cup?"

"The contents were disgusting. I poured everything down the toilet and put the containers in the dishwasher." At my exclamation of surprise, she said, "You're probably wondering why I didn't just throw them out, but my youngest is collecting containers for a school project."

"Did you run the dishwasher?" Dodie asked.

"Right away."

I couldn't bring myself to tell Sherrie she had destroyed not only tens of thousands of dollars' worth of semen, which was probably still viable, but also concrete proof that Tess had stolen it from Grizzly Gulch. Instead, I said, "Tess is one of our guests, and seems a little unstable. Would you mind sharing more about what makes her tick so I can understand how we can best deal with her?"

Sherrie scrutinized our faces. We must have passed the test because she started talking. "By all accounts, her father, my grandfather, was a brutal man who abused my grandmother until he died in a tractor accident. He likely abused Mom as well, but she refuses to discuss it. Every time I mention Granddaddy Phil, she shuts down."

I nodded. "That makes sense." At Sherrie's surprised expression, I explained, "Dodie, my other sister, Clara, and I know more about abuse than we like. My therapist explained that an abusive environment is often associated with psychopathy in the victims. From what I've seen, Tess exhibits many of the classic signs of a psychopath."

"Yeah. I know," Sherrie said. "I had a therapist too. Let's see. There's egocentricity, lack of empathy, manipulation, hostility, and impulsivity. They can also be extremely charming if it serves their purpose." Her eyes filled with tears, but she dashed them away. "Sorry. I refuse to shed another tear over her. She'll never change."

To break the tension, I nudged Dodie in the ribs. "With our upbringing, it's amazing my sisters and I dodged the bullet."

With a perfectly straight face, Dodie said, "Well, Clara and I did. We're not so sure about you."

"Very funny," I said and returned to questioning Sherrie. "How is your mother's overall health?"

Her brow wrinkled in confusion. "As far as I know, it's fine. Why?"

"She told us she was diabetic. She carries all the paraphernalia in her purse and never goes anywhere without her glucose tabs."

Sherrie hid her face in her hands. "Mom's an addict. That's the main reason I keep my daughters away from her. Those glucose tabs are coated in cocaine so she can give herself a quick fix whenever she needs it."

Everything clicked into place. She was using the doctored glucose tabs to drug our horses. No wonder poor Lancelot acted up. She'd dropped a handful in his stall. "Of course," I mused, more to myself than anyone else. "I can't believe I never noticed."

"Mom's a talented actress," Sherrie admitted. "You're not the first person she's fooled."

I fervently hoped I would be the last.

Dodie leaned forward, her eyes brimming with sympathy, and said, "You're doing the right thing, keeping her away from your children."

"I know, but it doesn't make it any easier."

It also made it all the more likely Tess was Luc's murderer, but for the life of me, I couldn't figure out her motive.

A moment later, two little girls who looked to be between eight and ten ran inside, their laughter breaking the tension. After introductions, the conversation centered on the girls' day at school. After they left, Dodie and I floated our ideas for collaboration between the two ranches. Sherrie shared a few of her own.

It was late afternoon when we left The Crazy Cow, satisfied the two ranches would increase their profit margins through cooperation. I tried phoning Zeke to warn him about Tess before their date. He didn't pick up, so I left a message.

I hoped he was right, that he didn't need any help protecting himself tonight.

Chapter 23:
Saved by an Axe

ODIE AND I DISCUSSED TESS's crimes the whole way home. On our arrival we discovered she'd bragged about her date to everyone within earshot. It was common knowledge that Zeke was taking Tess to dinner in town this evening. As far as I was concerned, I'd done everything possible to warn him. Recent events had taken their toll on me, both physically and emotionally. Chastising myself for zonking out during the big date, I went to bed early, proof that I trusted Zeke.

Although I fell asleep quickly, a sound jerked me awake during the dead of night. I bolted upright in bed and listened. A hoarse cry raised goosebumps on my arms. With a sense of déjà vu, I leaped from bed and rushed to the window. There was enough light for me to see water sloshing over the sides of the pool. No llama this time and not so much as one goat, hallelujah. The moon cast enough light to reveal that the swimmer was a man and, from the splashes and strangled shouts, definitely in serious trouble. Steam rose from the surface into the chilly night air, concealing his identity.

Without stopping for a robe, I raced out my kitchen door and galloped down the stairs toward the pool area. Wearing only my zebra-striped nightie, I stopped at the pool's edge. Ribbons of steam combined with geysers of water caused by his frantic movements concealed the man's features. Acting on instinct, I jumped into the water, which was surprisingly warm, and attempted a duck dive to determine the problem.

I remained bobbing on the surface, head down, zebra-striped hindquarters rearing skyward. Surfacing and hacking up chlorinated water,

I reflected that a butt attached to a woman of a certain age was an amazing flotation device. I needed a decent dive to propel myself deeper.

Emerging from the pool, I reminded myself to try the Atkins Diet. Again.

At the exact moment I poised at the edge to dive, a light breeze cleared the steam for one split second. The man appeared to be anchored in the deep end by a heavy object. Turning toward me, he released an incoherent shout into the night air while flailing his arms, creating a minor tsunami as he went under. Surfacing again, he coughed and sputtered while writhing in the water like an eel. It seemed another attempted murder was well underway.

The man would drown before my eyes if I didn't rescue him. My brain whirred in panic. I wasn't strong enough to pull him out of the water, anchor and all, so I needed to think outside the box. A glimmer of an idea took shape. There was an axe in the pool shed, right? I could use it as a lever.

"I'll be right back with an axe," I informed him over his garbled cries. "That'll make this easier."

Strangely enough, my words only seemed to increase his agitation, but I couldn't let myself be sidetracked. As I whirled and ran, my nightie wrapped itself around my ankles, a clammy shackle. Stumbling into the shed, I tossed chairs aside, pawed through mountains of fluffy towels, and rummaged through a box of pool toys. At last I spied the axe. Someone, likely Zeke, had placed it on a wall bracket out of the twins' reach. Mine too.

I dragged a step-stool to the wall, climbed onto the second level, and made a grab for the axe. The razor-sharp edge sliced my finger, but I scrambled down, my prize cradled in my arms. Ignoring the cut, I gripped the axe with both hands and returned to the pool, prepared to dive in.

The man swiveled in the water to face me. Thrashing around like a harpooned whale he coughed while uttering incoherent cries. I started to get a really bad feeling. A breeze cleared the mist for one split second. I recognized Zeke's distraught features.

Approaching footsteps alerted me to company. Reassurances would have to wait. What if this was his attacker? I needed a solution fast, before he drowned. My frantic gaze landed on a jumbo plastic trash can inside the pool enclosure. I dropped the axe and raced to the can to whip out the plastic trash bag. Seconds later, a dive propelled me to my target, who tried to clobber me. Fortunately, I was an inch beyond his reach. His fist connected with water instead of my nose.

Losing patience, I whispered, "Can it, Zeke. It's me. I'm trying to rescue you." I swung the trash bag overhead in an attempt to inflate it with as much air as possible.

He stopped struggling immediately and helped me hoist the plastic bag up and over his head like a diving bell helmet, only without the breathing apparatus.

Tess staggered into the pool area at that moment, no doubt hunting for Zeke to finish him off. She wore a zebra-striped nightie that looked exactly like mine, only a gazillion sizes smaller. Clearly, we both appreciated a Walmart bargain.

She also hefted a gun.

"Slow, shallow breathing," I warned Zeke in an undertone. "With luck, there'll be enough oxygen to keep you alive until she leaves." With that, I splashed around and positioned myself between Zeke and Tess, agitating the water as much as possible, hoping to hide his presence.

On noticing me, Tess did a double-take. Slurring her words, she said, "You again. What are you doing in the pool at this time of night?"

"I couldn't sleep, so I decided to take a walk," I explained, nerves turning my voice shrill. "Then I noticed a trash bag floating in the pool. People are so messy. I have to get it out before the guests wake up and see it." I smacked alternate palms against the surface while staying afloat by scissoring my feet like a duck.

"Have you seen anyone else?" Tess asked, gesturing with her gun.

I shook my head. "Nope. The water's lovely. Why don't you join me for a swim? You wanted to go skinny dipping the other day. We could do it now."

Tess shook her head and muttered, "I must be more stoned than I thought." Her shrill giggle confirmed her condition. "I have to make sure the bastard's dead. *No one* rejects Tess Jenkins."

My heart raced. Zeke must be running out of air.

"I guess he found a way to cut the chain, but I'll find him," Tess murmured before hurrying away, zebra stripes flapping.

As soon as she disappeared, I turned to Zeke, who was motionless. The plastic bag was plastered against his face. With grief clawing at my throat, I peeled the bag away. I'd killed him while trying to save his life.

Panic tripled my strength. I tipped his head back as best I could, making sure he floated with his nose above the surface, and did some speed swimming to retrieve the axe. Returning to Zeke, I took a deep breath and muscled my way underwater. Using the axe, I levered the weight, which appeared to be a cement block, toward the shallow end. Attached to it by a chain, Zeke bobbed along behind me. At last, we reached the concrete stairs. My chest heaved as I dragged him onto the top step.

Drawing on a faint memory of the CPR class I'd attended at the Rainbow Point Seniors' Center, I placed my mouth on his and started mouth-to-mouth breathing interspersed with chest compressions. After what seemed like a century, he coughed and moaned, causing my heart to somersault in my chest.

"You're alive." I said, aware that tears streamed down my cheeks.

In response, Zeke turned his head and hacked up a gallon of water. Once he recovered, he croaked, "Thank God it's you. At first, I thought you were Tess because of the nightie. Worse, you told me you were getting an axe to make things easier."

I narrowed my eyes. "Why was Tess wearing a nightie?"

"I'll get to that later. Nice save, by the way. I couldn't see or hear anything underneath the plastic bag, so I kept my mouth shut and tried to breathe. Guess I passed out. Next thing I knew, someone was cracking my ribs while conducting mouth-to-mouth. I knew it had to be you."

I went all gooey. He recognized the touch of my mouth. "How did you know?"

"I smelled your body wash," he said through chattering teeth. "That stuff has staying power."

Huh. So much for romance. Once I helped him from the pool, he convulsed with shivers. His legs were manacled at the ankles. A chain attaching the shackles was looped through a concrete block's opening.

"Stay put," I ordered.

Sprawled on the ground, he looked at me ruefully. "I'm not likely to run off."

I ran to the pool shed, returning with a couple of towels. While I was busy, he'd managed to pick up the cement block and shuffle onto the grass, where he'd flopped down. In no time, I had him wrapped in soft, fluffy warmth.

I hefted the axe. "I'll hack the chain off so you can walk."

"Oh, no. I don't think so," he said in a voice loaded with apprehension.

"Trust me. Back in the day, I lived off the grid for a year when I joined a commune. I used to split wood all the time." I gestured to his feet. "Spread your legs. There's a foot or so of yield."

"Not a huge margin for error."

"I've never missed. Trust me."

He scrunched his eyes shut, heaved a gusty sigh, and spread his legs as wide as the chain allowed. "Have at it."

I raised the axe over my head and brought it down in one smooth stroke. The chain parted with a metallic clink.

Zeke cleared his throat and said, "Nice job," as he stood and we started walking.

"Thanks. So what happened on your date? Keep in mind I'm holding an axe."

The faintest wisp of a smile touched his lips as he shuffled beside me toward the pool house. "Tess insisted on going into town for dinner, said she didn't want to see your face across the table. After that, we went to her cabin. She disappeared into the bathroom and emerged wearing a zebra-striped nightie exactly like the one you're wearing. I can't believe you have the same taste in lingerie. Any more similarities you care to share?" I steadied him as his foot tangled in the chain.

"Don't push your luck. What happened next?"

"She offered me some cocaine, which I refused. She snorted a couple of lines. I had a beer. While we were chatting, she stood up and slipped off the nightie."

"Son of a peach," I muttered, tucking the trailing chain over his arm. "And I let you go on another date with her."

"Relax. She wasn't naked. Exactly. She wore a leather harness affair under the nightie. She's into what she calls 'rough stuff', which involves riding crops and restraints."

"Like chains."

"Yep. Which reminds me, I need to find the key. It's in her cabin. Anyway, according to Tess, I'm a submissive who needs domination. When

I laughed in her face, she got all huffy and tried to handcuff me. I shoved her away."

"I bet that annoyed her."

"You have no idea. She went crazy, airin' the lungs and throwing stuff. Then she demonstrated some rough stuff of her own."

"How so?"

He hesitated, then continued his shuffling gait. "It's kinda humiliating. She whacked me over the head with her purse, knocking me out cold. I didn't regain consciousness until she tossed me in the pool and left me to drown, attached to a cement block by one of her custom-made restraints. Lucky I'm tall. I discovered if I balanced on my toes on the cement block, my nose would break the surface and I wouldn't drown—at least if I didn't make any waves."

"The cocaine must have given her enough strength to haul you all the way from her cabin to the pool, cement block and all."

"That's not all. Before I passed out, I heard her yelling about how it was time she closed this place down. Permanently."

A shudder ran through my entire body. "I wonder where she went," I said.

"I reckon she returned to her cabin to get dressed. I've got to stop her, but first, I need to find the key for these shackles before I trip on the chain."

I studied his shivering form. "You're not going anywhere. You've been knocked unconscious, suffered hypothermia, and nearly drowned. You're in no shape to bring down a toddler, never mind Tess on a drug-fuelled rampage."

He studied my face and frowned. "Oh, no. Definitely no. You're not going after Tess alone. Don't even *think* about it."

I eyed Zeke's determined expression. "Tell you what. Let's go to my apartment and throw on some warm clothes."

"Sure thing. I've always coveted one of your caftans." Zeke batted his eyelashes.

I uttered a groan. "The lost and found box is in the main lodge. You should find something that fits. Then you can grab some rest in my guest bed. I'll neutralize Tess."

"There will be no neutralizing without me by your side."

I nodded my agreement. I intended to give him the slip once assured of his safety, but only after waking Dodie with instructions to call a doctor for Zeke and notify the authorities about a dangerous situation at Grizzly Gulch.

He wouldn't like it, but I refused to lose him at the hands of a psychopath.

Chapter 24:
Harmony Speaks Out

ZEKE FOUND DRY CLOTHING IN the lost and found box. As soon as we entered my apartment, I found a note sitting on the hall table. I'd missed it earlier because I'd used the kitchen door in my race to the pool.

I scanned Dodie's scrawl and turned to Zeke in dismay. "Dodie's gone line-dancing. If she doesn't meet anyone interesting, she'll be home soon and will drop by to chat." My sister's decision to end her long, dry spell couldn't have come at a worse time.

We entered my apartment and used separate rooms to change into dry clothes. When Zeke emerged, I noted he'd found a way to remove the shackles, likely using the nail file I'd left in the guest room. He looked remarkably sexy in white sneakers, a muscle shirt imprinted with "Only in Canada, Eh?", and a pair of gym shorts. After that, he stuck to my side as if skin-grafted. I would have been flattered, except I suspected he'd guessed my plan to give him the slip. Not that it mattered. He'd follow me to Tess's cabin anyway.

After opening the front door to leave, I turned to face him, drawing one finger down his cheek. The rasp of stubble caused my heart to make a crazy jump. Collecting my wits, I took a stab at talking some common sense into him. "I want you to go lie down. There's an excellent chance you have a concussion."

"I'm not letting you go in alone, Abby. Tess is too dangerous. End of discussion."

He stalked beside me all the way to my truck. When I unlocked the driver's side, he nudged me aside and climbed in, crawling across the console to slide into the passenger seat. His folded arms and the stubborn jut of his chin warned me that nothing I said would change his mind. Seeing no other choice, I hopped behind the wheel. Ignoring his triumphant smirk, I floored it. Thirty seconds later, we screeched to a halt in front of Tess's cabin. The door stood ajar, a bad sign. Our cursory search revealed that the place, although in shambles, was empty.

As we shot away into the darkness, I muttered, "I'm adding damages to the bitch's bill."

"Don't get your hopes up."

"We need to find Tess so I can beat the snot out of her before turning her over to the Mounties."

"Where are we headed?" Zeke asked.

"The barn," I said, noting the way he white-knuckled the grab bar.

"Look out!" he yelled.

I swerved and stomped on the brake. The truck squealed to a halt inches away from a figure who'd darted out of the darkness and was waving at us to stop.

"Pluck a duck, Harmony," I yelled, sticking my head out the window. "I nearly killed you. You're lucky I have excellent reflexes."

"Something bad's going down," Harmony said. "You've gotta stop her."

Zeke and I exchanged a worried glance. "Stop who?" he asked.

"Tess, of course." Harmony giggled as she swayed from side to side in the middle of the road. "Whoa. The road's moving. I do believe I'm more than a little stoned." She stumbled onto the grass. "Ah. That's better."

We climbed down. Zeke rushed over to support her before she toppled over.

"What's happening? Start at the beginning," I said, tamping down my impatience.

Harmony stared at me. "I love the way your nose is melting. Reminds me of a Shih Tzu. Um. What's up? Let's see. I was conducting a little investigation, trying to nail Muffy and Franklin for Luc's murder. I went to the barn tonight, looking for drugs. Got more than I ever expected." She released a screech of laughter. "PETA will beg me to join them now."

I wanted to kick her. Zeke must have sensed my intention because he stepped between us. "What did you find in the barn, Harmony?"

She dialed down her braying laugh to a shrill giggle. "Tess was amped up on cocaine—probably the same stuff I'm stoned on now. She told me she'd had a real busy night and was in no mood to deal with an idiot animal rights activist on top of everything else. Then the bitch reaches into her purse, pulls out something, and jabs me in the stomach. Hurt like crazy. Then she informs me that the insulin pen contained enough to knock a bull elephant to its knees, and instructs me to haul ass onto a hay bale."

"I thought insulin took time to kick in."

"She must have used the rapid acting kind, because right away, I get the jitters, rapid heartbeats, you name it."

"Clearly you survived," I pointed out.

Harmony looked around and lowered her voice. "I feigned the symptoms and pretended to pass out quickly. Must have been convincing because Tess covered me with straw, I guess to hide me in case anyone came in. Next thing I knew, she was stacking hay bales in front of the tack room door. That is one brawny woman, eh?"

"But you survived the insulin," Zeke reminded her gently. "How?"

""My sister has diabetes, so I knew I needed carbs to counteract the insulin. Remember the glucose tabs Luc knocked from Tess's hand the first day? Well, I found some in the straw she used to cover me. So I chewed those tablets, to hell with sanitation. It wasn't enough, but it was a start. As an added bonus, they also made me stoned. I bet Tess doctored them with cocaine. No wonder poor Lancelot went ballistic. They landed in his stall. He probably ate some."

I remembered the rubbery candy I'd found in Lancelot's stall. I would get it tested for cocaine. What if Luc had discovered Tess's secret and threatened to report her? That would be a motive for killing him.

"I feel dizzy." Harmony plopped down on the grass to continue her story. "I was going in and out of consciousness, but as luck would have it, I still had four butter tarts I'd filched from the dining room. I'd wrapped them in a napkin and stuffed them into my pocket—that's why I like cargo pants—so I ate them, too."

While I pondered Harmony's revelations, Zeke continued questioning her. "Didn't Tess notice what you were doing?" he asked gently.

"She was too busy yelling and opening all the stalls to release the horses to pay attention me, so I snuck out the rear door. That's when I started getting cold sweats and chills. I knew I was in trouble." She paused. "I think I might be forgetting something."

"Dear God," I whispered as pieces of the puzzle clicked into place. "Tess is behind everything that's happened. I bet she even killed Luc."

"Whatever she's planning to do, we've got to stop her," Zeke said.

I studied Harmony's ashen face. Sweat dripped down her forehead.

"I don't feel so good," she said.

"First we drop Harmony off at my apartment," I said. "We can't leave her alone. Her condition's worsening. I read somewhere that she should drink juice or pop and eat carbs, lots of carbs, as much as possible. I have cookies and some Coffee Crisp chocolate bars at home." I reached inside my truck and came up with a can of Coke. "I always keep a soft drink in my glove compartment. This should help until we get to my place." I popped the tab and handed the can to Harmony.

After glugging down the drink, she tried to stretch out on the grass.

"No you don't. No passing out here." I grabbed one of her arms and hauled her upright while saying to Zeke. "Let's get her into the truck right away. I'm sure Dodie's home by now. While she's calling a doctor and the Mounties, we'll return to the barn to stop Tess."

Zeke nodded, and between us, we muscled Harmony into the passenger seat. Zeke hopped into the back while I drove us back to the main lodge.

We were halfway there when Harmony latched onto my arm. I swerved, and we skidded off the road sideways, ending up at a crazy angle in a gulley. "Hey. What do you think you're doing?" I yelled, gunning the engine and concentrating on getting us back on the road without tipping.

"I know what I forgot."

Once we were on solid ground, I floored it and asked, "What was it?"

"Wes and Coop were there too."

I nearly swerved off the road again. While I wrestled with the steering wheel, Zeke's gentle voice behind me asked, "What about the twins? Are they okay?"

"I think so. At least, they were still alive when I left."

A chill crawled down my spine as we tore around the final curve. Surely Tess wouldn't hurt the twins. They were mischievous, sure, but they were only little boys.

"Tell us everything you know," Zeke said.

"Okeydokey," Harmony said in a sing-song voice. "When I was playing dead under a heap of straw, the next thing I knew, I heard kids yelling. They were somewhere inside the barn begging Tess not to hurt them, but she didn't stop screaming at them long enough to listen. Man, that woman's off her rocker."

"And why did Tess want to hurt them?" Zeke asked in a strained voice as the lights of the main lodge shimmered into view.

"From the exchange of insults, I figured the twins had decided to get even with Tess for accusing them of releasing the goats into the kitchen when all the time, she was the one who did it. After their parents were asleep, the boys snuck out of bed and squeezed into her cabin through a window she'd left open. Seemed she heard them and crashed out of her bedroom waving a gun." Harmony paused, "I'm gonna puke."

"Finish your Coke," I said, careening up the laneway. "We're nearly there."

As Harmony obeyed, Zeke said, "What happened to the boys next?"

"They escaped. I guess she didn't want to fire the gun and wake everyone up, but she followed them to the barn, nearly caught them too, except they ran into the tack room and locked the door on her. That was when I arrived, looking for evidence against Muffy and Franklin. After Tess jabbed me with the insulin pen, she stacked hay bales against the tack room door. I guess that was to prevent the twins' escape. Shortly after that, I heard her releasing all the horses, screaming something about saving them before she set the barn on fire. That's when I snuck away to get help."

"Pull a U-turn, Abby," Zeke yelled. "We have to rescue the boys."

In spite of the chill gripping me, I forced myself to remain calm. "We will, but Harmony's in real bad shape. We have to get her inside or she could die." I skidded into the drop-off zone and screeched to a halt in front of the lobby.

Between us, we hoisted Harmony down and into the foyer. Zeke loaded her on a luggage trolley, and I tossed him my keys. "You're faster than I am. Take the elevator. Coke's in the fridge. Call the doctor. And the authorities." I pushed the door open for him. "Hurry or she might slip into a coma."

He started pushing the trolley into the lobby. "Don't you dare leave without me."

As I turned to go, I shouted over my shoulder, "Stay with Harmony. I'll keep Tess busy until the Mounties arrive."

"Hey, you can't go in alone."

I blew him a kiss and raced for the truck.

Chapter 25:
Flattery, Bribes & Lies

I STEPPED ON THE GAS, LAID some rubber, and sped toward the barn. Two minutes later, I stomped on the brakes, causing my truck to fishtail before stalling. In spite of the indignant neighs filling the air, I risked sticking my head out the window to make sure I wasn't hallucinating. No such luck. Our entire herd of horses milled around in the barnyard. Since I couldn't drive closer to the barn without taking out a horse or two, I climbed down.

Driven by an urgent need to rescue the twins, I ignored the impulse to flee, and edged cautiously into the barnyard. With luck, I wouldn't end up crushed to a bloody pulp beneath dozens of razor-sharp hooves.

A firm nudge against my shoulder made me yelp. Grabbing a fence post for support, I found myself nose-to-nose with Alamo. He whickered a greeting.

"Aw, gimme a break," I whispered, scooting away.

The horse ambled alongside me.

I stopped walking to give him a long look. "So we're friends again, are we?"

Alamo gazed at me, his eyes liquid with adoration.

My heart softened. I stuck out a hand and rubbed his nose. "I've gotta go, fella, but I appreciate the support."

He blew out a snort, as if saying, "No problem," before clip-clopping away.

With my heart thundering in my chest, I headed for the barn. The double doors were ajar, so I slipped inside. The lighting was dim. As I crept down the corridor, I realized a jumble of hay bales at the far end was a new addition.

Comprehension slammed into me. The hay bales barricaded the tack room door, blocking the boys' only exit. There was no way they could escape without help. I suppressed a despairing groan. There would be plenty of time later to fall apart.

A moment later, someone stepped out of the shadows. Although the figure was facing away from me, there was no doubt in my mind it was Tess.

The unmistakable rasp of a lighter made me pick up the pace. No wonder she needed the hay bales. They would act as kindling. A fire would destroy any evidence that might incriminate her.

Repeated lighter flicks suggested her luck had ended. A stream of highly inventive cursing revealed her mood. A moment later, the lighter flew through the air accompanied by a screech of rage.

I patted my pockets to find my bear spray before remembering I hadn't transferred it after I'd changed into dry clothes. Pluck a duck. I needed another way to subdue Tess until the Mounties arrived. My idea was definitely a long shot, dangerous too, but it stood a fifty-fifty chance of working. I intended to make a pit bull on steroids look mellow.

I moved closer until I gauged the distance was correct. "Hi, Tess," I said. "Whatcha doing?"

She whipped her head around. A glare of pure hatred instantly dissolved into a brilliant smile. "Hey, Abby. I thought I was the only one with insomnia." She slung her purse over one shoulder and turned her body to face me.

I moistened my lips before speaking. "The barn's supposed to stay locked during the night. You can't stay. Please leave immediately."

"Aw, you're a big meanie. I thought we were friends." She took one step toward me, then another.

The positioning was perfect. Success hinged on her underestimation of both my skill and my determination.

Drawing on my sketchy karate training, I spread my feet wide to lower my center of gravity then bent my knees as far as they would go, which wasn't as far as I'd hoped.

Tess giggled. "Don't tell me you're going all kung fu on me. Be careful, hon. A woman your age could hurt herself." Her hand inched its way into her purse, no doubt where she'd stashed her gun.

Ignoring Tess, ignoring the gun she'd slipped from her purse, I angled my body while tightening my slack core muscles to gain stability, balanced slowly on my front foot, and drew up the other as high as I could without falling. Tendons protested, muscles shrieked. Pain no longer mattered. Focusing every ounce of my energy on achieving power and speed, I released my battle cry while snapping that rear leg out to the side.

The resulting side kick—a move I'd never quite mastered in class—connected with Tess's chin in the most satisfying way. The gun flew from her hand and into a stall. Her eyes rolled back in their sockets, and she collapsed onto the floor, motionless.

My happy-dance was short-lived. What if I'd killed her? I forced my feet to move until I stood close enough to see the rise and fall of her chest.

Relief weakened my knees. She was merely out cold. I scanned the area frantically, looking for something, anything I could use to immobilize her.

A whisper of air preceded the sledgehammer blow that connected with my wrist, making me stumble. Tess stood before me, swinging her purse. The same purse she'd used to take down Zeke.

I cradled my throbbing wrist and said, "Gee, Tess. I'm impressed. You're quite the expert at faking stuff."

"Really? What stuff?"

"Oh, being friendly, having a conscience, losing consciousness, boobs."

She released an amused tinkle of laughter. "The boobs are real."

The chillingly normal sound made the small hairs on my arms stand at attention. Yep. Tess was a psychopath. Refusing to show fear, I said, "You need help. Maybe a good shrink—"

"Don't you trouble your pretty little head about me, hon." She slipped the massive purse off her shoulder. "Let's play a game." Although she was smiling, her gaze was cold and empty, as if the soul behind her eyes had fled.

I backed away.

Her trill of laughter bordered on hysteria as she swung the purse around her head like a lasso.

I tried to dodge, but my reflexes weren't what they used to be. The purse connected with my shoulder. It was a glancing blow, but hard enough to make me lose my balance. I made the most of my fall, dropping to the floor and rolling, screeching as if she'd broken every bone in my body. Let her think she'd incapacitated me.

Tess continued to toy with me, using gentle purse swings and boot prods, which I dodged easily. "Fun, right?" she said, laughing. "We're bonding at last."

Knowing the killer blow would arrive any second, I welcomed the flicker of movement that appeared in my peripheral vision. I squinted into the shadows. Yeah, we had company. Luckily, Tess was too busy tormenting me to notice.

To keep her distracted, I gave her a friendly smile. "No wonder you're so stressed, hon. It's a shame your daughter refuses to let you near your grandchildren." I rolled away before the purse slammed into the concrete where my head had rested.

Where was the cavalry when I needed it?

Sprawled on the floor, I laughed in an attempt to buy more time. "Did I mention Sherrie and I had a nice chat? No? She told me about the gift you delivered last night. Nothing says mother-love like stolen semen."

"It's a legacy for my granddaughters." Tess whipped the purse around her head, warming up for the kill shot. "Let's hear you beg."

Not in this lifetime.

Hoping to confuse her, I threw back my head and released a belly-laugh. After a moment, her giggle joined my laughter in a macabre duet. With each revolution, her purse inched closer to my head. She was clearly crazier than an outhouse rat. When Zeke finally materialized behind Tess, his face was a mask of rage. To give him cover, I increased the volume.

At the exact moment her purse reached its apex, he wrenched the strap from her grasp and used it to trip her. Her scream of rage echoed through the stable as she stumbled and hit the ground. Although sprawled on her back, she aimed a kick at his shin, laughing in triumph at his grunt of pain.

He dropped to his knees and positioned himself behind her head. Using both hands and considerable muscle, he stretched the purse's strap across her neck, pinning her thrashing body to the floor.

Panting, he said to me, "Check for duct tape in her purse."

As I lowered myself to unzip the purse, I enjoyed the gagging sounds Tess was uttering. Picking through the jumble, I used my sense of touch to locate a roll of duct tape, which I extracted. Pushing myself upright, I dangled the roll in her face.

She bared her teeth in a snarl. "You're both thugs and thieves. Wait until the police hear about this."

Zeke tightened the strap across her neck, cutting off more threats. "I don't dare let go," Zeke said. "She's meaner'n a trapped weasel. Tape her ankles together, then I'll help you with her hands."

I ripped off a length of tape and started in on the thrashing feet. Once I was done, he wrestled her hands together, and I taped her wrists.

With Tess immobilized, I staggered to my feet and pulled Zeke to one side for a private discussion. "What about the boys?" I whispered.

"I met them on the way here. They'd found a stepladder in the storage area, and managed to squeeze out the narrow window near the ceiling. Luckily, neither of them broke an ankle, or worse. I dropped them off at their cabin with a quick explanation to the parents, and said I was sending a doctor over to make sure they were unharmed. It wasn't easy to get away, but I told them we would explain everything later."

"Oh, thank God," I murmured. "So you called the authorities?"

"Yep. Help's on the way. Harmony seemed okay, but who knows how much insulin she received? Dodie's taking care of her until Doc Shearer arrives. When I left, she'd polished off a case of soft drinks and was chugging a bottle of maple syrup. Once she's out of the woods, Doc Shearer will go take a look at the twins."

"Thank you," I breathed. "Now we have to make the most of our time before the Mounties arrive, and get her confession."

"How? If we coerce her into talking, the courts will kick it out."

"I have an idea. It involves flattery, bribery, and lying. Just follow my lead."

Tess, who lay flat on her back exactly where we'd left her, stared at us stonily. "What were you two cooking up? You'll never prove I did anything wrong." She directed her gaze at Zeke. "Like I said, I cover my tracks."

For my plan to work, I had to get myself into the right head space. After letting out a breath, I smiled a wide, admiring smile at Tess. "That's why I admire you so much, Tess. Your intelligence is one of the things I respect most about you. You're too smart to leave any loose ends."

She narrowed her eyes at me. "Are you for real?"

"I know we haven't been the best of friends, but that was my fault. I guess I felt intimidated and, well, terribly, terribly jealous of you."

She darted an appraising glance at my face and followed up with a pathetic groan. "I'm afraid I don't feel so good right now. I'm tired and I can't concentrate." With that, she closed her eyes and whimpered.

Sure enough, sweat beaded her forehead and tremors wracked her body. Combined with fatigue, these were classic signs of cocaine withdrawal, especially for highly-addicted users. My spirits soared. Tess had crashed and needed a fix.

I let my eyes soften with sympathy. "You poor dear. Could it be the flu?"

"No. It's my diabetes." She opened her eyes and looked at me with a steady gaze that was so intense I found it impossible to look away. "I'm such a silly goose. I didn't eat much dinner. Now I've got hypoglycemia. Would you be a dear and give me a couple of my glucose tabs? They're in my purse." She sighed and turned her head to eyeball her purse with the intensity of a starving wolf eyeing a juicy porterhouse steak.

I pretended to look for them, then dumped the purse's contents onto the floor. I had to admit she was well-stocked with the "necessities" for her "mission." I gave her an A+ for efficiency. The glucose tabs had spilled from the box and rolled almost close enough for her to touch.

"What a mess," I said, ignoring her request. "Don't worry. We'll tidy everything up for you, hon." I re-packaged the tablets and placed the box in my pocket, while Zeke, who'd caught my subliminal head nod, returned everything else to the purse and slung it over his shoulder for safekeeping.

I turned to her and patted my pocket. "There we go, all safe and sound. I'll keep these things handy, shall I?"

"Please give me one."

I crinkled my forehead. "I don't know anything about diabetes. What if I gave you too many? What do you think, Zeke?" I locked gazes with him and mouthed, "Say no." His minuscule nod indicated message received.

"Don't listen to Tess," he said to me. "She'll survive until the authorities arrive."

Tess's reaction was to squirm into a sitting position while trussed like a Thanksgiving turkey. I envied her those abs.

"Please?" she pleaded, "Look at me. I really need a glucose tab." She looked so pitiful, if I didn't know better, I'd give her as many as she wanted.

"I am so sorry, but I don't dare." I glanced at Zeke. "You know how he is."

"I sure do. Don't listen to him. I need a glucose tab." With that, Tess butt-walked over to me and flipped herself into a kneeling position to grope in my pocket.

The move was so sudden, I froze. Even Zeke took a couple of seconds before he peeled her away. Without ceremony, he dragged her, howling like a lunatic, across the corridor. After he positioned her in a sitting position with her back against an empty stall, he backed away as if he couldn't escape fast enough.

I had to hand it to Tess. Her core muscles were amazing.

I wandered over and placed a hand on Zeke's arm. Projecting my voice so it would carry, I said, "Poor Tess was only trying to reach her glucose tabs. Did you need to be so rough?"

Her howling stopped. I knew without a doubt she was listening.

"As I recall, she tried to kill me tonight." Zeke said.

"Come on. Poor Tess doesn't have a mean bone in her body."

Diving into his role of bad cop, he yelled, "Why don't you ever believe a word I say? She tried to drown me."

I waved an accusing finger under his nose. "A big, strong man like you? What on earth did you do to make her so angry?"

He shrugged. "Nothing. That's my point. Nothing"

Tess rose to the bait. "He's lying, Abby. If I were you, I'd dump this loser. He asked me for a date, then pushed me away when I opened my heart to him." Malice glittered in her eyes as she glared at him. "You're a lowdown piece of donkey dropping. I even gave you a second chance, and you screwed up again. I had to teach you a lesson."

I had the wits to say, "Men are heartless animals. Am I right?"

"Can't argue with that."

I smiled my encouragement. "What did you do to teach him a lesson?"

My exclamations of admiration punctuated Tess's description of her attempt to drown Zeke, ending with a shriek of laughter.

"What an amazing story," I exclaimed. "I have so much respect for powerful women like you." To keep her off-balance, I added, "By the way, I don't blame you for barricading the twins inside the tack room. They annoy me, too."

She nodded in agreement. "They're bad to the bone."

"They're just little boys." Zeke's voice vibrated with genuine anger.

"They snuck out of bed to spy on me. I caught them in my cabin, looking through my purse. I felt violated. What was I supposed to do?"

Maybe not murder them?

"Anyone would feel violated," I assured her, hoping I hid my revulsion.

"They deserve to die along with the stupid activist woman I jabbed full of insulin. What's her name?"

"Harmony," Zeke answered curtly. "She'll be fine. We got to her in time. The boys too."

Tess turned on him. "I should have hacked the door down and killed them then and there, instead of giving them the gift of another hour of life." She thrashed her head from side to side.

"Sweet baby Jesus," Zeke muttered. "You are one sick puppy. Everyone escaped. No one's dying tonight."

She fixed him with a flat, reptilian stare. "They must die, and they will. A fire leaves no evidence. I've thought of everything."

Except a decent lighter.

Good grief. Before Tess totally lost it, I said, "Of course you thought of everything. You're the smartest woman I've ever met." I paused for effect. "In fact, I believe you're a genius."

There. The bait was out there. If Tess needed a fix badly enough, she'd talk. I wanted to hear the truth from her lips.

She slid a sly sideways glance at me. "You do?"

"I do." I lowered my voice to a confidential murmur. "I think you've turned those glucose tabs into, you know, special treats. In my book, that's a stroke of genius."

She swung her emotionless gaze to me. "How did you know?"

"Because we're on the same wavelength." I kept my voice low. "Don't be modest. Admit it. If you tell me how you did it, maybe I'll give you a couple." I held my breath.

Fortunately, Tess wanted her fix. "You're right. I am a genius. Those are my special treat. I doctored them with cocaine."

"You should patent the idea," I gushed.

Her smile looked tainted to me, perhaps because of her basilisk stare. "Cocaine-coated candies. They're discreet, delicious and highly effective. Best of all, they're handy whenever I need a fix. Matter of fact, I could use some right now. Would you mind popping a couple of them into my mouth?"

I glanced at Zeke, and he took over. "Don't look at Abby for your fix. You won't get anything, at least not until you tell us the truth about why you brought a separate suitcase full of doctored glucose tabs for a one-week stay."

"Duh! To feed to the trail horses so they'd go wild."

A muscle jumped in his cheek. "Someone might have been killed."

She rolled her eyes. "Exactly. Bye-bye stellar reputation, bye-bye Grizzly Gulch. I wanted to get started before registration, but the barn was like Grand Central, so I gave up. I tried again with Lancelot during the guided tour, but it didn't work." She scowled. "Luc slapped the tablets from my hand, sending them flying. They disappeared, mostly into Lancelot's stall. I had to find them. If someone else did, I'd be convicted. My chance to destroy Grizzly Gulch would be over. I didn't dare hunt for them at the time."

"You're not really a diabetic, are you?" Zeke said, catching me by surprise.

Tess shot him a look that was so cold, so expressionless, it would've caused a lesser man to empty his bladder. "Why do you say that?"

"I trained to be a vet. Animals get diabetes too, so I understand the disease. I should have noticed you never do a self-test. I also know something else. Any diabetic who uses cocaine would be in danger of crashing on a regular basis."

"Well done. You know your diseases. Diabetes makes a good cover for a lot of things, including my glucose tabs." She paused and appealed to me. "So I've told you the truth. Now can I have one? Before I jump out of my skin?"

I dropped my voice to a confidential whisper. "Later. Zeke's watching us right now." I resumed my normal voice. "Why don't you tell us about the sabotage," I suggested. "Only someone with your intelligence could have done all those nifty things. You were behind every incident at Grizzly Gulch this week. But why?"

The words gushed out. "I had to stop you from stealing customers from The Crazy Cow, so I signed up for your symposium. I wanted to cause enough trouble to shut Grizzly Gulch down for good. I was protecting my granddaughters future."

I said, "Your granddaughters are adorable. And so clever, just like their grandmother."

While Tess preened, I explained to Zeke that Tess's daughter owned a guest ranch in the next county.

Showing no reaction, he said to Tess, "You brought wire cutters to cut the fences, didn't you? I spent hours patching them up."

"You must have worked like stink on those repairs," she said. "I made sure I did a thorough job of it."

Zeke arched a brow. "Tell us about releasing Lancelot."

Veins popped out on her neck as she raised her head to stare at him. "That's your own stupid fault."

I suppressed a smile at his bewildered expression. "How so?" I asked.

She addressed her explanation to me. "After a dud evening with Lover-Boy here," she jabbed a thumb at Zeke, "my feelings were hurt. When everyone was asleep, I returned to the barn, still trying to recover my glucose tabs. The doors were locked, but there was a light on in his office. He really should close the window and lower the blinds at night. I found him asleep at his desk beside the keys, so I helped myself and went into the barn. Lancelot was in a foul mood, most likely amped up on my special glucose tabs. I released him so I could search his stall. I hope he enjoyed his freedom."

"I can guarantee that he most certainly did. Then what did you do?" I asked.

"I got sidetracked."

"You expect us to believe that?" Zeke asked.

"I tend to lose focus when I'm coming down from using blow. I forgot all about the glucose tabs, but remembered I wanted to ruin the ranch's reputation. That's when the idea of leading the goats into the pool came to me. I still had the master keys."

"That was you?" Zeke asked, his voice incredulous.

"Sure was," Tess gloated. "A couple of quartered apples did the trick. The goats followed me, and Larry followed them."

Zeke's expression was murderous, so I nudged him and took over the questioning. "That was absolutely ingenious," I gushed, hoping to draw her out. "Let me guess. I bet you stole the semen from the demo, too." At her hesitation, I patted my pocket with the glucose tabs.

She nodded and resumed talking. "I needed that semen to help my daughter start a new career. The door to the outbuilding was locked, so I cut the padlock using my hacksaw, tossed the lock, and went inside. Good job I'd had a fix. Even then, I thought my arm would fall off. Then along came Clay. I bet he was after the semen too. I lied my ass off about the door being open when I arrived. You arrived next. I sure didn't expect you to kick me out."

I beamed a smile at her. "I really wanted to join you for a drink, but I had something to clear up with Clay."

"Then you tried to kill Abby," Zeke said in a matter-of-fact tone.

"That's her fault. I hid outside, waiting for them both to leave, but Abby had to stick around and play detective. Instead of leaving, she crawled around in the bushes trying to find the padlock. I couldn't let that happen because my fingerprints were all over it, so I whacked her with a tree branch."

"The branch was rotten. You missed killing her by a hair."

"Yeah. Too bad. But at least I gave it the good old college try. I found the padlock and took it away. No one will ever find it. I always cover my tracks."

Zeke didn't acknowledge her foresight. "What did you do with the semen?"

"I placed it in an insulated container containing liquid nitrogen and used a handful of carrots to distract Lancelot when I hid it in his stall." Tess sounded proud of her accomplishment.

By then, I was practically frothing at the mouth. Abandoning my role of good cop, I said, "It was you in the barn last night. You nearly killed me with a punch to the solar plexus then tried to kill me for real by tossing me into Lancelot's stall."

"Who knew the horse would take a shine to you? There's no accounting for taste." With that, she released a stream of foul language that offended even my liberal sensibilities.

I smiled. "Now you're showing your true colors."

She ignored me. "Good job I managed to get the insulated container out of there before you arrived. That horse does love a nice, ripe apple." Tess's voice softened. "My daughter will use the semen to start her own horse breeding business."

"No, she won't." I offered a triumphant smile. "She didn't want your gift. She told me she dumped the contents down the drain."

Tess didn't take the news well.

While she ranted and swore, I got antsy. The Mounties would arrive any minute, and I still needed Tess's full confession that she murdered Luc.

Using my outdoor voice, I said, "You haven't told us everything about the first day. Start with stealing my phone. Maybe you need some incentive to talk." I rattled the box of glucose tabs.

"Give me one of those."

"Only if you tell us everything."

After a prolonged silence during which I could actually hear the gerbils in her brain scampering, she said, "I accompanied the group to the main lodge to sign up for a free spa treatment. I pushed to the front of the line to make sure no one noticed me returning to the barn." She grinned at me. "Nice free facial by the way."

"Keep talking."

"I needed to collect those glucose tabs before anyone else found them and discovered they were laced with blow. You were dumb enough to leave your pink phone lying on the check-in counter, so I grabbed it. Luc was at a meeting with Clay, but there was a slew of wranglers in the barn. I figured I could clear the barn by texting about a fire, then retrieve those glucose tabs without anyone knowing." She started to laugh. "You should have seen everyone run from the barn like rats from a sinking ship."

"You deleted the text you sent, erased the call log, and left my phone sitting on the hay wagon."

"I also wiped it down. I always cover my tracks. It's a matter of pride."

"Then what."

"I used the barn's back door so no one would see me. I'd brought carrots to keep Lancelot busy, but I didn't need them. Luc's meeting with Clay was short. He returned and caught me opening the stall door." She stopped talking and chewed her lip.

We were closing in on Luc's murder. "Keep going," I urged.

"He read me the riot act. I flirted a little, but it didn't go anywhere. He told me if he caught me in the barn again, he would make me a very sorry woman." She let loose with another loud laugh. "Ironically, the whole time we talked, Lancelot was rooting around in the straw and came up munching a glucose tab."

"What did you do next?" I asked, wanting to hear Tess confess to killing Luc.

"Nothing. Figuring Lancelot would go nuts from the coke kicking in, I got out of there as fast as I could. Luc was very much alive and kicking when I left."

"Seriously?" I tossed the box of glucose tabs from one hand to the other.

Not taking her gaze off the box, Tess said. "Yeah, seriously."

I shook a pink tablet into my palm and pretended to examine it. "So who killed Luc?"

"I don't know," she yelled, focusing on the tablet. "Ask Muffy. She was headed to the barn. I passed her while returning to my cabin."

Zeke crouched and got in her face. "Why didn't you mention this sooner?"

"Why on earth would I?" Her surprise seemed genuine. "You told everyone his death was accidental."

My heart thundered in my ears. Was it possible Tess had nothing to do with Luc's death? To be fair, Muffy did have an excellent motive to kill him. What if she'd found him drugging her horse?

"I have one last question," I said. "Why did you release the horses tonight?"

"My granddaughters would never forgive me if I hurt them."

I rolled my eyes. "Prepare for life behind bars."

"Bitch. I told you everything. Now give me a couple of glucose tabs."

She struggled to stand, but Zeke pushed down on her shoulders. "Abby's not giving you anything. Let's see what the Mounties have to say." He straightened and moved closer to me.

Her mouth twisted into a snarl as she glared at us. "None of this will stick, you know. It'll be your word against mine. There's no proof. For my granddaughters' sake, my daughter will hire a good lawyer for me. Wait and see. I won't even serve time."

"Oh, but I guarantee you will," Zeke replied with a certainty that surprised me.

He clasped my hand and drew me close. I expected him to kiss me, but a distant siren announcing the Mounties' approach ruined the moment. I hoped whoever was behind the wheel had the common sense to silence it before the racket awoke the guests. I'd no sooner had the thought when the siren cut out.

We dropped hands and stood together listening to Tess curse a blue streak while waiting for the RCMP to arrive. This would be the second time in less than a week.

Chapter 26:
Plenty of Proof

TWO FIGURES BURST INTO THE barn ahead of a third, this one shorter and definitely plumper, who struggled along in the rear.

"RCMP," the tallest figure shouted as they closed in, their heels echoing on concrete. "Don't anyone move."

"Abby?" came Dodie's breathless voice, identifying her as the short, plump figure. "Are you okay?"

I should have guessed Dodie would insist on guiding them. I bet they told her to wait outside. "I'm fine," I hollered.

As they drew closer, I recognized Inspector Brody Tate, and heaved a sigh of relief. There wasn't a Perkins brother in sight. Brody was Zeke's friend and an outstanding cop, not to mention one of my fans. I'd met him and his lovely wife at a fundraising event in Calgary, and we'd hit it off.

His grin flashed beneath a well-groomed moustache. "Your emergency sounded too important for the Perkins brothers to handle, so here I am. This is my colleague, Sergeant Francine Simard."

Dodie interrupted the introductions by throwing her arms around me, squeezing hard. "I was terrified Tess would kill you," she said, her voice muffled. "From what Zeke told me, it sounds as though she may have experienced a psychotic break."

Tears prickled behind my eyelids. I told myself they were merely a delayed reaction, totally understandable given the circumstances. Blinking them away, I said, "It takes a better woman than Tess to kill me. When the bitch tried to bludgeon me to death with her purse, I clobbered her with my karate moves."

"Well done," Dodie said. "Where is she? Tell me she's still alive."

I pointed to Tess, who was seated against the stall, legs stuck out in front.

We all formed a semi-circle around her. She gazed up at Brody, her eyes brimming with unshed tears. Wisps of loose hair framed her face. She looked fragile and pathetic. Meryl Streep would be green with envy at the performance.

The inspector peeled off Tess's duct tape and helped her to her feet. In a calculated move, she wobbled so much he had to steady her.

Ignoring everyone else, she gazed up at her saviour while glomming on to both his arms. "Thank you so much, Officer. I'm afraid there's been a huge misunderstanding," she said, her voice breathy.

Brody's face remained inscrutable as he pried her hands away. "It's Inspector, and don't thank me yet." He nodded at the sergeant, and she snapped handcuffs on Tess's wrists.

It didn't take long for us to get seated in the tack room, the two Mounties flanking Tess, presumably to thwart any escape attempt.

Without preamble, Brody said, "Let's start at the beginning."

"This is a witch hunt," Tess announced, glaring at me. "I didn't do anything wrong."

In an icy tone, Brody said, "Ms. Jenkins, please don't interrupt again. You'll get your turn." He pulled out a recording device and asked her, "Is it okay if I tape this session?"

Zeke and I said, "Yes," simultaneously.

Tess remained silent.

"Tess?" Brody prompted.

She scowled. "If you must, but don't expect to hear much from me."

He nodded his thanks and pressed the start button. "Go ahead, Abby."

I looked at Dodie. I could tell she was impatient to get to the big reveal—Luc's murder, so for Brody's benefit, I led with a description of his death, followed by the revelation that Tess might not be the murderer.

"Is that true?" Brody asked Tess.

"Of course," she replied.

My sister gripped my arm. "Shut the front door. If not Tess, then who?"

I repeated what Tess had told us about Luc kicking her out of the barn, and how she'd seen Muffy approaching the barn's back door shortly before his death.

"And you believe Tess?" Dodie demanded, her voice rising in disbelief.

Tess turned to Brody. "See? I told you. Witch hunt."

Dodie was halfway out her chair and looked ready to rumble when Brody said, "Settle down, ladies. We'll interview Muffy once we're done here."

Dodie subsided, looking sheepish.

Tess sat there, motionless and expressionless, while Zeke and I described Tess's role in the events of the past week, including several attempted murders, property damage, cocaine use, and ending with tonight's showdown. Dodie offered her comments while Brody asked pointed questions to keep us all on track.

Once we wrapped up, Tess gazed at Brody with the intensity of a narrow-beam flashlight. Her wobbly smile came off as a tad incongruous. "Good golly, these people should write crime fiction. I hope you don't believe a word they said, Inspector. They're trying to frame me."

I visualized my foot connecting with Tess's face in another snap-kick.

The sergeant patted her arm. "Why would these people try to frame you?" she asked.

Tess bathed the sergeant in the glow of a conspiratorial smile. "It's a girl thing. Abby sees me as a rival for Zeke's affections. I'm sure you'll agree there's nothing more pitiful than a cougar, or, more accurately, a saber-tooth, who'll lie and cheat to control her boy toy. Dodie hardly counts at all because she falls in line with anything Abby says. And don't get me started on Zeke."

I came close to levitating from my seat. "What about Zeke?" I shrieked. "I oughta—"

Zeke leaned close, saying, "Don't react. It's what she wants."

Tess played to the crowd. "Zeke's out to get even. To be blunt, the poor man couldn't perform in bed. Okay, I may have made light of his situation, but it was just a little good-natured ribbing, a joke to lighten the moment. I'm afraid my teasing backfired. I was afraid he was going to hurt me, or worse."

I couldn't help it. I jumped to my feet and got in her face. "Take that back. You were all over Zeke like a dirty shirt. He's smart enough to see right through a viper like you, and you can't deal with his rejection. Besides, if I'm a saber-tooth, you are too. You're older than I am."

Zeke hauled me back down. "Shush. She's trying to throw you off-balance."

"Well, it's working," I grumbled.

I forced my fists to unclench. Aware that Brody was recording every word I uttered, I warned him, "Don't believe a word Tess Jenkins says. If her lips are moving, she's lying."

Brody addressed me. "Would you please tell us your assessment of this woman's mental state."

I cleared my throat. "I'm convinced she's a psychopath, which, by extension means she's also a narcissist. I was married to one, so although I'm not a psychiatrist, I'm only too familiar with the condition. I've read up on mental illness and personality disorders. I also underwent extensive counselling to deal with the effect my ex had on me. Tess exhibits most of the clinical signs of a psychopath, such as lack of empathy, pathological lying, lack of remorse or guilt, grandiosity, and many more. But as I said, I'm not a shrink."

"Thanks, Abby," Brody said. "That was a real clear and concise summary." He turned to Zeke and Dodie. "Do you agree with Abby's assessment?"

"Yep," Zeke said.

Dodie gave me a thumbs-up. "Couldn't have said it better myself."

Tess gave the inspector a seductive smile, which didn't reach her predatory eyes. "I'm perfectly sane. Please don't believe any of Abby's nonsense. There's no proof of any wrongdoing because I'm innocent."

"See, that's where you're dead wrong," Zeke drawled. "We have plenty of proof, more than enough to convict you." He pointed to an electronic device installed on a beam above us. "Check it out."

Everyone stared at the ceiling.

"What's that?" I asked, craning my neck. "It wasn't there yesterday."

"It's a motion-activated camera with embedded sound technology. Each has a sign beside it advising that the equipment is a motion-activated recording device. That way, any recording it takes won't be classified as surreptitious and tossed out of court. The recording it made tonight falls under the "one party consent" exception, meaning, that if one of the parties to a conversation consents to being recorded, then the entire conversation may be recorded. If memory serves, everyone, even Tess, consented."

Brody eyed the equipment and slapped Zeke's back. "Good man. I'm impressed. You've done your homework. If the surveillance equipment checks out, Tess Jenkins will be sent away for a long, long time."

"What prompted you to install them?" I asked.

"On the morning he died, Luc complained about the security situation at Grizzly Gulch. He was absolutely correct. I scheduled the installation of several cameras in the barn for earlier today, one at each door, one in the tack room, and three in the main stable area. They've been recording since dusk."

Everyone stood, except Tess, who continued sitting in stony silence.

Brody concluded our session with, "There's more than enough evidence to book Tess Jenkins. In the meantime, I want to interview," he checked his notes, "Muffy Walton. Sergeant Simard, please stay here with Ms. Jenkins and make sure she doesn't escape. Duct tape her ankles to the chair." Brody turned to Dodie. "Ms. Foster, I would be grateful if you would keep Sergeant Simard company."

I read that as, *Don't let Tess manipulate Sergeant Simard.*

"Abby, I want you and Zeke to come with me and help interview Muffy."

"Wait," Zeke said, halting Brody's exit. "Before we leave, I need to get something. After that, I want you to follow me and witness what I'm about to do."

As we waited in confusion, Zeke took five minutes to fetch a large manila envelope, a pen, and a stepladder. Once he returned, we witnessed his extraction of the cameras' microchips and the subsequent placement in the envelope.

Sensing he was about to seal it, I retrieved the bag of glucose tabs from my pocket. "Here's something else for the envelope. A simple test will prove they're loaded with cocaine. I think you'll find them identical to this one, which I found in Lancelot's stall." I pulled out the tablet I'd picked up.

Zeke sealed and labeled the envelope and handed it to Brody. "This should satisfy the chain of evidence."

Brody nodded his thanks and said, "Let's go talk to Luc Lacroix's killer."

Chapter 27:
The Truth About Luc

THE MOON DISAPPEARED, LEAVING THE starless night inky black. I was grateful Clara had insisted on installing the solar garden lights edging the pathways. During the walk to Muffy's cabin, Zeke and I brought Brody up to speed on the relevant background information. When we reached our destination, one of our upscale log cabins, Brody pressed the doorbell.

Muffy opened the door immediately. She looked terrible, well, terrible for Muffy. She'd scraped her blonde hair into a lank ponytail, her regal nose was red and shiny, and the haggard expression spoke of a sleepless night. An uneasy conscience, perhaps? I gave her top marks, however, for the silky turquoise robe draping her elegant frame.

She greeted us with, "I heard sirens. I've been expecting you."

After introductions, she led us into the spacious sitting area, which was separated from the kitchenette by a quartz counter. My teeth were chattering, so I switched on the gas fireplace before sitting.

Muffy offered drinks. Brody declined but Zeke and I felt free to accept. Booze might soften the distress of what we were about to do.

Muffy took a slug of her drink before saying, "I assume this is about Luc's death."

"It is," Brody agreed.

"Why me?"

"Ms. Jenkins told us she passed you on the pathway shortly before his time of death. You are likely the last person to see him alive as you were headed for the barn."

Muffy put down her drink. "You believe I killed Luc."

Brody got right to the point. "Ms. Walton, I have some difficult questions I must ask. I hope that's okay."

She nodded and said in a small voice, "Please. Call me Muffy. It's friendlier."

He nodded. "This must be upsetting for you, Muffy, but we're trying to figure out how Luc Lacroix died. We think you might be able to shed some light on the situation. Please tell us everything you know."

She downed some whisky. Ice clinked as she set it down. "Franklin—he's my husband—insisted I fire Luc for horse drugging. I pointed out that Luc was a friend of mine and the best horse trainer in the province. Franklin gave me an ultimatum. Fire Luc or face divorce. Oh, not in so many words, but his meaning was unmistakeable. After that, he immediately took off on a business trip." She glanced at me. "Abby heard everything because our argument took place in the lobby shortly before guests arrived to register for the week."

"You were in a tough spot," Brody said.

She looked at him gratefully. "Exactly. But as it turned out, Franklin didn't go on his business trip. In fact, he stayed home." Muffy recited the tale of finding him working at home, their happy reconciliation, and his continuing insistence that she fire Luc.

"I promised to fire him right away," she said, "so I returned to Grizzly Gulch and headed for the barn. I was so focused I barely noticed passing Tess along the way."

Brody praised Muffy for the clear and concise summary of events leading up to Luc's death. "Now, I must ask you," he said, "what happened between you and Luc in the barn?"

Zeke leaned forward, all his attention focused on Muffy.

She took a deep breath and moistened her lips. "When I arrived, Luc was terribly angry, banging things around and cursing. He mentioned something about kicking Clay's ass and getting rid of some old broad who'd come on to him. He was so nasty, he made it easy for me to fire him." She stood and wandered over to the window, her back rigid.

"What was Luc's reaction?" Brody asked, while Zeke never took his eyes off her.

Muffy turned to face us. Her mouth trembled and her blue eyes swam with tears, but she pulled herself together. "He warned me that if I followed through with the firing, he would let Franklin know that I'd begged him to drug my horses because I wanted them to win. I lost my temper and started yelling at him." She stopped talking, her face pinched.

"Go on," Brody said.

"Lancelot was agitated by our argument, so Luc entered his stall to calm him down. I followed him inside and begged him not to lie about me to Franklin. It would be the end of our marriage. Luc laughed at me. Lancelot freaked out. I screamed at Luc that I'd never asked him to drug my horses. He couldn't betray me like that." She started pacing as if working up the courage to finish her confession.

"You're in the home stretch," Brody said gently. "If you tell us everything, it'll be a weight off your shoulders."

She continued her pacing, not looking at us. "The horse was rearing up and screaming. Luc turned his back on me to calm Lancelot down. I was so angry, I pushed Luc as hard as I could. He staggered, slipped, and fell. One hoof caught him on the back of his head. By then Lancelot was in a frenzy, so I backed out of the stall. Luc didn't move." Tears streamed down her cheeks. "I accept full responsibility. I killed Luc. I couldn't let him destroy my marriage."

I was close to tears as well. Her despair touched my heart.

"I knew Luc must be dead," she continued. "I panicked and ran. I should have confessed when the Mounties arrived, but I was afraid Franklin would leave me if he learned the truth." She covered her face with both hands. "As long as I live, I will never forget the sound of Lancelot's screams."

Before Brody reacted, Zeke stood and walked over to Muffy. For the first time since entering the guest cabin, he spoke, and his words rang with sincerity. "I am so sorry to learn the truth, Muffy. Love is a demanding master. I hope you can come to terms with what happened in Lancelot's stall." He leaned down and hugged her. After a beat, she clung to him and sobbed uncontrollably. He held her until she quieted down before letting go and moving to my side.

By the time the Mounties left with a subdued Muffy and a defiant Tess, a new day spilled over the eastern horizon. A glory of red and magenta streaks filled the sky. The horses awakened from their barnyard snooze with snorts and a shuffle of hooves.

Dodie, Zeke, and I stood silently, watching the Mounties' red tail lights disappear around a curve. Dodie broke the tension. "The horses are fine, and the wranglers will be along any moment. I suggest we all try to grab an hour or two of sleep."

Zeke wrapped an arm around my shoulders and drew me close. I recognized the heat in his gaze as he looked down at me. His warm, understanding smile made my decision easy. Life was too short to waste another minute by wallowing in cowardice.

Dodie's gaze shifted between us. "Okeydokey. Is there more you or Zeke care to share with me?"

"Nope," I replied, feeling my face go incendiary. I peeled myself out of Zeke's embrace and dragged Dodie a few feet away. "Shhhh," I whispered. "He'll hear you. We haven't resolved anything one way or the other."

"Well, I hope you resolve it the right way." She held out her hand. "Keys, please. If you're as smart as I think you are, you'll stay here. I'll drive your truck back."

I relinquished my keys. "You're the best. Please make excuses for my absence to the guests and the wranglers."

"Don't worry. I'll take good care of her," Zeke said from behind me.

I turned to face him, and he took my hand easily, as if it was the most natural thing in the world, which it totally felt like.

Dodie smoothed over the awkward moment by addressing practicalities. "The guests may have questions," she warned, "especially about the twins. I'll explain everything to Big John and Sheila, even offer to make sure Wes and Coop receive a couple of counselling sessions to help them deal with their emotions, though chances are the boys are fine."

I gave her a warm hug. "That's a generous offer. After breakfast, I'll let everyone know that Tess had a breakdown and had to leave Grizzly Gulch, and that Muffy was called away by a family emergency. Later, we should hold a private de-briefing with every guest.

"What about the rest of the symposium?"

I thought about it. "There are only two workshops left to deliver—*The Problem Birth* and *The Post-Partum Mare*."

"I'll deliver those workshops," Zeke's volunteered. "Believe it or not, I trained to be a veterinarian before I joined the military. I've delivered more foals than I can count, and treated the mares as well."

I studied him in astonishment. Zeke brimmed with surprises. And I lost another chunk of my heart. "That's very generous," I said. "I don't know how to thank you."

"Oh, we'll figure something out." He waggled his eyebrows.

Dodie grinned. "Okay, then. Make the most of what's left of the night, children." She waggled her fingers at us and headed for the gate, stepping nimbly between curious horses.

"Wait, Dodie" Zeke shouted to her. "Would you call the head wrangler? Tell him I said to make sure the boys clean out Lancelot's stall before they do anything else. They have to find every glucose tab first. I'll check in later."

My entire heart melted. This man was so caring, he'd remembered the poor horse needed TLC.

"Sure thing!" Dodie shouted back, and walked away, leaving me alone with Zeke.

Any lingering doubts fled. This wonderful man was my Mr. Right. I needed to tell him how I felt. I didn't want to live with regret the rest of my life.

Clueing into the fact he was staring at me with concern, I gripped his hand tighter and swallowed hard. "I, um, don't know how to say this. I've never been in this position before."

"Easy there, tiger. You can tell me anything." Gently, he disengaged his hand.

Gah! I hoped my grip hadn't done any permanent damage. "Well ..." I sucked in a deep breath. "To celebrate our takedown, I was going to offer you some, um, fooling around, but here's the thing..." I hesitated, knowing my face was scarlet. What was wrong with me? I didn't do bashful. Ever.

He gripped my shoulders and stared so deeply into my eyes, I felt myself drowning. "Do not leave me dangling or I'll explode," he said.

I gazed into the lovely, unshaven, and, I realized, *worried* face of a man who cared deeply for me. Running my fingers down his weathered cheek and reveling in the stubble rasping against my fingers, I said, "Life is short. I nearly lost you tonight. I don't want to waste another minute, so I'm offering you, um, the real deal."

He went still for a moment. "Do you mean what I think you mean?"

I laughed softly. "All the way to home plate, baby."

A light of pure joy filled his eyes, and my insides gave a funny little tremor. I might have melted to the floor in a puddle of lust if he hadn't wrapped his arms around me. I tilted my head to give him better access to my lips.

Zeke settled his mouth against mine, igniting a flame that threatened to consume me two seconds in. He had me clinging to him, but actually, the clinging might have been mutual.

"You do realize I have a terrible track record with men," I blurted.

Way to push him away before we get started.

"And me, with women," he countered.

"I've had more relationships than I care to count, but none of them worked out."

Yeah, definitely making a huge fool of myself.

"Guess you didn't meet the right man, eh?" His slow, easy drawl wrapped me in warmth.

"I'm bossy, opinionated, and touchy," I continued. "And in the interests of full disclosure, I have an inappropriate sense of humor, a mean streak with people who piss me off, and I'm too old to change any of it, even if I wanted to, which I don't."

"Babe, I don't want you to change anything."

"Not even my weight? I hate diets."

"I think you're perfect exactly the way you are."

I didn't waste any more time on trying to push him away. "I'm crazy about you," I whispered, hoping it would be enough. Would he say it back?

He used his thumb to smooth away the worry-lines that tended to appear between my brows. "I'm crazy about you, too. Truth be told, I've never felt this way about a woman." I must have looked shocked, because he said, "Don't worry. I'm as scared of this as you are. Together we'll make it work."

He lifted me up and swung me around as if I was a featherweight. My girl parts gave a slow, hard tug. When Zeke cared, he gave it everything he had. Damn, but that was appealing.

He set me down gently and pulled me into an embrace. Electricity sizzled up my legs, circled twice, and landed on the bull's eye. When he let go, I lifted my chin to peer at him. He looked so hopeful, I kissed him. How could I not?

The kiss deepened. It was the kind of kiss that melted the hard, cold knot that had occupied my heart for so long, I'd grown accustomed to its presence. In a thick, hoarse voice, he murmured a few words, which I didn't quite catch. My pulse quickened, and he kissed me again.

When we broke apart, we were both breathing hard.

He was warm. And he smelled delicious, like sexy man and something better. He was also honest, kind, compassionate, understanding, and loyal through and through. And best of all, he wasn't expecting me to change. He accepted me for who I was.

All my doubts fled as we clasped hands and walked to his quarters.

Epilogue

OUR AND A HALF MONTHS later, Dodie and I welcomed Clara back to Grizzly Gulch with open arms and a ton of guilt. Our youngest sister was finally home. Her daughter's recovery from a bad fall had taken four months longer than anyone, including the doctors, had anticipated. During Clara's absence, we'd glossed over Luc's murder and skirted other unpleasant events to avoid adding to her stress. Tonight, we planned to reveal the unvarnished truth of the equine breeding symposium week. The good, the bad, and the ugly.

After giving Clara two days to settle back in, I found myself arranging a pitcher of lemon drop martinis and a tiered stand of Chef Armand's cupcakes alongside three glasses, plates, and napkins on my coffee table. As I waited for my sisters' arrival, I soothed my nerves by strolling onto my balcony to watch the fiery September sun dip below the mountains. With my gaze fixed on the snowy peaks backlit with gold against the deepening purple sky, I decided the best way to handle the revelations would be to announce the good news first, then hit Clara with the truth.

Dodie and Clara arrived promptly at eight o'clock. I led them into the living room where I filled the martini glasses and handed them out. Taking a deep breath, I announced, "Ladies, I have news."

"Martinis and cupcakes," Clara said, eying me closely. "Either we're celebrating or we're drowning our sorrows. Please tell me it's good news because if not, I'll never forgive myself for leaving Grizzly Gulch in the lurch."

"It's excellent news." I raised my glass with a flourish. "We're fully booked and have been ever since our equine breeding symposium week. I've crunched the numbers. At this rate, we'll be able to pay off our debts in no time."

Grinning like idiots, we all clinked glasses, sampled our martinis and sat. I selected a maple cupcake and bit into the decadent, buttery sweetness. No wonder guests loved them.

"That's amazing news," Clara said reaching for a red velvet cupcake. "Before I left to help my daughter, I thought we might be finished. What happened?"

Dodie blurted, "I bet it's because every guest from the symposium week posted glowing reviews on multiple travel sites."

Clara quirked one eyebrow as she licked cream cheese frosting off her fingers. "Seriously? They enjoyed the week? From the little you told me about Luc's death, I assumed they'd be less than enthusiastic."

Little did she know we'd conducted an undercover murder investigation while hiding the truth from our guests. I smiled brightly. "We made a point of holding a private de-briefing with every guest to explain everything and apologize. To seal the deal, we offered everyone a free weekend to make amends for any inconveniences encountered during the week."

Like attempted kidnappings and drownings, or learning a murderer was on the loose.

Dodie's bark of laughter sounded forced. "It helped that Abby's drunken first-night speech was a huge hit."

Clara's shocked expression prompted me to jump in. "Hey, the semen collection demo was the unanimous favorite. But we digress. Whatever prompted the five-star reviews, every single symposium guest is returning next year, some for two weeks. The reviews attracted dozens more. We're fully booked for the fall and winter seasons."

Clara reached for a chocolate chunk cupcake. "I'm so sorry I wasn't here to help."

Dodie chugged the rest of her martini before saying, "No problem. We rose to the occasion."

"There's something you're not telling me." Clara bounced a determined stare from my face to Dodie's and back to mine. "Describe the symposium week again. This time, tell me everything. I'll know if you don't." When I protested, she said, "I'm well aware that whenever either of you phoned me, you minimized any difficulties because you believed I had enough worries taking care of Wendy and her family."

I drew in a deep breath before saying, "Okay. Full disclosure."

"About time," Clara muttered.

Taking turns, Dodie and I gave a detailed recap of the entire symposium week up to the moment the Mounties carted Tess and Muffy away. Once we wrapped up, Clara surprised me by saying, "You guys were awesome. Zeke, too."

We all stood for a group hug before returning to our seats and draining our glasses. I lifted the pitcher and topped everyone up.

"I'm glad Tess and Muffy's court trials are over," I said. "They were both astonishingly brief. Muffy pled guilty to a reduced charge of manslaughter, and Tess's was pretty much open and closed. Zeke's surveillance equipment sealed the deal."

"I can't believe it all happened so quickly," Clara commented. "It usually takes years before criminal cases come to trial."

"Brody Tate, Zeke's RCMP buddy from Calgary, has friends in high places," I said.

Dodie wrinkled her nose as if detecting a bad smell. "Tess got what she deserved. She's going away for a long, long time with no chance of parole for two decades."

Ice clinked as we raised our glasses.

"Here's to justice," I said. "The jury found her guilty of five charges of forcible confinement, seven charges of attempted murder, one count of grand theft, cocaine possession, multiple counts of property damage, possession of an unregistered handgun, and cruelty to animals."

Clara said, "I never met the woman, but she sounds twisted. I can't believe I missed all the excitement."

"I ran into Franklin last week. He quit the oil business and has thrown himself into ranching. He told me Lancelot's producing gallons of semen and winning races under a new trainer. In fact, Franklin's so happy, he sent Clay twenty doses of Lancelot's semen to make amends for Luc's scam."

"Thank goodness he's hanging in with Muffy," Dodie said. "I figured he'd head for the hills at the first sign of trouble. I guess he really does love her."

We discussed the other members on our suspect list, chatting about each one. After doing Clay and Veronica, who'd tied the knot and were enjoying married bliss, we moved on to Harmony. She'd phoned to thank me because PETA had hired her as a full-time employee, mainly due to the glowing reference I'd sent.

"I talked to Sheila last week," Dodie said with a grin. "She and Big John have signed up for a series of parenting workshops. They decided to get their act together with the twins, particularly because they'll be hitting adolescence in no time."

"What about Zeke?" Clara smiled at me.

"What about him?"

"I've seen the way he looks at you. When are you two getting married, or at least moving in together?"

I glugged down the rest of my drink. "We're not. At least, not yet. I'm not ready to commit to another man. Too many trust issues." I set my glass down. "Speaking of Zeke, we've got a date tonight. He'll be here any minute."

"In that case, you'll need privacy. I'm sure we'll find a way to entertain ourselves," Clara said, polishing off her drink and placing a half dozen cupcakes on her plate. "For the road," she explained as she got to her feet.

Dodie eyed my tunic top, which hid a multitude of sins. "I see you're not wearing that tummy-taming teddy again," she said, standing and turning to Clara. "Wait until you hear this story. You're gonna love it." She placed two more cupcakes on Clara's plate and picked up the pitcher of martinis.

They both hugged me before departing, taking the goodies with them. Before the door closed behind them, I heard Dodie ask Clara, "Have you ever heard of a Super-Deluxe Fat Buster Thigh 'n' Butt Toner?"

THE END

Acknowledgements

Although writing a novel is very much a solitary pursuit, few, if any, books worth reading are written in isolation. In my case, I had a whole village to support me.

First, I must thank Maggie Jagger, my amazing critique partner, who got the ball rolling, so to speak, with her anecdote about her days as a vet's assistant. Maggie, your hilarious description of your attempt to collect horse semen was the inspiration for a chapter in Horsing Around with Murder. Hey, I couldn't make this stuff up.

Next, I want to offer huge thanks to Louise Clark. You took my first chapter, turned it inside out, and basically saved the book. Not only that, you accomplished this feat gently and with great kindness.

Boundless gratitude to editor Stacy Juba. You were the first person (other than myself) to read the entire book. Your developmental edit was so awesome, I enjoyed the re-write it triggered.

Also, many thanks to my beta readers: Allison Booz, Wendy Burch Jones, Cora Von Hampeln, Peggy Rasmussen, Linda Lou White, and Boni Wagner-Stafford. Although you may not realize it, you provided much-needed support, especially by 'getting' my warped sense of humor. On top of that, you offered numerous insightful suggestions, ones I would not have imagined. You made the book so much stronger.

And last, but far from least, heartfelt thanks to my husband, the best (and toughest) editor on the face of the earth. Nothing, and I mean *nothing*, slips past you. You edited Horsing Around with Murder not once, but twice, even when your own responsibilities weighed you down. I love you with all my heart.

And many thanks to the readers who have chosen to read this book. Words cannot express my gratitude for taking the leap of trust to spend your precious time with my literary offering.

Other Books by Maureen Fisher

Cold Feet Fever (The Fever Series, Book 2): 'One for the Money' with steamy romance meets 'The Sopranos'. A bad boy gambler and a mortician-turned-event-planner find romance while overcoming obstacles such as a goofy dog, ruthless thugs, exploding trucks, an eccentric granddaddy, disappearing corpses, an unfortunate synchronized swimming episode, and the threat of live cremation.

"An exciting novel that left me doubled over in laughter"
"a wonderful hilarious comedy … a warm and enjoyable read"

Fur Ball Fever (The Fever Series, Book 1): This romantic crime mystery features romance (sizzling hot), a second chance at love (hope and heart), crime (dastardly), an aging aunt (bawdy), dogs with personality (many), and humor (may cause mascara to run).

"It entertains, it heals, it delivers a message."
"… hilarious, moving, and sexy."

The Jaguar Legacy: Romance, suspense, and adventure explode in the steamy Mexican jungle. A secretive archaeologist guards his discovery, the ruins of a hidden Olmec city, while a journalist on the trail of an ancient Olmec curse experiences flashbacks to her past life where shapeshifting is a reality.

"Fisher has redefined paranormal romance…
magnificent characters and scenarios."
"An intricately woven tale of mystery, romance
and occult. Definitely a keeper."

About Maureen Fisher

After eons in the I.T. consulting world, I live with my husband in Ottawa, Canada's beautiful capital city, where I write fresh and funny novels featuring romance, mystery, suspense, and always an animal or two. I'm also a besotted grandma, a voracious reader, the Gardening & Landscaping Coordinator for our community, an avid bridge player, yoga enthusiast, seeker of personal and spiritual growth, pickleball player, and infrequent but avid gourmet cook. My husband and I love to hike, bicycle, and travel. I've swum with sharks in the Galapagos, walked with Bushmen in the Serengeti, sampled lamb criadillas (don't ask!!!) in Iguazu Falls, snorkeled on the Great Barrier Reef, ridden an elephant in Thailand, watched the sun rise over Machu Picchu, and bounced from Johannesburg to Cape Town on a bus named Marula.

Please feel free to keep in touch with me using the following links:

Website: http://booksbymaureen.com/

Twitter: https://twitter.com/AuthorMaureen

Facebook: https://www.facebook.com/MaureenFisherAuthor/

Goodreads: https://www.goodreads.com/author/show/845094.Maureen_Fisher

42354254R00132